He held the orange segment out to

JARRETT, Miranda

The lady's
hazard

THE LADY'S HAZARD

Miranda Jarrett

MILLS & BOON

Pure reading pleasure

All the cha   nation
of the auth   he
same nam
individual   re
pure inven

All Rights   le or
in part in   ith
Harlequin   or
any part th   rm
or by any   ying,
recording   ise,
without th

This book   ay of
trade or otherwise, be lent, resold, hired out or otherwise circulated without the prior consent of the publisher in any form of binding or cover other than that in which it is published and without a similar condition including this condition being imposed on the subsequent purchaser.

® and TM are trademarks owned and used by the trademark owner and/or its licensee. Trademarks marked with ® are registered with the United Kingdom Patent Office and/or the Office for Harmonisation in the Internal Market and in other countries.

First published in Great Britain 2007
Harlequin Mills & Boon Limited,
Eton House, 18-24 Paradise Road, Richmond, Surrey TW9 1SR

© Miranda Jarrett 2005

ISBN: 978 0 263 85194 6

Set in Times Roman 10½ on 12 pt.
04-0907-84686

Printed and bound in Spain
by Litografia Rosés S.A., Barcelona

Miranda Jarrett considers herself sublimely fortunate to have a career that combines history and happy endings, even if it's one that's also made her family regular patrons of the local pizzeria. With over three million copies of her books in print, Miranda is the author of more than thirty historical romances, and her bestselling books are enjoyed by readers around the world. She has won numerous awards for her writing, including two Golden Leaf Awards and two *Romantic Times BOOKreviews* Reviewers' Choice Awards, and has three times been a RITA® Award finalist.

Miranda is a graduate of Brown University, with a degree in art history. She loves to hear from readers at PO Box 1102, Paoli, PA 19301-1145, USA, or MJarrett21@aol.com For the latest news, please visit her website at www.Mirandajarrett.com

Recent novels by this author:

PRINCESS OF FORTUNE
THE SILVER LORD
THE GOLDEN LORD
RAKE'S WAGER*

*A *Penny House* novel

For Abby
With many thanks & much appreciation
for your wise suggestions & constant good humour.
Hee!

Chapter One

St. James's Square, London
1805

William Callaway stood in the shadows of the iron fence and thought again of how much he hated weddings.

The guests were arriving now for the wedding feast, clustered along the pavement before Penny House as they waited for the new husband and wife to appear. The gentlemen laughed and joked, already drinking, while the women preened like gaudy exotic birds in the late afternoon sun, the plumes on their hats nodding as they gathered in chattering little groups on the pale stone steps. Their laughter rippled across the summer afternoon air, bright with excitement.

William hunched his shoulders deeper into his coat, ignoring the boy who'd guided him here. Too much joy, he thought grimly, too much happiness and optimism for all the suffering and misery that filled the world. Didn't these fools understand that this couple was as doomed as any other? Couldn't they see that what the beau monde called love was only a fool's solace, temporary and empty?

The steady procession of carriages had slowed along St. James's Street, and gentlemen leaned impatiently from the windows to see the cause of the delay. William slipped further back into the shadows, ducking his head beneath the yew branches that overhung the wall. Almost as an afterthought, he hooked his arm around the boy and pulled him back into the shadows, too.

"Best not to let them see us gaping, Twig," William warned. "They'd rather folks like us kept our eyes to ourselves."

"In the gutter, you mean, Guv'nor?"

"I mean out of their sight," William said. "Poor people are an eyesore to the rich, a blight they'd like swept from their pretty streets."

A woman in one of the carriages noticed them, lifting her scented handkerchief to cover her face and nose, and William's expression hardened. How far would the gentry go to rid London of those who didn't share their good fortune? Workhouses, transportation, gaols…

Or poison?

"A pox on what them want." Twig rubbed a grimy, defiant thumb across his nose, ready to challenge them all. "I say a cat may look at a king, an' them swells an' ladies, too."

That made William smile. "No ladies in that troop, Twig. Penny House is a gaming house, a private club for gentlemen only, with no true ladies welcome."

Twig craned his neck to look back at the women with fresh interest. "Then they all be whores?"

"After a fashion, yes." William wasn't in a humor to discern the good women from the bad. Once, long ago, he'd been part of this world, and he hadn't forgotten how such women had fluttered around him in his bright new regimentals, or how heady their perfumed scent had been beneath his nose, their soft breasts pressed against his chest.

"The only difference comes with the prices they command for their company."

"All whores, then." Twig whistled low. "Even the lady-bride, Guv'nor?"

"She cannot be a lady," William said firmly. Everyone in London had heard of the three Penny sisters, the clever, beautiful daughters who ran this fashionable gambling club near St. James's Square. Though the gossip claimed they were the daughters of a Sussex minister, William doubted it, just as he doubted the great virtue that they tried to claim for themselves. The great sums they supposedly gave to charity were likely exaggerated, too, or perhaps some stipulation of their inheritance. There could be no other explanation. How could a true generous spirit exist in a place like this?

"No real lady could live in such a house, Twig," he said. "Not catering to the follies of gentlemen as they do."

The boy glanced up at him, his dark eyes full of doubt. "Beg pardon, Guv'nor, but not Miss Bethany Penny. You'll see. She don't be like them. She be kind, an' gentle, an' good to everyone, not just to fine gentlemen. She be famous for it. Her 'flock,' she calls us at her door, like we be special to her. She be a true lady, all right and no mistake."

But William didn't answer. Bethany Penny was the reason he'd hired Twig to bring him to Penny House. The streets and poorhouses were full of talk about her generosity to the unfortunate, but William didn't give a damn if she were twice, even three times the paragon that Twig and the others claimed. All that would matter was whether she was guilty, or innocent.

"You'll see, Guv'nor," Twig insisted. "Once you—ah, there be the bride an' groom now!"

The open carriage was a glossy pale blue and decked with garlands of white flowers that made the women squeal and clap their hands with delight. Blue silk ribbons were braided into the manes and tails of the matched greys, and riding on the box behind were two trumpeters in old-fashioned livery and powdered wigs, their gleaming silver instruments heralding the arrival of the newlyweds.

"They say th' groom be richer than th' His Majesty himself." Twig's voice rose, eager to share his own information. "Mr. Blackley. That be his name. Mr. Richard Blackley. They say he made piles an' piles of gold in the Indies, growing sugar."

"How fortunate for him," William said dryly. "From the looks of this, I'd guess he must be spending at least one of those piles today."

All gallantry, the groom waved aside the footmen who hurried to open the carriage door. He gathered up the bride in his arms, kissing her to more applause and cheers, then carried her up the stairs in a froth of ruffled white muslin. The bride tipped her head back against his arm and laughed with joy, not caring at all that her coppery hair was tumbling loose from her headdress or that her slippered feet were kicking so high among her skirts that she displayed her legs clear to her blue garters.

"Lor'," Twig said with open admiration. "Now that do be a show, don't it?"

William grunted with disgust. A show, yes: a vulgar, self-indulgent, ostentatious display of the worst and noisiest sort. No wonder Penny House's more staid neighbors complained to the watch, if they were often forced to suffer through this sort of low rigmarole. How many of London's orphans could be fed tonight simply for the cost of the silk ribbons trailing from the carriage and horses?

"That be Miss Bethany," Twig said, stepping away from the wall as he pointed toward Penny House. "There, near the bottom of the steps, her an' her sister Miss Amariah."

With new interest William looked to where the boy was

pointing. From this distance, all he could see was that Bethany Penny shared the same red-gold hair as her sisters, and that she was the same height, too, tall and slender and graceful. Beyond that he had only a vague impression of a simple but elegant—and no doubt very costly—bright blue gown that fluttered about her legs and hips with a provocative sway, and a matching bonnet whose wide brim hid her face. She carried herself with a beauty's confidence, sure her every move would draw attention.

Or was it the arrogance of a woman who dabbled in poison under the guise of charity? A clever woman whose cookery could nourish, or kill?

He sighed restlessly, refusing to let himself be drawn into her spell. Four men, good men, had been murdered since spring. William couldn't let himself be lured into thinking better of Bethany Penny just because she was beautiful.

As if she could hear his thoughts, she ran her fingers flirtatiously along the edge of the sweeping brim of her hat, then hooked her arm through her sister's. Their heads nodded toward one other, sharing some secret between them, as they climbed the steps after their now-wed sister, with the rest of the guests following.

"So much for the public diversion, lad," William said. "The rest of that party's only for those with an invitation."

He reached into the pocket of his waistcoat for a coin to pay Twig for his time. He was more tired than he wished to admit, the scar in his leg aching from having kept pace with the boy. He shouldn't have let his pride make him leave his walking-stick at home, not when the consequences were that every nerve in his body groaned in angry protest.

He glanced back to the steps where the woman had

stood. Seeing her and the other revelers of Penny House had brought back too many old memories that he'd rather keep safely in the past, and the effort of shoving them further back into his head had been just as exhausting as the long walk to this part of London.

"We'll return tomorrow, Twig," he said, purposefully turning away from Penny House, and his own past. "Better to give this foolish lot plenty of time to sleep away their celebrating."

"Oh, no, Gov'nor, not at all!" Twig flung his arms out, as if offering William the world. "Miss Bethany won't be above stairs with them others. She never goes there. She always be below, in the kitchen an' at her door for us."

William frowned, skeptical, the coin tucked between his first two fingers. "On her sister's wedding day? I am sorry, lad, but surely a woman like that will have other ways to occupy herself this evening than giving scraps to poor folk."

"Beg pardon again, Guv'nor, but you don't know Miss Penny," Twig insisted. "She gave her word yesterday that she wouldn't forget us tonight, and she won't. She *won't.*"

William shook his head. "With this lot, 'tonight' could mean noon tomorrow."

"Not with Miss Penny." With the nerveless audacity of London street-boys, Twig grabbed William's arm to lead him toward the back of the gaming house. "I'd wager there already be a line to her kitchen door. Come with me, Guv'nor. I swore I'd take you there, an' I will."

William shifted his weight from one leg to the other, wincing at the sharp, fresh pain. But this time the pain wasn't limited to his leg, instead shooting straight to his conscience as well.

He was still alive to feel that pain, still alive to worry over a pretty woman's reaction to his ravaged face and body. Too many others were not as fortunate, including the four dead men who had died not on the battlefield, but alone and unlamented on these London streets. He had been their major, their leader, and they had always followed him with unquestionable courage.

And he would not fail them now.

"Very well, then, Twig," he said softly. "Lead away."

The boy knew the way exactly as he'd promised, guiding William from the affluent public face of St. James's Street down the narrow alley that ran behind the grand houses. Used for deliveries or emergencies, the alley was unpaved and muddy, lined with high walls to protect the tiny city gardens. Heavy locked doors kept outsiders away and the ladies safe within, along with their whitewashed Chippendale benches, a bed of carefully tended flowers and perhaps a nodding crabapple tree or two.

But there was no genteel ladies' garden behind Penny House, nor was there a heavy padlock to bar the alley. Instead the door was propped open, so welcoming that even Twig marched boldly beneath the arch. Inside these walls, the ground was worn bare, with only a pair of halfhearted yews in planters beside the door, and several rough benches.

Yet what William noticed first wasn't the lack of a garden, but the crowd of people, more people in this little yard then had likely been in all the others on the street combined in a year. They stood in a queue that began at the back door and snaked back and forth until it nearly reached the alley, and they stood patiently, quietly, with the resignation of those who'd seen too much of the raw end of life. Sad women with fretful, ailing babies, old men bent with age, grimy, hollow-cheeked girls and boys like Twig—they all had their places in line.

But the ones that caught William's attention were the men who should have been in their prime: men still young in years, but old in the ways that only war could cause.

Whether they'd once been soldiers or sailors or marines, the damages were grimly the same—a missing limb or eye, a crippling wound that twisted the body into a wasted mockery of itself, the tremors from a fever that never cooled. Worst of all were the scars that showed not on the skin, but in the eyes, blank reflections of minds emptied of reason by what they'd been forced to see. They were ridiculed by others in the street, shoved aside as halfwits or cowards by those who could never know.

But William—William understood. He understood it all. This was where he belonged now, among these people in this yard, and not with that overdressed pack of useless jackals upstairs.

Twig sniffed extravagantly, his eyes closed to savor the scents drifting through the open windows. The kitchen ran the entire length of the big house's ground floor, with at least a score of cooks, maids and footmen racing back and forth at their tasks inside.

"Didn't I tell you how it be at Penny House, Guv'nor?" he said. "Don't it smell like th' finest things in th' whole world, stirred up together in one big pot?"

"Indeed it does," William murmured, not really noticing the cooking smells from the kitchen with so much else to be considered. He pressed the coin into the boy's palm. "Thank you, lad."

"Lud!" The boy's eyes widened at the coin in his fingers before he quickly stuffed it away inside his clothes. "Thank *you*, gov'nor!"

But William had already turned away, intent on joining the others. Of course to have a list of the names of the men he sought would have been simpler, more efficient, but the

army didn't believe in such niceties. Whether a man died
in battle or from disease, whether he'd been discharged and
cast out: it was all the same to the clerks on their high
stools, the end of their interest and their records. Once
gone from the service, a soldier ceased to exist, except by
this way that William had found, searching one by one by
one, and praying he'd find the survivors in time.

Now he made his way along the line to a man missing
both his left arm from the elbow and his leg to the knee,
supporting himself on a homemade crutch.

"Good day to you, friend," William said to him.
"What ship?"

It was an easy guess to mark the man as a sailor. The
tattered striped trousers and the waist-length pigtail would
have been enough, even without the amateur tattoo of a
ship across his biceps.

The man squinted up at William, his expression
guarded. "The *Hector,* twelve, Cap'n Robeson, may his
black soul forever rot in hell."

"Ahh." William nodded, his voice gruff and noncommittal. "What was your last action?"

"Scarce an action at all," the sailor said, not bothering
to hide his disgust. "Robeson nigh ran us aground in the
fog off the coast, making us easy pickings for the lugger
that raked us good."

William nodded again, knowing the value of listening.
"No satisfaction from the admiralty?"

"Not worth the pot to piss in." The man studied William shrewdly, his gaze sliding from William's battered
wide-brimmed hat to his lopsided body beneath the worn
greatcoat to the twisted hand that his sleeve couldn't quite
hide, to, finally, the leg forever shortened in the ambush.
"Where'd the Frogs take you, mate?"

William didn't flinch beneath the sailor's scrutiny, the

way he'd hide himself away from the inspection of his family and old friends.

Or from the young woman inside with the copper-gold hair....

"The Peninsula," he said quietly, almost a whisper, but more than enough to explain things to this man that a thousand more words couldn't explain to his own family.

"Rough luck, mate," the sailor said. "Rough luck."

William's smile didn't reach his eyes. "But we survived to be here now, friend."

The sailor nodded, the bitter joke shared between them. "Aye, that we did, such as this life may be."

They shared enough that no more needed saying. "Did you ever see a man here with sandy hair and a withered arm, and a saber scar across his face like a bolt of lightning? A man named Tom Parker?"

The sailor screwed up his weathered face, thinking. "A mate of yours?"

"He was in my regiment, yes."

"Can't say I've seen him." The sailor sighed, sorry not to have been more helpful. "Leastways, not here."

"London's a big sea for us small fish," William said, not letting his disappointment show. He found another coin in his pocket, and slipped it without fanfare into the canvas bag with his belongings that the sailor wore slung over his shoulder. The man looked up, surprised.

"I'd luck at dice last night, friend," William explained, "and I believe in sharing."

He clapped the man gently on the shoulder, taking care not to skew his balance on the crutch. "May better luck come your way as well."

He turned and limped along the line until he found the next crippled man. This one had been a soldier who'd long ago cut the gold lace and buttons from his uniform coat to sell, and the wool that was left was now faded and tattered. The man wasn't from William's own regiment, but that didn't matter. He might still have seen or spoken to one of the others in this very yard.

"Good day, friend," William began. "I trust you're not—"

"Guv'nor!" Twig reappeared, scrambling his way through the others. "Guv'nor, look! There be Miss Penny, just as she promised!"

William took a deep breath and straightened, and turned toward the kitchen door.

And toward the woman who could either be a saint, or a murderer.

Chapter Two

"**O**h, Pratt, *look* at all the people waiting today!" Briskly Bethany tied a fresh linen apron over her gown, trying to balance the number of faces turned toward her with the amount of food she'd had prepared. "I've never seen so many this early in the afternoon. I hope we have enough to feed everyone."

Pratt, the club's manager, sighed with resignation, and blotted his face with his handkerchief. The day was warm, made warmer still with every fire and oven in the kitchen in use for the wedding preparations. "You can't feed all of London's beggars, miss, especially not today."

"They're not to be called beggars, Pratt," she said firmly as she turned back to the kitchen. "How many times have I told you that?"

"More than you should, miss," Pratt said, unconvinced. "I know that your late reverend father believed in catering to the poor, but Sussex poor aren't London poor."

"They are indeed different, Pratt." She swung a heavy iron pot on its crane away from the fire and critically sniffed the chicken fricassee inside it while one of the cooks hovered anxiously beside her waiting for her verdict.

"The London poor are infinitely more in need of whatever assistance my sisters and I can offer with our work here. You *know* that."

"Giving money from the gaming table's not the same as putting food into some pox-ridden mouth, miss," he said primly. "A lady like yourself should consider the dangers, miss."

"A lady should first consider her moral responsibilities." She nodded to the cook, who began ladling the fricassee into a rooster-shaped tureen. "I'm not so many steps removed from those people waiting outside."

Pratt pressed his lips together, keeping a disapproving silence, but still Bethany knew what he was thinking.

"You can make all the sour faces you want, Pratt," she said as she ducked to avoid a huge covered dish passing by on the shoulder of a footman. "I'd wager there's not a single person in our yard today who'd rather not be earning his or her supper instead of having to take it from us."

Pratt grumbled, no real words. "What will you say when they come creeping inside to steal the silver, eh? Or up the stairs to murder in our beds?"

"Oh, Pratt, hush," she said, glancing back over her shoulder, out the open door. "Do you see any murderers among the women and babies?"

"My London eyes see more, miss," Pratt said gravely. "Behind those rags I see pickpockets and cutthroats, and you should, too, miss, before it's too late."

"Then I'm glad I've Sussex eyes instead," she said, pausing to tweak the paper ruffles that capped the legs of a roast turkey before she called to one of the other cooks. "Letty, have one of the boys help you with that soup. Our flock outside is waiting."

"Your guests upstairs are waiting, too, miss," Pratt said, trailing after her. "Peers can also be hungry."

"They're thirsty, not hungry." Bethany took a spoon to taste the steaming soup in the kettle held by one of the cook's assistants. "A bit more salt, I think, Betty, and another palmful of sage, and then it is ready to serve."

"Please, miss—"

"Pratt, as long as the gentlemen upstairs have their liquor, they won't care a fig what or when I feed them," she said. "Most of what I'll send up will come back untouched, anyway, no matter how delicious it might be. You know that."

Pratt stepped from the path of another man bringing the cans of fresh milk that Bethany provided for the children in the yard.

"But this *is* your sister's wedding feast, Miss Bethany," he protested. "This is not one of our ordinary nights. Miss Amariah sent me down here specifically to tell you—"

"I know perfectly well why she sent you, Pratt." Bethany sighed impatiently, tucking a loose strand of hair behind her ear. Just as she was responsible for Penny House's kitchen, Amariah oversaw the club's public rooms upstairs, making sure that the gaming tables were fair, the servants efficient and that every gentleman left Penny House convinced he'd had the most enjoyable evening of his life.

And while Amariah believed in charity, too, she would not believe that it should come before Cassia's wedding feast, especially not when so many of their guests were also favored members of their club.

Pointedly Pratt cleared his throat. "Then what shall I tell Miss Amariah in reply?"

"Tell her the first courses will be up directly," Bethany said, and only partly because that was the only answer Amariah would accept. She nodded at the boy with the stack of tin plates for serving the soup, and selected the long-handled ladle she'd use to serve it. "And tell her I am not neglecting any of our guests."

"And what of yourself, miss?" Pratt asked. "Miss Amariah wished to know when you would be joining them as well."

Bethany sighed again, tapping the bowl of the ladle lightly against her palm. Of course she wanted to be part of Cassia's celebration, but she wished Amariah hadn't decided to mix their personal life with their private one, and invite some of the club's more prominent guests to the wedding. It didn't seem appropriate, and besides, she didn't share Amariah's gift for making charming conversation with people, especially not with powerful titled gentlemen who often had little charm themselves.

"Tell my sister I'll join them as soon as I can, the very minute my responsibilities here are done," she said finally. "Tell her I promise I'll be upstairs in time for the cake."

Pratt looked back at the line of waiting poor, sniffed, then finally bowed. "Very well, miss. We shall see you upstairs directly."

Bethany was glad to see him go, and joined Letty at the door. The routine was the same: each shallow plate received two ladles-worth of the thick soup and a chunk of bread—a plain, hearty meal, but one that Bethany took every bit as much care preparing as she did with the more exotic dishes that went upstairs. Children were offered a cup of milk, and the adults cider.

There was also a basket of whatever fruit was in season, and today, in honor of the wedding, another basket held tiny bundles of sweet almonds, tied with the same blue thread as those for the guests upstairs. Knowing how rare a treat such sweets must be, Bethany didn't care how many disappeared into pockets for later, or for friends. With her flock, she was certain that not one scrap of food was ever wasted.

"We can look after this for you, miss." Letty was already

at the door, breaking the bread into rough chunks and tossing them onto a platter. "You wouldn't want to splatter on
your fine gown."

Bethany glanced down at her skirts, frankly having forgotten she was wearing the elegant gown that Cassia had
chosen for her. Just as she lacked Amariah's social skills,
she also lacked Cassia's innate sense of style.

"That's the reason for aprons, Letty," she said, filling the
first plate with soup. "I'll join them upstairs soon enough.
Here you are, lad, careful not to spill."

She was able to greet many of those who came before
her by name, people who came here every day for what was
often their only meal of the day. As she ladled the soup,
she paused long enough to smile, and ask after babies, listen to grievances and laugh over a silly story.

Yet there were always new faces, too, some that would
only come once, then vanish forever. Today, near the end
of the line, stood one of these: a tall man in a slouch-
brimmed hat that shadowed his face. He walked slowly,
with a limp that dragged at his steps, and though his greatcoat was worn and ragged and hinting at a better, finer past,
there was still a darkness to him, almost a menace, like a
wolf whose wounds had made him more dangerous. The
others sensed it, too, the men deferring to him, the women
inching away, all treating him with wary respect.

"Here, lamb, here you are," she said, handing one of the
little bundles of wedding-almonds to a small red-haired girl
who was always one of the first in line. "And don't your plaits
look fine today! You must have taken extra care with them."

"For th' wedding, Miss Penny," the girl whispered, cup-
ping her hands together over the almonds as if they'd somehow try to escape. "For th' bride."

Bethany grinned, and patted the girl's cheek. Yet from
the corner of her eye she still followed the tall man, watch-

ing him. He held no place in the line for himself, instead moving among the others to talk only to the men who'd been crippled by the war. She tried to tell herself that he was likely just another poor battered sailor or soldier, but there was something different about this man that separated him from the others. Her uneasiness growing, she remembered Pratt's warnings about cutthroats and thieves.

"Good day to you, Mrs. Till," she said to the next woman waiting. "Careful now, the soup's hot. And please make sure your son gets a cup for the milk, too."

The man was coming closer now, inching along with the others at the very end of the line. She'd feel much better if she could see his face, to know if he smiled or not. Especially since she had the oddest sensation that he was watching her in return from beneath that hat's brim, studying her, judging her, making her feel self-conscious and awkward and—

"Oh, no, miss, not on your best gown!" At once Letty bent to blot the fresh splatter of soup on the hem of Bethany's skirts. "I hope it's not ruined, miss!"

"It's only a scrap of cloth, Letty." Quickly Bethany crouched down to take the cloth from Letty and wipe at the spreading greasy blot. "Fetch a clean ladle, and go on with the serving. Don't stop on my account, Letty, please."

"Then you'll be wanting this."

Bethany looked up just far enough to see the ladle she'd dropped, now rescued from the ground and held out to her, and she didn't have to raise her gaze any further to know who was offering it. His voice, low and rough and impossibly male, was too much a match for his appearance for it to belong to anyone else.

"Thank you, sir." Quickly she rose, uncomfortable on her knees before him. But it wasn't enough; she was tall for a woman, but he was even taller, and she scarcely reached the brim of his hat. Yet still she did not meet his eye. She hadn't taken the ladle from him, either, instead leaving it dangling from his fingers between them. "Fortunately my kitchen is full of other spoons and ladles."

"Of course it is," he said, giving the ladle a little swing, as if it were a pendulum. "You wouldn't want any less, not for Penny House."

"No, sir." She hadn't expected such sarcasm from him, nor had she expected the public school accent that was layered over it. "We feed many folk from Penny House, both rich *and* poor. We couldn't do that without a properly outfitted kitchen. Here, let me serve you your soup."

"Thank you, no." He stopped the swinging spoon, holding it crossways like a bar against her offered soup. "I didn't come to eat. I came to see you."

For no reason at all her cheeks grew warm, the empty tin soup plate clutched in both hands. This was ridiculous. She had met hundreds—thousands!—of men standing here on her kitchen step, and not one had ever disconcerted her like this one did. How foolish she must look with a soup plate as her makeshift shield, defending herself as if he held a broadsword instead of a ladle!

"I cannot make you eat, sir," she said, striving for her usual brisk efficiency, "though I should venture that a good meal would do you a world of good. But if you choose against it, then I must ask you to yield your place to the next person, who might be more hungry than you."

"But there is no next person, hungry or otherwise," he said. "I made sure that I was last, so I wouldn't make anyone else wait for his supper."

Her flush deepened. How had she not noticed that he was the last in line? And when had the two tall footmen come to stand behind her, just inside the doorway and within reach of the block of cleavers if she needed rescuing?

Letty hoisted the near-empty kettle from the step to take it back inside. "I'd say we're finished for today, miss, and a good thing, too, considering how much we've still to do for the celebration upstairs."

"You forget yourself, Letty," Bethany warned. "I know my responsibilities without you telling me."

"Then forgive me, miss." Unrepentant, Letty glared pointedly at the tall man. "But then you know, too, miss, that you can't be dawdling out here all the day long."

The tall man shook his head, unconcerned by Letty or the footmen. "Miss Penny's not dawdling," he said. "She's conversing with me."

"Please do not mistake generosity for familiarity, sir," Bethany said indignantly, grabbing the ladle back from his hand and passing it to Letty to take inside. "They are not the same."

"I never said they were, Miss Penny." He might have chuckled, so low she couldn't tell for sure. "And though you might be…confused, I assure you that I'd never make a mistake like that."

"Nor would I, sir," she said tartly, and at last she looked him square in the face.

And caught her breath, stunned by what she found.

Once he must have been a handsome man, the kind that turn heads at the theatre. Some might say he still was. His jaw was strong with a slight cleft to the chin, his nose straight and his mouth full but firm, equally capable either of resolution, or seduction. His hair was dark, unruly beneath his hat and flecked with early grey.

But it was the man's eyes that made her gasp. Pale blue eyes, without a hint of warmth to soften their iciness: eyes as ruthless as a wolf's and with as little emotion. She'd thought she'd seen every kind of face among those who'd come to her kitchen door—those who couldn't hide their physical pain, or their misery, or their hopelessness—but never one like this man's.

What must his eyes have seen, she wondered, or was it what he had done that had made him this way?

"You're precious quiet," he said, his voice so low only she would hear it over the noise of the kitchen behind them. "And here I'd heard you Penny women were a glib lot."

That jerked her attention back where it should have been. "My sisters and I pride ourselves on expressing our thoughts more often than is common among London ladies, sir, but also perhaps with more care and precision than the word 'glib' implies."

"Then you won't mind defining a word for me, Miss Penny." He smiled, a slow, predatory smile that didn't come close to reaching his eyes. "Truth? Can you tell me the meaning of that word, Miss Penny? Of truth?"

She frowned, disturbed not so much with the question, but whatever lay behind it. "Of course I know the meaning of truth."

He hadn't moved, yet she still felt as if he were somehow intruding, even threatening. "Then you will tell me, yes?"

"No, sir, I will not." She dropped the tin plate in her hand onto the small stack of others left beside the step, then bent to gather the whole clattering stack into her arms. "I've far better use for my time than to waste it here playing riddles with you."

"No riddle, lass," he said, still keeping his voice at a level where she was the one who was forced to make the effort to listen. "All I want is the truth, the names of those who come here for your charity."

"Then you shall have a long wait for nothing," she said, her chin high and determined. "I make no judgments and ask no questions. They come because they are hungry, not to be interrogated."

"Yet you addressed most of these people by their names."

"My memory, sir, is notoriously short," she said, adding an extra sniff of disdain. "Dinner will be served here again tomorrow at the same time. Everyone is welcome, and no one is turned away, so even you may come join with the others."

He turned his head a fraction to one side, his pale eyes turning shrewd and maybe amused, too. "Even me?"

"Yes." He was studying her so closely she had to concentrate on not flinching beneath his scrutiny. "So long as you expect no answers to riddles."

"Then one of us, lass, is bound to be disappointed." He touched the brim of his hat. "Good day to you, Miss Penny."

"Good day to *you*." She turned on her heel and marched back into the kitchen, the plates rattling in her arms.

The truth, the truth: what kind of nonsense was that? There was nothing in her life that was false or untrue, no secret shame that she'd hidden away to nibble at her conscience, which was likely what came of being a minister's daughter. She'd certainly not erred by defending the privacy of her flock.

She'd no reason to duck her head or blush before anyone's accusations, and certainly not before a man like that. He had no power over her except what she gave to him by letting herself be affected by his strange ways.

So why, then, had it felt as if he'd had the last word—as if he'd *won*—when he hadn't? And why, really, should she care one way or the other?

"Is everything to rights with you, miss?" Letty was watching her closely, her mouth pursed with concern. "As it should be?"

"Of course it is, Letty." Bethany set the plates on a table and began inspecting the row of covered dishes waiting to be carried upstairs. "We are very busy today here in the kitchen, that is all."

"We are always busy in the kitchen. It was that rascal bothering you, miss, *that* is all," Letty said darkly. "Eyes like Lucifer, he has, and if Mr. Pratt says there are villains pretending to be otherwise prowling about the yard, then that one'd be the first I'd point out to the magistrate, and—"

"We have never questioned the circumstances of the unfortunates at our door, Letty," Bethany said, "and I've no intention of doing so now."

Letty's scowl deepened. "Even if they mean you harm, miss, like Mr. Pratt said? Even if they threaten you with their foolish questions?"

Determined to be reasonable, Bethany snapped another of the covered lids in place, and nodded to the footman who would take it upstairs.

"You saw that poor man, Letty," she said striving to think only of the man as a tattered, pitiable pauper, and not as broad-shouldered and well-spoken and as dangerously handsome as the devil himself. "He is broken and scarred, doubtless by the same war that has broken and scarred so many other Englishmen, and I would not be surprised if he is also more than a little mad. We should be understanding and charitable toward him, not suspicious of his motives."

Even to Bethany's own ears, the argument sounded as hollow and unconvincing as a seminarian's sermon, and Letty didn't accept it any more than Bethany did herself.

"And what murderer isn't mad, miss, I ask you?" she demanded. "He wasn't so broken that he couldn't snap you in two like a matchstick. Murder and madness at your dear sister's wedding!"

The wedding. Swiftly Bethany glanced up at the small

brass clock that hung near the stairs. She knew that more people than usual had been waiting in the yard today, but she'd had no idea nearly two hours had passed since Pratt had left her.

She yanked away her apron and tossed it over the back of a chair. "I must go upstairs, Letty. Everything should go smoothly now, but don't hesitate to send for me if it doesn't."

With her skirts clutched to one side, she ran up the back stairs, remembering at the last moment to smooth back the fuzzy stray hairs around her face. Likely her face was flushed from the heat of the kitchen as well, and there were the fresh stains on the front of her gown, but it was far too late to change any of that.

She took a deep breath at the top of the stairs, then plunged in among the well-wishers that seemed to fill the club's ground floor. This was her sisters' domain, not hers; by choice, she almost never left the kitchen, no matter how busy the club was.

And it was extraordinarily busy tonight. The majority of the wedding guests were members of the club, rewarded with invitations for being loyal supporters of the sisters from their first days in London. There was also a faint smattering of family, and a handful of the groom's rakish friends and sea captains from the East Indies.

But to Bethany's eye, this mostly male crowd looked no different than any other evening at Penny House, nor was there much difference in the way that most of these same gentlemen already appeared to have drunk every toast offered to the happy couple. With their fine linen neckcloths untied and their silk waistcoats half unbuttoned, they roared and staggered and slapped each other's backs, and as Bethany slipped between them, she couldn't help but think of how much better behaved the poor folk—at least all except the tall man with the pale eyes—had been than their betters.

Slowly she made her way down the hallway to the dining room, where the long table had been spread for supper. She caught her breath when she saw what remained of the wedding cake, a spun-sugar extravaganza now reduced to a buttery rubble of yellow cake and crumpled orange blossoms. That cake had taken her two days to bake and build, and she hadn't even been here in time for its cutting and destruction. All she could hope was that Cassia and Richard had enjoyed it, and that—

"Bethany!" Cassia flung her arms around Bethany's shoulders, hugging her with affectionate joy. "Oh, duck, where have you *been?* I felt sure I'd have to come drag you away from the fire myself!"

"Well, you didn't." Bethany untangled herself from her sister's froth of skirts, laughing but also feeling oddly close to tears. "You're the most beautiful bride, Cassia. I'm so, so happy for you and Richard both!"

"Thank you, Betts." She smiled, a little blob of white frosting on her cheek, and Bethany realized that tears glittered in her sister's eyes, too. Their lives were changing. Although they'd always be close, once Cassia left Penny House today, she'd forever be Richard's wife first, and a Penny sister second. "And the cake you made—oh, the cake was glorious!"

"And now it's rather not." Bethany glanced back at the table and smiled ruefully. With her finger she reached out and swiped away the frosting from Cassia's cheek. "I trust it was better to eat than to wear."

"Do not say that to Richard." Cassia chuckled, full of newly acquired worldliness. She pulled Bethany with her into the arch of one of the windows, where they could speak more privacy. "He has already said the most *scan-*

dalous thing! He told me he would ask you to make a big bowl of the icing so he could spread it all over me and nibble it off."

Bethany blushed with startled embarrassment, unable to think of a reply to such a suggestion, and just as unable not to picture her sister and new brother-in-law behaving so outrageously. Slathering one's spouse with icing did not quite seem to fall into the sanctified idea of marriage that her father had taught them.

"Oh, now I've shocked you." Cassia laughed again, but at least she was blushing in sympathy. "I was, too, when Richard first suggested it, but then once he whispered exactly what he would do, and how he would do it, and how much we'd both enjoy it, why, it seemed like it could be the most…*delicious* pastime imaginable!"

"Perhaps," Bethany said faintly. She and her sisters had always shared their secrets and dreams, but this was rather more sharing than she wished. "I suppose most anything could become agreeable if one loves one's husband sufficiently."

"It's not just 'one's husband.'" Cassia leaned closer, placing her hand on Bethany's arm. "It's *Richard*. Oh, Bethany, some day when you find your own true love, you shall understand, too. I know you will!"

But Bethany had heard enough, and she gave her shoulders a small shrug of impatience. When they'd still lived in the country, she'd had her share of followers who'd beg for a dance at the Havertown assembly, but now that all seemed frivolous and inconsequential, and forever in the past.

"I've too many other responsibilities for that, Cassia," she said firmly. "What we're doing with Penny House is *important*. You should know that as well as anyone. I'm far too busy with our work here to go hunting about London for a husband."

"I was working, too, but I didn't have to hunt for Richard," Cassia declared. "He simply found me."

"Richard would have found you if you were in China." Bethany smiled indulgently. She couldn't imagine a better matched couple than her sister and new brother-in-law, or one more in love, either. "But what was right for you is not necessarily right for me. I've a family that loves me, a good roof over my head and a useful purpose to my life. Why should I wish to clutter that with a husband?"

"Oh, Bethany, that's what every unattached woman says until she finds her love," Cassia said with a dramatic sigh. "What if it's a gentleman who can offer you a more agreeable roof?"

Pointedly Bethany glanced about at the crowds of gentlemen around them, men that, to her mind, had far more money and rank than they had wit or conscience. "I'm hardly a fortune-hunter, Cassia. Mind how you wed Richard in spite of his estate, not because of it."

"Then why won't you? He could just as well be a poor man as a rich one, if he can share your heart," Cassia said. "Why don't you want the happiness and joy that comes with love? You, being you, will think you're above love, beyond men, until some fine fellow appears to sweep your heart away. Unless, that is, he already has."

"Oh, yes, up he popped like a weed in the garden, right beneath my nose."

"Perhaps." Cassia tipped her head slyly to one side, the ribbons in her hair curling over her cheek. "*I* know why you were so late coming upstairs. It was a gentleman that kept you, wasn't it?"

"Wherever did you get such a notion, Cassia?" Bethany tried to sound indignant, even as she remembered the pale-eyed man's face. "I was serving supper to my little flock, which you know perfectly well."

"But I heard that today your flock included a certain tall and handsome ram." Cassia's blue eyes sparked with impish glee. "You can't deny it, Betts. The staff is chattering of nothing else. They say this man waited until everyone else in line had gone ahead, just to speak to you."

"He was only another unfortunate, Cassia," Bethany said as firmly as she could, "another poor soldier who lost a share of his wits in battle. He waited to speak to me, yes, but what he then said made no sense."

"That's not what the servants were whispering." Cassia wasn't ready to give up. "They said he was dressed poor, yes, but that he spoke like a gentleman, an officer, and that he—"

"Please, Cassia, don't," Bethany said softly. "It's only because it's your wedding day that you've turned matchmaker. Love has no place in my life, not now. That poor man deserved my compassion and my assistance, if I could give it, but nothing else."

She squeezed Cassia's hand, then began to turn away. "Have you seen Amariah? I should—"

But Cassia caught her arm to draw her back. "Do you believe that with your heart?" she asked, searching Bethany's face. "The truth, now, Betts, and don't pretend otherwise."

The truth. Bethany's face grew warm as she thought again of the man who'd asked for—nay, demanded—the same from her. She tried not to think of how broad his shoulders had been as he'd stood before her, or how adversity had only made his features more defined, more masculine, or how his gaze had been enough to unsettle her so. He'd more presence than the entire lot of gentlemen in these rooms. The servants' gossip had been right: once he must have been an officer, a leader, a man with power, to have caught such a hold on her imagination.

But that was all, wasn't it? Wasn't it?

"The truth, Bethany," Cassia whispered. "Tell me, and I'll never ask you again."

Bethany took a deep breath. "I am content as I am, Cassia, on my own," she said. "And that, so help me, is the truth."

Chapter Three

William sat in his usual chair near the front window of the Gold Lion, a chop on his plate and a tankard of ale at his hand. The Lion was crowded, the way it was most nights, the watermen from the Whitehall steps and the workers from the docks adding to the blue-grey haze of tobacco smoke and raucous laughter. But still no one dared join William at his table, nor was his prime chair by the window ever challenged. No one ever did. Without saying a word, William had long ago made it clear that he liked his solitude, if not his own company, and by God, he'd earned both.

He ate with the common broadsheet folded on the table beside him, and pretended to read while he listened to the conversations swirling around him. Any word could be the clue he might need. But tonight there was nothing new, nothing useful, only the same ancient indignities and boasting and ill-treatment by women, and with a sigh, he finally tossed his coins to the keeper and pushed his way back into the street.

The lanterns were lit now, the long summer day done and the blurred sliver of a moon rising through the clouds over the chimney pots and roofs. But William's thoughts were still too unsettled to head for home, so he turned his steps slowly toward the river. In the shadow of the abbey, Westminster Bridge was nearly quiet now, the wagons and drays gone for the night. The air felt heavy and damp: rain tomorrow, in from the east.

At the center of the span, William rested his arms on the rail to ease the weight from his leg, and stared down at the water running beneath him. Though the stench of the Thames could clear anyone's head, it was in the ever-shifting patterns of the currents that he could usually find some manner of peace.

Yet tonight was different. Tonight when William stared down at the dappled water, he saw only the face of Bethany Penny, as changeable and perplexing as the quicksilver river itself.

He had gone to St. James's Street with her as one of his most likely suspects. A clever woman who knew the intricacies of seasoning a dish would find the leap to poison an easy one, and he knew that any of the dead men could have eaten their last meals in the yard at Penny House. He'd imagined how she'd look, too, a hard, chilly beauty without a soul or a conscience, the kind of woman who mined the pockets of hapless rich and idle fools.

Then she'd come to her kitchen door, a homespun apron over her Bond Street gown and her cheeks flushed from the kitchen fires, and every wrong notion he'd formed of her scattered to the winds.

She was young, impossibly young for such responsibility, her round face still fresh with the glow of a country childhood and her copper-colored hair soft around her face like sunshine itself. The elegant carriage that he'd first noted from a distance softened into a self-assured ease at closer range, the confidence that came more from talent than appearances. He'd recognized that at once: she ruled her kitchen and staff with the same sure touch that every good officer had, efficient but without bullying.

But the real proof of her beauty had come in a kindness too sincere, too genuine, for even the most accomplished actress to feign. She could deny it all she wished, but there it had been. If William hadn't witnessed her actions for himself, he would never have believed it, and even so he'd still found such unabashed generosity difficult to accept.

Every person who'd come to her step had received the same sunny smile from her to go with their bowl, every ragged child and old man had been treated with the same regard she must show to those others who entered Penny House by the front door. She'd welcomed many by name, and all with a greeting or question that had, for that moment, made each feel special.

When at last it had come to be William's own turn, she'd held steadfast against his questions, deftly defending herself. She'd even tried to include him in that same circle of her smile—a smile he had firmly resisted. She'd been good that way, too, warm and winning, so good that he'd almost weakened and smiled back.

Almost...

But the smile of a pretty woman no longer had any place in William's life, especially not if it hid a darker secret. Trust was a luxury no soldier could afford, not if he wished to live another day. With one taste of that fragrant chicken stew, he could have been the next to die, and as he stared down at the water he saw the faces of his old comrades rise out of the currents as well, finally obliterating the smile of Bethany Penny, until—

There. His wandering thoughts halted at once, his instincts taking over. Without turning, he knew someone was behind him, someone different from the other straggling walkers and mongrel dogs.

Someone who'd come for him.

He tensed in defense, mentally cursing himself for being so careless. Standing as he was, there'd be nothing easier than toppling him over the railing and into the river, one more waterlogged corpse to wash ashore with the dawn.

As slowly as William could, he shifted his weight backward, more onto his legs and away from the railing. He could see no one on either side; the two of them were alone on the bridge. Inside his coat, he carried both a knife and a pistol. Would he have time to reach for either one? Could he still be fast enough to save himself?

He turned his wrist a fraction, just enough so that the brass button on his cuff caught the pale light from the lantern farther down the bridge. The light, and the dark shadow of whoever it was behind him. Not as close as William had thought, but there, inching closer with his hands slightly raised, waiting for his moment.

But William was done with waiting. The French and the Spanish between them hadn't been able to kill him. He'd be damned if he'd let this skulking coward have the honor.

He spun around as quickly as he could on his good leg and grabbed the stranger, locking his arm across the other's man chest. He yanked his knife from the sheath inside his coat and pressed the long blade against the man's throat.

"What do you want, eh?" William demanded hoarsely. "My money? My life? Why have you followed me here?"

The man gurgled with fear, his feet scuffling over the ground. He was larger than William had thought, nearly as large as William himself, and he struggled hard to break free, arching back to avoid the knife.

"Answer me." Breathing hard, William kept the blade

steady, pressing into the man's skin as he fought back. The leverage, the skillful use of force: ah, how readily the old ways came back when he needed them. "Answer me now! What do you want from me?"

"No—nothing," the man gasped, his breath sour with drink and fear. "Nothing!"

William relaxed a fraction, trying to judge if the man could be telling the truth. "Then why not tell me outright? Why creep up behind me in the dark like some damned cutpurse?"

"Mercy, M'Lord Callaway, please! I—I swear it be so!"

William grunted with surprise. There were few people left in London would call him now by name, and fewer who would recognize his face to do so. London: aye, he was in London, not Spain. "You know who I am?"

"You—you was shown to me, at the Gold Lion!" the man gasped. "Mercy on my miserable soul, Major, My Lord, mercy!"

"You deserve nothing from me," snarled William, yet the red clouds of violence were beginning to lift from him. With practiced efficiency, he ran his hand along the man's body and through his pockets, searching for any weapons. When he found nothing, he raised the knife from the man's throat, and dragged him around so they were face-to-face.

The man shuddered, and swallowed again, gingerly feeling his throat as if he expected to find it already slit. He was younger than William had first thought, but his doughy face and unsteady hands were those of a habitual drunkard, the kind of shiftless coward that most disgusted William.

"What else did they tell you at the Lion?" he demanded. "That I carried a sack of coins like a moneylender, enough to keep you in gin for a week, a month, a year? Did they tell you I was a cripple, easy pickings for a man who had the nerve?"

"He told me you was a lord," the man said without answering the question, which was answer enough for William. "He said you was rich, and—and—"

Abruptly the man lunged forward, his arms raised and his fists clenched to knock William down with one last desperate effort.

But William stepped to one side, letting the man stumble and pitch forward, landing hard on the ground. The wind flew from his lungs at the impact, making him writhe and gasp for air, and quickly William knelt beside him, pinning him down with his knee.

"You're a damned bloody coward," he snarled furiously in the man's ear. "You would rob me and kill me and my men for—"

"Here now, what're you two about?" The watchman ran toward them, holding his truncheon high over his head as the light from his lantern bobbed over the pavement. "Back off, I say!"

"You're just in time." Quickly William slipped the knife back beneath his coat and out of the light. He stood, wincing at the strain on his leg. "This bastard meant to kill me."

"Did he, now?" The watchman raised his lantern to squint up at William. "That's not how it looks."

"But that's how it is." William took a deep breath, then another, struggling to regain control. Damnation, how had it come to this again? He could not afford to let his anger get the better of him, to let his temper rule him like a madman from Bedlam. He had to keep it down, keep it down where it belonged. "This man attacked me first. I am Major Lord William Callaway."

"Are you, now." With his truncheon still poised, the watchman looked him up and down, and William knew he was trying to reconcile William's claim with his appearance. A small ring of other passersby had gathered just outside the circle of light, watching and giving their own opinions in muttered whispers. William was used to that sort of judgment by now, but that still didn't make it any easier.

"A soldier would know how to do this to another, wouldn't he?" The watchman lowered his lantern over the other man, and prodded the other him with his toe. "So what tale do you have to tell?"

The man groaned dramatically without answering, aware of his audience.

"He's feigning now, to win your sympathy," William said with disgust. Hell, if only he'd kept his own temper, then the circumstances wouldn't look so damning now. He'd be of no use to anyone if he were hauled off to gaol. "The rascal tried to attack me, then tripped and fell by himself. I didn't have to lay a finger upon him."

"He's yowling, for certain." The watchman looked back at William, and at last lowered his truncheon. "Not a finger, you say?"

"Do you question my word?" Bitterness filled William's voice. He'd done this to himself, tripped and twisted by his temper. "I fought in the Peninsula. I know a hundred ways to kill a man, and I've seen more die than you can count. But I lived, you see. I *lived*."

The watchman's expression turned wary in the lantern's light, as he looked from William to the other man and back again. Finally he nodded, and touched the brim of his hat.

"As you say, Major," he said. "As you say. I'll look after this blackguard for you, so you can be on your way home."

The watchman turned away from William, and toward the other man still lying on the pavement.

But William wasn't ready to be dismissed like this, not by a mere watchman. "I'll swear a complaint against him if you wish, and—"

"Oh, that's not necessary." The watchman had set his

lantern down on the pavement, and was prodding at the other man with his truncheon. "He don't look to be much trouble."

"But if I can—"

"No, no, m'lord." He smiled, and William heard the shift in his voice, slight, but unmistakable, with the kind of emphasis on his title that reduced it to a shared jest. "But you take care on your way home, mind? Some nights these streets don't be fit for dogs, m'lord, let alone a gentleman like yourself."

"Damnation, I don't need—"

"'Course you don't, m'lord," the watchman said with maddening patience, not above playing to the audience, too. "But if you have a wife or daughter I could call to come fetch you, why, then I'd—"

"To hell with your fetching," William snarled. "To hell with everything."

He forced himself to turn from the watchman, forced himself to place one foot after the other, step by step by step, across the bridge, past the old Abbey and away from the wrongheaded anger that once again had flared too fast, too hot, for any sensible man.

But he'd heard it there in the watchman's voice, seen in his eyes by the wobbling light of his lantern and on the faces of the others who'd stood and gawked.

Pity.

They'd thought he was mad, or drunk, or maybe both. They'd thought he needed to be indulged and looked after, and taken from the streets where he might be a danger to himself and others. They'd thought he *was* the miserable beggar he pretended to be, overwhelmed by the horror of his memory and stripped of his dignity, and fit only to be tended by dutiful women.

That was how it had been when they'd shipped him

back home. Neither his mother nor his sisters had been at his bedside, nor had he expected it. No peeress would perform such sordid duty, especially not for a younger son like him. Even if they'd been willing, Father would never have permitted it.

Instead grim-faced women brought from Edinburgh had tended to him, the best nurses his father's money could buy and the ones whose faces had haunted him throughout his fevers and pain. No wonder, not when they had been the ones who'd held him down on the bed while the London physicians had tried to repair his shattered leg.

He looked down at the worn toes of his boots as they trudged the filth-covered cobblestones, at the way his limp had worn the leather sole unevenly, the way it would for the rest of his life. If his company had been ambushed any closer to the front and the field hospitals, then the surgeons there would simply have amputated his leg altogether. He should be grateful for what he had, instead of lamenting what he'd lost. No soldier had any right to expect more.

But tonight his thoughts kept wandering down another, more confusing, path. What if he'd been nursed with kindness and devotion instead of duty? What if the woman bending over his bed to wipe his brow had smiled like sunshine, and whispered words of compassion and encouragement?

What if she'd been Bethany Penny?

Pity, that's what he would have had, pity piled high and served to him on a battered tin plate at the kitchen door. Nothing would have changed. Nothing would be different, and he was the greatest fool in the kingdom for dreaming otherwise.

He wanted justice, not pity. He pulled the brim of his hat lower over his face and dug his hands deep into the pockets of his coat, and turned down the darker street.

Justice, not pity: what he wanted, what he needed and all he deserved.

* * *

With a dish of pekoe tea balanced in her fingertips, Bethany stood before the window of their upstairs private parlor and gazed out at the falling rain. She and Amariah had agreed to keep the club closed for another day, to give the staff a day to recover after the wedding, and now at midmorning, the large house felt oddly silent around her. The last of the guests had not left until three, and Bethany knew that if she had any sense, she would still be asleep in her bed now.

But habit was stronger than sense, and because on every other day she would have risen early to go to the market stalls at Covent Garden, she'd wakened at her usual time, just before dawn. Although she had tried to use the extra time wisely, her mind was still too weary from yesterday's excitement, and watching the fat raindrops sliding down the glass seemed all she was fit to do.

Summer rain was not so bad as winter snow, but still she worried about the people in her flock, especially those who were very young or very old. Most would take cover wherever they could, of course, or simply ignore it and go about their usual day, letting the damp settle into ague and chills. If she could rouse any footmen, she'd have them rig the sheets of canvas across the yard to serve as makeshift shelter, though she knew the crowd would be half because of the weather. She watched the rain beat against the glass, thinking.

Would the grey-eyed man be among her flock again? So many came once, and never returned. Was he gone now, too, or would he come back to ask again for truth instead of food? Would he—

"I thought I smelled breakfast." Amariah yawned, tying the sash around her flowered silk wrapper as she joined Bethany. She paused at the table, raising the lid on the covered dish to peek inside. "What is this, Betts? Grilled onions beside the eggs?"

"Shallots, with a scattering of snipped herbs." Bethany set her tea on the table. "They were left from yesterday, but I thought they'd suit the eggs. Now that you're awake, I'll toast you a muffin or two here over the fire, and—"

"You'll do nothing of the sort." Amariah took her by the arm and gently pressed her down into one of the chairs. "Recall that today is to be our day of rest, and most deserved it is, too. Running down and back up three flights of stairs to toast me a muffin does not qualify as rest, not even for you."

"I wouldn't have to go clear to the kitchen. I brought the pans from there, yes, and the eggs and such, but I've prepared everything here, on the parlor fire." Bethany tried to wriggle free of her sister's hand. "It's no trouble at all. You must eat, and I must cook, and that's an end to it."

"Not today, it isn't," her sister said firmly. "Here, let me freshen your tea. You've already done more than enough with eggs and shallots already, and *that* should be the end to it."

Bethany sighed impatiently, her hands clasped in her lap as she watched her sister pour tea from the little pot painted with irises. "I can't help it if I woke as usual, Amariah, nor is it in my nature to be idle. I've done a few small tasks to fill the time, that is all."

"Small, ha." Amariah flipped her long braid over one shoulder and reached for one of the oranges, piled in a silver bowl. "Your few small tasks would fair exhaust Hercules himself."

"They *were* small," Bethany protested. "I prepared the club's menus for the next week and I reviewed the bills for Pratt to have paid."

Amariah's expression remained skeptical as she worked

her thumb inside the orange's skin, freeing the peel from the fruit. "That is all?"

"Most all." Bethany wished the grey-eyed man who'd questioned her truthfulness could see her now, unable to hedge even on such a trivial question. "I began to work my way through that new cookery book that Mr. Sillinger brought back to us as a souvenir from Rome. Many of the words were similar to Latin, or even to English, and if I glossed them against Father's old dictionary, I was able to make translations of the first recipes for made dishes, and if—"

"Oh, Bethany, that is exactly, *exactly* what I mean!" Amariah cried with indulgent exasperation. "Father raised us to be industrious, but he also wished us to lift our noses from the grindstone long enough to enjoy what else life has to offer. Consider how much you missed of Cassia's wedding feast yesterday, hiding yourself away in the kitchen below stairs."

"I wasn't hiding," Bethany protested. "I was needed there. How else was that grand wedding feast to appear? From beneath a cabbage leaf?"

"That is what that staff of yours is for, Bethany." Amariah frowned, pulling the first segment of the orange free. "Each of us worked hard to make Cassia's wedding a success, but by evening most of the toil should have been done. Surely you could have been spared earlier to come join the company upstairs."

Bethany frowned down at her tea, running her fingertip lightly around the rim of the saucer as she remembered the crush of guests last night, the heat and the noise of so many raised male voices enough to make her head spin. "I'm not like you and Cassia. I don't enjoy company."

"You never stay long enough to give any of the gentlemen a chance to be agreeable," Amariah said. "Most of them can be quite amusing, while others are every bit as shy as you are. You know Lord Harleigh was asking after you again."

"Oh, Lord Harleigh." Bethany wrinkled her nose with distaste. "Lord Harleigh's only met me once, no matter what gibberish he tells you. He wants a cook, and hopes to acquire one on the cheap by asking for my hand."

"I've no wish to find a replacement for you here at Penny House, either." Amariah pulled another segment of the orange free, licking the juice from her fingers. "But there's nothing wrong with a gentleman appreciating your talents as well as your beauty."

"Father left us Penny House so we could help others, not find rich husbands!"

"I haven't exactly forgotten, Betts." Amariah smiled. "We were to be his lady Robin Hoods, taking from the too-full pockets of the rich to help those less fortunate in any way we could. What other father but ours would concoct such a legacy?"

"What other daughters but us would accept it?" Bethany's smile was bittersweet. Not even a year had passed since Father's sudden death, pulling weeds in the kitchen garden behind the rectory in Woodbury, and the grief had struck them hard. But the shock of his loss had proved to be more of a beginning than an end, exactly the way that Father, being Father, must have planned.

"What others, indeed?" Amariah sighed, not bothering to hide her sorrow. "But since Cassia and Richard found one another, I've begun to think that Father had an even grander design for us. As much as he wished us to do good in the world, he also wanted us to be happy, as happy as he was with Mama."

"Of course he did," Bethany said indignantly. "But I do not see how that gives you the right to play the matchmaker for me."

"I've no desire to make any matches for you or anyone else," Amariah said, jabbing a piece of orange at Bethany for emphasis. "Overseeing the faro table alone takes more energy than that. But I do believe now that Father forced us to move from Woodbury to London so we would be able to widen our acquaintance among marriageable gentlemen. He wished us to find love, lasting love, with the proper gentlemen to bring us happiness. And that includes you, too, Bethany Penny."

"But *not* with that dreadful Lord Harleigh." Bethany flushed, and pushed back her chair to stand. She hadn't realized how different things would be between her and Amariah once Cassia was gone. Now there was only big sister Amariah and little sister Bethany. The whole give-and-take of their relationship felt changed and turned about, and not necessarily for the better.

"You are *so* matchmaking, Amariah," she said, "and if you think for a moment that I have nothing better to do than to—"

"Than to scrub pans and chop onions?" asked Amariah, unperturbed. "Rain or not, I'm going to take you out to the shops today, Bethany. Clearly the only way I can take your mind from the kitchen is to remove you from it by force. We'll make a day of it, just the two of us."

"But I can't," Bethany protested. "My flock will be waiting."

Amariah bit the last of her orange, wiping her fingers on her napkin. "I thought we'd decided weeks ago that Penny House would be shut today. I thought we agreed that the staff—and we—needed a day of rest after the wedding."

"We agreed to keep the gaming rooms dark, yes," Bethany said, "but I never said I would shut my kitchen door to those in need."

Amariah looked up, clearly surprised that she would

challenge her like this. "Bethany, please, if you will only consider—"

"No." Urgency made Bethany lean toward her sister, her palms flat on the table between them. "The members of Penny House will dine elsewhere, or go to the theatre, or even, Heaven forbid, stay home with their families in their grand houses for the evening. But my stews and apples are all the food many of my poor people will have in a day. If I go with you to the shops, then they must go hungry. And the kitchen staff will still have their day. My flock will be small today on account of the weather, so I can do everything myself."

"Oh, Bethany." Amariah reached out and rested her hand over her sister's. "When Father wished us to do good in the world, he never intended for us to try to save *all* of it by ourselves."

Bethany slipped her hand free. "I'm not trying to save the whole world, Amariah, or even all of London. Just my hungry little scrap of it."

Amariah sighed, and shook her head. "I had hoped to save this conversation for tomorrow, but it seems you're determined not to have a day of rest. Pratt has told me things that—"

"Oh, no, not again!" Bethany folded her arms defensively over her chest. "First Cassia, and now you, too! What sort of tattle did he bring to you? What nonsense did he tell you of that poor man yesterday?"

"What man?" asked Amariah, her face such perfect surprised innocence that Bethany realized she'd blundered. "Whatever are you talking about?"

"A man who was at the door yesterday," she said hurriedly, turning away so her face wouldn't betray—well, betray whatever she didn't want it to betray. "It doesn't signify at all. The poor fellow seemed different from the usual men—his speech was more suited to one of your gentlemen at the gaming tables than mine in the yard—and because he waited to speak with me after the others had left, the servants were all a-flutter. I vow it must have been the wedding that made them see intrigue and assignations where there were none."

"What did this man want from you?" Amariah's voice was more curious than judgmental. "Did he ask you for money?"

"Nothing as rational as that," Bethany said with a dramatic sigh, shoving the memory of the man out of her mind. "Instead he kept asking me over and over for the truth, as if it were something I kept in a cupboard. Most likely he'll never return. That is the way with so many of them."

"It could be for the best as well," Amariah said. "I know we've come far and fast from our old cottage in Woodbury, yet we're still not as clever in worldly ways as we might wish. I don't wish to frighten you, Betts, but you must begin to be more careful with those you feed—your flock. Pratt has told me that there have been several unhappy murders connected to charity houses."

"Deaths?" repeated Bethany with concern, not surprise. "Was it fighting, then? I have heard that several of the charities in Seven Dials can be—"

"Not fighting, no," Amariah said carefully. "Those who died had been poisoned, dead from a poison buried in the food they received."

"I cannot believe that!" Shocked, Bethany turned back to face her sister. "My work, what I do, is a way of giving life, not taking it! To steal the trust of some poor soul and murder them instead of offering the sustenance they expect—why, that is the worst, the very worst, sort of villainy!"

"But it is true," Amariah insisted. "And there is no telling when or how such a villain might act again. We must take care, Bethany. Your safety comes first, of course, but we must also guard the reputation of Penny House against scandal, so that—"

Bethany shook her head, reaching around behind her waist to tie her apron strings more tightly with short, sharp motions. "I'm not going to stop, Amariah. My flock needs to know there's a safe place for them."

"Only for a little while, Betts." Amariah wasn't pleading, or even asking, but stating a fact, as if it had already been decided. "A fortnight or so, until the magistrates can find the culprit."

"How hard will the magistrates be searching, when the victims had no name nor station in life?" Bethany demanded. "The death of a poor man or woman signifies nothing to this city."

Amariah tapped her fingers on the table with impatience. "Meaning you now would like to serve as magistrate, too?"

"Meaning *you* would rather us be cowards, and let yourself be intimidated by the cruel actions of another." Bethany's voice warmed with anger. "Meaning you would rather hide away and do nothing, than offer a haven to those who have no such choices. That is not what Father would do, Amariah. You know he wouldn't."

Now Amariah was standing, too, there on the far side of the table with a teaspoon pinched incongruously in her fingers.

"Father would not want you or your kitchen slandered," she said with maddening conviction, "just as I don't want anyone here at Penny House to be put at risk."

"Father would never be so—so *suspicious,* Amariah." With both hands, Bethany shoved her chair back under the table. "Especially not of those who most need our help."

"Bethany, please, I only—"

But Bethany was already on the stairs, her skirts bunched

to one side in her hand and the heels of her mules clicking on the bare wood as she fled. For once *she'd* have the last word, and besides, she was so angry right now whatever word she said to her sister would be one she'd later regret. But when had Amariah become so uncaring, so much more concerned for the welfare of the wealthy, overfed gentlemen of the club? Since when had she become so—so *complacent* about the suffering of others?

She stormed into the empty kitchen, muttering to herself to help fill the silence. She put fresh kindling on the banked fire and fanned the embers to bring it back to life. The wood began to crackle and pop, matching the staccato of the rain splattering against the windows, and Bethany turned to the cupboards, drawing out bowls and pans with the leavings from yesterday's feast. As usual with the upstairs meals, the guests had drunk more than they'd eaten, and there was plenty left to inspire her. Savory pies, she decided. A treat for her flock, and easier for her to manage on her own than a large, heavy kettle of stew or soup.

With brisk efficiency, she began stripping the meat from the goose carcass and then the ham. She tossed the scraps together on a large board and chopped them into a fine mince. In her hands the large kitchen knife had the same kind of elegance of motion that a swordsman had with his saber, the blade's rhythm calming her, settling her. By the time she'd turned to the onions, she was humming in time to her work. Amariah could talk all she wanted about time away; *this* was where she belonged, and where she always found her peace.

She was so preoccupied that she didn't hear the first knock at the door behind her, nor even the second. Not until she turned with a bowlful of chopped onions to put on the fire did she see the shadowy movement on the other side of the glass. She gasped, and dropped the wooden bowl back on the table with a clatter. Swiftly she seized the long-bladed kitchen knife and turned back toward the door, her heart pounding and her sister's warnings fresh in her ears.

"Who goes there?" she called out through the bolted door as the stranger knocked again. "What do you want?"

The stranger moved closer to the glass, his features now coming into focus: broad shoulders, dark hair beneath the wide-brimmed hat, and the pale eyes she'd never forget.

"It's me, Miss Penny," he said, barely raising his voice at all. "And all I want is to see you."

Chapter Four

William had come to Penny House early, telling himself that he would have a better chance of finding Bethany Penny less busy and more willing to talk. He'd told himself that all he wanted was to ask her about the poisonings, ask her about his men, and nothing more. He'd told himself exactly that, as if the telling could make it so, as if he hadn't sat awake long into the night thinking of how closely her bright blue gown had fitted her body, how she'd moved with both purpose and grace, how her eyes had flashed blue fire at him when he'd challenged her, how such beauty couldn't possibly mask the soulless chill of a murderer.

But most of all, he'd thought—selfishly, shamefully—of how soon he could see her again.

Now water streamed from his hat as if the brim were a rainspout, and though he'd turned the collar of his greatcoat up against his neck, still the raindrops slipped inside, soaking the back of his shirt like a chilly hand on nape.

Once again, he rapped his knuckles on her kitchen door.

"I give you my word that I mean you no harm, Miss Penny," he said to the heavy wood, and with luck to her as well. "I'm as wet as a toothless old dog that's fallen in the river, and no more dangerous."

"More like a wolf, prowling through the rain." Her voice was muffled, wary. "You're too early for supper by hours."

"But not too early for you," he countered, "and that is why I'm here. My word of honor that I mean no harm, Miss Penny, my word as an officer of the king."

She didn't answer, and he squinted through the rain-streaked glass of the sidelights, trying to see her response inside the murky kitchen.

"Is that what you were?" she asked at last. "An officer in the army?"

"I still am, lass, so long as I'm on this earth," he said softly, so softly that he wondered if she'd even hear. "Even under it, when it's my time."

"You are not like any king's officer I have ever met."

That made him smile. "I did not realize your acquaintance was so vast among military men. That is not the reputation of Penny House."

"No, it is not," she said, the tartness of her words slicing through the oak panels. "We prefer wastrel lords with deep pockets in place of a conscience, and younger sons intent on burning through their inheritance as fast as they can."

"So there are limits to Miss Penny's famed generosity." Better not to let her know that he could qualify in either of those categories. "Who would have thought the hospitality of Penny House was so mercenary?"

"The club is a business like any other," she said. "The difference is that what comes in the front door helps support those who wait at the back."

Before he answered, she'd drawn the bolt on the door with a metallic scrape, and opened the door, standing back to let him enter.

"Five minutes, that is all," she warned. "I've too much work to squander more."

He paused in the doorway, surprised. "You shouldn't let me in. You don't know anything about me."

"I'm proving my sister wrong."

"What if she's right about me?"

"I don't believe she is, which is why I'm going to trust you this far," she said. "And I'll have you know that the footman and the butler should be returning here from the wine cellar at any moment, so do not consider taking any advantages."

She was lying. He'd looked in the other window before he'd knocked, and there'd been no servants anywhere in sight. Not that he'd been considering any of that advantage-taking, especially not with her brandishing that kitchen knife big enough to slaughter an ox.

"Thank you," he said, always the safest answer. He stepped inside and shook the rain from his hat before he hooked it on the back of a nearby chair. "Five minutes, no more. And you can put down the knife, if you wish."

"I don't." She smiled, but the way she tightened her grip on the horn hilt told him she'd have no compunctions about using the knife to carve him as neatly as any goose. "And I won't."

"How charming." She was wearing some sort of soft green gown that clung to her body in all the most interesting places, and made her blue eyes brighter, even on this drab, grey day.

"I'm not trying to be charming, sir," she said. "And you're wasting your five minutes. If you've something to say, pray, say it."

"I will." He opened the front of his greatcoat, drew out his own knife, and tossed it onto the table beside them. "There. If my word isn't enough, then I'll disarm myself, so you will do the same."

Her eyes widened with surprise as she looked down at his knife. He hoped she realized that he was every bit as skilled with it as she was with hers—something he had to admit he'd never considered about any other woman as beguiling as this one.

"Have you a pistol, too?" she asked, the tremble in her voice betraying the bravado of her question. "Or is the knife the sum of your weaponry?"

"A good knife is all one needs," he said. "In the right hands."

"That is true." She glanced down at her own knife, then laid its blade across William's. "There. Now speak."

For the first time he smiled. He liked Miss Bethany Penny, liked her far more than he should. "You're a brave woman."

"Or a very foolish one." She folded her arms and tucked her hands beneath her armpits, unaware of the lush display her raised breasts presented. "I won't ask you who you really are, not only because that would be extraordinarily rude of me, but also because I respect the secrets of those who come here. But you are a puzzle, sir, a puzzle. You claim you are an officer, but you dress yourself like the shabbiest of costermongers in Green Park."

He ran his hand lightly down the front of his worn linen waistcoat. "Not everyone can be attended by doting servants, Miss Penny."

"Nor does everyone who could choose to." The blue of her eyes seemed to intensify as she studied him. "Your coat has holes and missing buttons, yet your hands and hair are clean and neat, and your jaw fresh-shaven. You stand in line for food, but take none for yourself, and your manner of speaking—why, your accent would be perfectly at ease among the dukes at our faro table upstairs instead of here among those without a farthing to their name."

She frowned a bit, her eyes narrowing as she continued her catalogue. "There is also a fresh bruise above your brow that wasn't there yesterday. You might simply have struck your head on, say, an inconvenient branch."

"An appropriate guess," he said cautiously. He must listen to her, *listen,* and not let himself be distracted by that soft green fabric pulling across her breasts.

"Appropriate, yes," she continued. "But the knuckles on your right hand are also grazed and swollen, which, in conjunction with the bruise, makes me conclude the culprits for those injuries were more likely another man's fist and jaw respectively than a branch."

She flashed a small smile of triumph, clearly expecting him to smile in return.

He didn't. "You are observant, Miss Penny." Observant, and clever and too damned inquisitive. Did she really expect him to confess he'd been brawling last night in the middle of Westminster Bridge?

"My father always said to judge a man not by what he says, but what he does, and what he shows of himself," she said. "Would you like a dish of tea?"

Surprised again, he cocked one brow. "What became of my five minutes?"

"More of my foolishness, I suppose." She turned her back to him, wrapping a cloth around the hot handle of the kettle as she swung it from the fire. With her hair pinned in a loose knot at the back of her head, he had a clear view of the nape of her neck, creamy pale and impossibly vulnerable.

How had he forgotten how complicated a woman's body could be, how much temptation could be found in even the slightest, sensuous curve?

"Sit here, if you please." She pointed to a massive oak armchair at the head of the table where the servants must eat. "You can be Mr. Pratt for now."

"Being William Callaway is more than enough."

She didn't turn. "So that is your name, Mr. Callaway?"

"So my parents told me." Even without the title and rank, his name sounded odd said in her voice, as if it really did belong to someone else. A damned shame it didn't, really. He crossed the room to the chair slowly, taking his time so his limp would be less pronounced. "You shouldn't have turned away from me like that."

"How else was I to fetch the kettle?" Finally she looked up at him, her smile reaching clear to her eyes, and he felt something lurch inside.

"It wasn't wise," he said, wanting to make her understand. "If I had wanted to harm you—if I'd been carrying a second knife—then that would have been the moment to use it. You wouldn't have had a chance."

"Perhaps not." She set a cup and saucer before him and filled it, the sweet-smelling steam rising in a curling plume. "But my father also taught me to trust others when I believed they merit it. Would you like sugar or cream, Mr. Callaway?"

"I have earned your trust?" He set his palms flat on the table on either side of the teacup, frowning a bit as he wondered if he were the one who was trusting too much. "What have I done of such an honor from—"

"Oh—*oh!*" Abruptly she reached out and pulled the dish away from him, splattering tea across the table. Her confidence had vanished, her speech rapid and rattled. "You think I mean to poison you, don't you, Mr. Callaway? You won't drink the tea because you think you'll die as those other poor men did? Oh, *what* was I thinking?"

William went very still. "What do you know of this?"

"I know that to take another's life is the greatest sin possible." Rapidly she fanned her fingers through the air, trying to cool her knuckles where the hot tea had splattered onto them. "But what to me is even worse is how it was done, poisoning food that had been accepted as a gift, with thanks and trust. And I know that I could never—*never*—do such a wicked thing."

Swiftly she poured a measure of William's tea into the saucer, raised it with both hands, and drank, emptying the saucer. She set it back down with a clatter of porcelain and another little gasp.

"There," she said, her voice as defiant as her eyes. "I've burned my tongue, but I have also proved that you've nothing to fear from me."

Silently he reached across the table for the cup, and refilled the saucer. With the fragile porcelain balanced between his fingers, he carefully turned the saucer so that the edge that had touched her lips now touched his.

He knew she was watching, just as he knew she understood what he was doing. She had to. Despite those wide blue eyes, she was an owner of this place, a worldly woman who likely saw more wickedness in a single night than most other ladies of her breeding saw in a lifetime. And he knew what he was doing, too: a challenge, that's what it was, a challenge between the two of them.

The tea was hot in his mouth; no wonder she'd burned herself. He let it slide over his tongue and down his throat to warm him inside. Lip to lip through the porcelain, as close as they could ever be. He'd done it to rattle her, to dare her, yet here he was feeling a connection he'd never anticipated. He sipped, and swallowed, and could not make himself break his gaze with hers.

"There," he said, setting the empty saucer back down. "Now you can trust me in return."

She flushed, finally looking away from him. She turned for the teapot, busying herself to fill the space yawning between them, and refilled his cup and a second cup for herself. She set his before him, then sat in the chair across from his with her own cup before at last she had composed herself enough to meet his eye again.

"If I didn't trust you already, Mr. Callaway," she said with surprising evenness, "you would not be here at my table."

He cleared his throat, though it didn't need clearing. "Is that more of your father's judgment?"

"Perhaps." She tapped one fingernail against the side of her teacup, a tiny, echoing *ping.* "But you didn't come here to speak of my father, did you?"

Why the devil did he need to be reminded of his own duty? And what was it about her that could make him forget?

"Last night I was told that Tom Parker ate his final meal here."

She gasped, shocked, and thumped her fist hard on the table between them. "That is an outright lie, sir, and whoever told you that should be ashamed, and horsewhipped, too!"

Part of him wanted to smile at that, remembering how close he'd come to the spirit of horsewhipping. "He may well have been both," he said. "What is your side of the tale? What do you know of the men who were murdered?"

"Only what I said before, that they were poisoned by charity food, and that that man did *not* eat here." Her nostrils flaring with agitation, she smoothed a loose strand of her hair back behind one ear. "My sister told me this morning, not an hour ago. She wishes me to stop feeding my flock for the next fortnight or so, until the murderer is caught."

He nodded; this much must be true, for there was no reason for it to be otherwise. "Your sister fears the constables will suspect you?"

"My sister fears for the reputation of Penny House." She rested her elbows on the table, leaning toward him. "The food that's cooked for charity and that for the gentlemen upstairs comes through this same kitchen. A death in either quarter would scatter our membership and destroy the club."

"To hell with the *club.*" His throat felt raw in a way that no tea could ever soothe. "I knew the men who died."

"I'm sorry," she said swiftly. "Oh, I am so sorry!"

He looked down at the tea in the dish before him, avoiding the pity he knew would be on her face. He wished he still wore his hat, to keep beneath the shelter of its brim. "They were good, brave men who had defended their country with honor and regard. They did not deserve to die like that."

"You served with them, Mr. Callaway?" she asked, her voice as gentle as a lamb. "They were your comrades in battle?"

"They were my men," he said hoarsely. "They did not fail me when I needed them most, and by God, I will not fail them now."

Her hand covered his without a word spoken, her fingers small but strong, her palm warm, her touch full of the same gentleness he'd heard in her voice, now laced with shared sorrow.

He jerked his hand free of hers as if pulling it from an open fire. He shoved his chair from the table and rose, grabbing his hat and then his knife, sliding it back into the sheath at his waist.

"I must go," he said, his words strained and harsh as he lurched toward the door. "I have stayed too long."

She stood, too, rushing around the table after him. "You came here because you thought I'd done this—this horrible act. That was the truth you were seeking yesterday, wasn't it? To learn if I were the one who'd poisoned your men?"

The truth, the damned *truth* about everything, pressing on him, an inescapable weight that seemed determined to crush him if he did not flee.

"Let me help you find who did this," she said, almost pleading. "I can help you, I know, if only you'll let me work with—"

"No." He kept his back to her, afraid his resolve would falter if he saw her again, and reached for the latch on the door. "Not you, not anyone else."

He could hear the *shush* of her skirts, the *click* of her heels on the stone floor. "But what if I do learn something? How can I find you again?"

"You won't," he said. "You can't."

He threw open the door, and at once the chill drops pelted against his face and hands. He yanked the brim of his hat lower and plunged back into the rain, away from the comfortable warmth of the fire, away from the hot tea, away from the dry, sweet-smelling kitchen.

Away from the truth, and away from her.

The next morning, Bethany climbed from the hansom cab, and hooked one of the large baskets of fruit and vegetables over each arm. She'd sent the rest of her purchases from the market back to Penny House with Letty and one of the kitchen boys, but the provisions in these baskets were reserved for another purpose. William Callaway might want no help from her, but he couldn't stop her from acting on her own.

Watching her from the cab's box, the driver tucked her fare into his waistcoat. "Are you certain you've got the right place, miss?"

"Oh, yes," Bethany said cheerfully, looking back up at him silhouetted against the flat grey sky. "This is St. Andrew's. I know it well."

But the expression on the driver's face said infinitely more. This small parish church had been old when King Henry had sat the throne, and the time since then had not been kind. Never grand, the church was now worn and shabby as well as humble, the carvings along its front broken off and shutters closed to guard what remained of its leaded windows. Grimy pigeons huddled along the edge of the porch, while a man still lost in last night's drink sprawled snoring on the worn steps, his ragged clothes stained with vomit.

No one noticed. St. Andrew's decline had mirrored the parish it served, and Bethany knew that such sights were more common than not. Now there were more low taverns and rumshops than all other trades combined, and once-respectable homes had been broken down into dank, overcrowded rooming houses. Despair and drunkenness were as much a part of this street as chamberpots emptied into standing puddles of filth, and as much at odds with Bethany's well-bred demeanor and neat, fashionable clothes. No wonder the cab's driver was confused.

"I thank you for your concern," she said, hoisting one basket a little higher against her shoulder, "but I shall be quite safe. I am a friend of the minister of this parish and his wife, and have visited here often."

"Very well, miss. If you are content, then so am I. Good day, miss." Clearly relieved to be dismissed, the driver touched the front of his cap and flicked his whip over his horse's back.

With brisk purpose, Bethany made her way around the back of the church, to the door of the parish house, and knocked. The older woman who answered was somberly dressed, her grey hair sleeked back beneath a plain white cap and her face lined with weary tension.

"Miss Penny, good day," she said, giving Bethany a quick embrace. "How comforting it is to see friends in such times of trial!"

"What trial, Mrs. Barney?" Bethany set her baskets

down on the bench in the hallway while the minister's wife shut the door. "Surely St. Andrew's has not been affected by these dreadful poisonings?"

"So you have heard?" Mrs. Barney sighed her sorrow, clasping her hands before her. "We are such a small parish kitchen, yet still we do good to the people we help. And then to have such a thing happen here!"

Bethany caught her breath. "The magistrates have not dared accuse you or Mr. Barney of any wrongdoing, have they?"

"No, no." She sat on the bench beyond the baskets, and patted the seat beside her for Bethany to join her. "There is no proof to link us to the death, nor can there be. The dead man did eat here, that is true, but there is no telling what else he might have eaten or drunk after that. Though the poor fellow died in convulsions and in great pain later that night, the constable who was called declared the death to be natural and unremarkable."

Her brows drawn as she listened closely, Bethany came to sit on the edge of the bench. "Then how can you be blamed for a murder that isn't one?"

"It's not the law that charges us, but the people," Mrs. Barney explained, her misery palpable. "The man died in Green Park, struck down on the grass in the center of a gawking crowd that began to whisper of poison even before his soul had left his body, may God have mercy upon him. With each telling, his death grows more grotesque, more horrible. No wonder those we wish to help most now fear us."

Bethany placed her hand over the other woman's. "It's not fair, Mrs. Barney, not at all."

But Mrs. Barney only shook her head. "Rumor and suspicion are hard foes, Miss Penny. Not one child has come to my little school since this happened. Not one woman or man has come for my suppers. Even the church itself was empty on Sunday, without a single soul there to worship with Mr. Barney. I've heard it's been the same at every other place where there's been a poisoning, and even some that haven't. I know this must be God's special way of testing our faith, but if this continues, I can only imagine what the bishop will say."

"I am sorry," Bethany said softly, longing to say something more that could bring real comfort. "Most sorry. But surely, something can be done to clear your name and prevent this from happening again."

"I do not wish to counter you, Miss Penny, but what could that something *be?*" The starched ruffled edges on her cap trembled. "This man and the others who have died were poor, without families or friends to cry for their vengeance, or even for justice. Mr. Barney has tried, of course, but no one with the power to help will listen."

At once Bethany thought of William Callaway, and of how sure he'd been that his old comrades had been murdered—so confident that she believed it now, too.

"Then we must do what those powerful men won't," she said, her voice firm with conviction. "If this happens to us all, then there will be no place left for the poor to turn, no place that they feel safe."

"That would be the true tragedy, isn't it?" Mrs. Barney ran her hand across the gleaming red skin of one of the apples that Bethany had brought. "First it was the almshouse near Cornhill, then St. George's near the river and now us. You are most kind to be so generous, but you might as well take it away with you. At least there will be someone at Penny House to eat it, so it will not be wasted."

"No!" Bethany swept to her feet, unable to sit any longer. "I won't let that happen, Mrs. Barney, and neither shall you."

Mrs. Barney raised her hands with hopelessness. "That is very kind of you, Miss Penny, but I told you before that there is nothing to be done."

"There is *always* something to be done," Bethany said with determination. "Tell me everything that you know of the dead man. Did he come here often? Did you know his name? Did he do anything that was remarkable, anything at all, that could be a clue for us?"

"His given name was Jemmy," Mrs. Barney began, though her expression remained more resigned than convinced. "Jemmy Reed. He was still a youngish man, though he'd suffered some sort of terrible injury serving in the army that had wasted his legs. He dragged them, you know, though he was quite clever with his crutches. Miss Penny, I do not see how this can—"

"Had he any special friends?" Bethany asked, undeterred. She thought again of William Callaway, and how this Jemmy's description fit with those of the men he mourned. "Any other man in particular who might know where he went after leaving here?"

Mrs. Barney almost smiled. "Oh, everyone was Jemmy's friend. He was very good at little conjurer's tricks, you know, making walnuts disappear and plucking handkerchiefs from the air. It was how he earned his pittance in the park, and it made him a great favorite with the children. But like most men in this street, he had a weakness for strong drink, and any coin he earned went straight to the barkeep."

Bethany began to pace, thinking. "Could he have left with another who offered him drink?"

"For a fact he did," Mrs. Barney said. "There was a man new to me, a stranger, who'd come right up to Jemmy, talking all about how they'd been together in Spain. Jemmy didn't seem to know him, but he was pleased just the same, the way all the poor old soldiers are, and after they'd had their bowls filled, off they went together."

"Would you recognize the man if you saw him again?"

Mrs. Barney shook her head. "It was odd about that man. He turned his face away and kept his hat pulled low so I never did see him clearly. There was nothing else remarkable to him at all."

"Except that he spoke of Spain," Bethany said, hoping that William could make some sense from that tiny scrap of information. "Do you know which tavern they went to?"

Mrs. Barney pursed her lips with disapproval. "I do not know, Miss Penny, nor would I wish to. Gin and rum are this country's true poisons, and those who sell it are the devil's disciples, not mine. Without them, even poor Jemmy Reed might still be alive."

"He might indeed," Bethany said, her mind already racing ahead. She didn't know the taverns that Jemmy Reed would have patronized any more than Mrs. Barney did. How could she, when the only drinking men she knew were the gentlemen upstairs at Penny House, downing hundred-guinea bottles of smuggled French brandy?

But William Callaway would. He'd know every low, dank place in London that would welcome a man with more thirst than coin, and he'd be eager to go there if it meant he'd be closer to finding Jemmy's murder.

Of course, all she'd have to do was find *him* first.

"I promise to do whatever I can to help, Mrs. Barney," she said, retying the ribbons of her bonnet beneath her chin. "I won't let this sorry business destroy all the good you and Mr. Barney have done."

"Then take care, Miss Penny," Mrs. Barney said, troubled. "I know you go with only the most honorable of intentions, but this city is not the same as your country village. Here you must watch yourself every minute."

"You know I shall, Mrs. Barney." Bethany said, bending to give her cheek a quick kiss of farewell. "Good day to you, and to Mr. Barney, and may God watch over you and your parish, too."

But such optimism was harder to keep glowing outside in the grey, dirty streets that were, as Mrs. Barney had said, so far from Bethany's old home in the green hills of Sussex, much less Penny House's fashionable address off St. James's Square. The drunken man was still sprawled on the steps of the church, though now several small, grimy boys were jeering and tossing pebbles at him to see if he'd wake.

Ahead of her the door to a tavern was already propped open, with several men lolling on the bench outside, and though she crossed the street to avoid them, she couldn't mistake the lascivious invitations they called after her. She *didn't* belong here, no matter how noble her intentions, and the sharp scrutiny of the few other women she passed were as pointed as the men's comments. Her cheeks hot, she walked faster, trying to keep her face impassive.

Last night's rain was threatening to return, the sky growing darker and sudden gusts of wind tumbling old newspapers and other rubbish against Bethany's skirts. With one hand on her hat to keep the brim from blowing back and the other clutching her reticule under her arm, she bowed her head and hurried away from St. Andrew's, toward the busier streets where she could find another cab. She should have thought ahead and asked the earlier driver to wait for her.

"What be your hurry, darling?" The leering red-haired man was suddenly there beside her, his step matching hers and his breath ripe with gin. "Stay, an' have a dram with me, eh?"

Her heart pounding, Bethany ignored him. Only two more blocks to go until she reached the broader thoroughfare, she told herself, only two. But this street had narrowed around them, lined with shuttered warehouses instead of shops or houses, and with rising panic she knew that even if she shouted for help, no help would come. Her steps grew faster until she was nearly trotting.

But the man walked faster, too, edging so close that she could smell the stale filth of his coat. "I told you, darling, no more hurrying. You come with me, and you'll forget everything about where you was going."

He grabbed her arm, jerking her to a stumbling halt, then hooked his arm around her waist to break her fall.

"Let me go!" Bethany cried, struggling and shoving hard against his chest, her reticule swinging from her arm. "Let me go at once!"

But the man only laughed, and yanked her closer. "So that's how you like it, do you? Carroty hair, and a fiery temper? Give me a kiss and let me judge."

"I will *not!*" As she twisted her face away, she saw him raise his hand, ready to strike her. She gasped with sick anticipation and tried one last time to break free even as she braced herself for the blow. God help her, it was nobody's fault but her own and—

"Let her go," ordered another man behind her. "Damnation, let her go *now.*"

Chapter Five

The ginger-haired bastard had the kind of face that William hated most in a man, weak-chinned and bug-eyed and full of mean-spirited bluster, a face that belonged only to bullies and cowards. But to see that face looming over Bethany Penny, intent on harming her, was almost more than William could bear.

He took another step toward the man, barely containing his anger. "Let her go now, you bastard, or you'll answer to me!"

But the man only laughed, jeering at William as Bethany frantically tried to pull free. "Why should I give her up to you? Off with you, you stinking beggar, and leave us in—"

William's fist snapped through the air with practiced efficiency, his knuckles striking the man's jaw in the precise place to silence him. He felt the soft flesh over hard bone, heard the little puff of the man's startled breath, saw his eyes bulge with surprise as the blow lifted him from his feet, just enough, and then slammed him back to the pavement.

The man twitched and twisted, his arms jerking as if pulled by a puppeteer's strings, before, at last, he lay quiet. It was over too fast, too easy, leaving William's fury unspent and his body still tense and coiled, waiting, ready if the man needed more.

What was it in him that made his temper so quick and hot, blinding his senses? What had the war done to him, to make him like this?

"Mr.—Mr. Callaway?"

Blast, how had he forgotten the girl? Her face pale, she stood to one side, gasping for breath while still trying to smooth the tangled ribbons on her bonnet with shaking fingers.

"Are you unharmed, Miss Penny?" He took a deep breath of his own to calm himself, then another, forcing himself to relax. "Did that bast—that rascal hurt you?"

"Oh, no," she said with an admirable effort. He liked a woman who didn't blubber and wail and feel sorry for herself when there was no need. "That is, yes, I am unharmed, but no, he did not hurt me."

"Then come, we must go." He glanced once again at her attacker, now groaning and beginning to twitch. All around them the curious were beginning to peek from their windows and pause in doorways. He couldn't afford to be caught again in such a situation, not after he'd already left another man in a similar state on the bridge two nights past. "Now, Miss Penny. We can't stay here."

"Now?" Surprised, she gulped again. "This isn't our fault! He was the one who seized me!"

"There's always the chance of a difference of opinion," he said, already beginning down the street. "Come *now*, Miss Penny."

"I'm not a pet dog to be summoned, you know," she said tartly. But still she hurried forward, her back as straight as her bonnet brim was bent, passing him with humiliating ease.

Damnation, he should just let her go. Down the street, into a cab, clear to the moon, if she pleased. He'd already been tangled in her life more than he'd ever meant to, even if it was by accident. If he'd any sense at all he'd simply let her go on her way and he'd go his—preferably in opposite directions.

But instead he pushed after her, forcing his scarred leg to move faster than it wanted until he'd caught up with her. She didn't turn to look at him, though he was sure she must have realized he was at her side.

"Do you know where in blazes you're going?" he asked, the ache in his leg sharpening his words.

She still didn't look at him. "I am continuing in the same direction as I first intended, with the goal of obtaining a hackney cab back to Penny House."

"Well, what a deuced fine *goal,*" he said. "I suppose that doesn't include pausing to thank me for saving you, does it?"

"You told me to hurry, and I am." She quickened her steps even faster, the color coming back to her cheeks. "You seemed most accomplished at—at striking that man. Did you learn that in the army?"

"That, and a good deal more," he said, irked that she still hadn't thanked him. Not that he'd acted with that in mind—that had been instinct, no more—but he'd expected a woman who prided herself on being such a damned lady to show a little gratitude. "You should be glad I did."

"I don't believe I can condone violent actions under any circumstances," she said primly. "Why were you following me, anyway?"

"*Following* you?" He couldn't believe she'd actually said that.

"Yes," she said, briskly turning the corner before stopping abruptly to face him, her confidence growing as the neighborhood around her improved. "How else would you have happened along at the precise moment that I was in need?"

Forced to stop too, he frowned down at her. "Perhaps I

should be the one to ask the same of you," he said. Likely she thought she didn't need him any longer, that she'd be safe enough on her own now. "What the devil were you doing alone near St. Andrew's, anyway?"

"Visiting a friend in need of comfort, and company." Her answer was so instant and defensive he knew she wasn't telling him everything. "And you? What excuse do you have for being there?"

"You weren't asking questions about the poisonings, were you?" he asked, though he doubted she'd admit it. "Nosing about in matters that don't concern you?"

"They *do* concern me, Mr. Callaway," she said, more answer than she realized. "Such villainy should concern everyone. And *you* should be interested to hear that your man Jemmy ate his last meal in the company of another man who'd also served in Spain."

"What man is this?" William demanded. "Give me his name!"

"I don't know it, not yet," she said. "But Mrs. Barney said that he was a stranger to the parish, and to Jemmy. It was the link with the army that made Jemmy trust him, and go with him to drink in a tavern."

"Why didn't you tell me this sooner?" he said, stunned that she'd keep something this important from him. "Why in blazes did you decide to keep such news secret?"

"I never meant it as a secret!" she exclaimed. "And it's as much my concern as yours. If someone were to perish after eating at Penny House, why—"

"Does it concern you enough to die for it yourself?" he said roughly. "Are you willing to be that concerned, Miss Penny?"

She squared her shoulders looking up at him and ignoring the other passersby forced to walk around them. "Pray do not be so dramatic, Mr. Callaway."

"Dramatic, hell," he growled. "What just happened to you here?"

She raised her chin a fraction higher beneath the bent brim of her bonnet. She'd stopped before a bakery, the window behind her piled high with loaves of fresh bread on wooden racks.

"Nothing that had anything to do with the poisonings, Mr. Callaway," she said with an extra little twitch to her head. "I can assure you of that."

"Can you now, Miss Penny?" he demanded, her willfulness irritating him. "Why are you so certain?"

"Because I don't believe that in this great city there is anyone intent on singling me out for harm simply because I feed the poor!"

"Trust like that is the comfort of fools."

"Fools!" she cried. "My father said that—"

"Your father never spoke of the peril you've blundered into now," he said, too frustrated to spare her. "Would you be able to use 'violent actions' to save yourself, or would you have been as helpless as you were just now?"

"'Helpless'?" she repeated, her voice squeaking on the single word. "Helpless? I do not consider—that is—that is, I—"

Abruptly her face crumpled. She pressed her palms over her mouth, squeezing her eyes shut as she tried not to weep.

"Oh, hell," he muttered. He hadn't expected her to cry, not now, and her tears made him feel like the worst bully in the world. "I thought you said you were unharmed."

"I am," she said without opening her eyes. "I don't know why I'm—I'm doing this, but I'm not—not *helpless*."

It didn't matter what she said. He'd never seen anything more pathetically helpless in his life than Bethany Penny, standing there with her bonnet bent and her shoulders quaking like a child's as she wept. Helpless, and forlorn, and poignantly in need of reassurance.

But damnation, not from him. No matter how desperate she seemed, he must not touch her, must not reach for her. He didn't need that kind of responsibility and he didn't want it. What kind of comfort could a man like him offer a woman, anyway?

"Not—not helpless," she whispered miserably, trying to convince herself, not him. "I am not."

How many times had he felt this exact way himself? How many times since the ambush had scattered his men beyond his control, since he'd been blinded by the flash of the explosion, since he'd fought to keep his consciousness even as the pain from his wound had begged for merciful oblivion?

How many times since he'd realized he was as mortal as any man?

"Don't cry," he said gruffly. "Damnation, you don't need to do that."

And before another fat tear began to slide down her cheek he was slipping his arms around her trembling shoulders, drawing her in against his chest, as gently, as slowly, with as much care, as he could muster.

She sank against him gratefully, curling her hands against his chest as she rested her cheek against his shoulder. She was smaller than he'd thought, more fragile, and he could feel her trembling, trying not to cry, yet not too proud to come to him.

How long had it been since he'd held a woman, any woman, in his arms like this? How long since one had looked at him with anything other than revulsion?

"Poor lass," he murmured, holding her as if he feared she might break. "I'd no wish to frighten you."

"You—you didn't," she said into the front of his coat. "And—and I'm sorry."

"Ah, well," he said, wishing he could remember how to

be gallant to ladies in distress, "there's no reason for apologizing, not really. All I want is for you to be safe, and watch yourself."

She didn't answer, her face still buried against his chest and obscured by the bent bonnet. Behind her William could see the women in the bakery window, watching, fascinated by the sight of the lady and the beggar. Let them damn well look; whatever this was, it was between him and Bethany Penny and no one else.

She snuffled and rubbed at the corners of her eyes with her fingers, and he fished around in his coat for his handkerchief, pressing it into her hands.

She took it with another sniff, and blotted at her eyes. Then she pushed back from his chest, staring at the neatly pressed handkerchief, the white Holland linen now smudged with her tears.

"It's clean," she said slowly. "And pressed."

He frowned, not following. "I wouldn't have given it to you if it weren't."

She turned the handkerchief in her hands, stopping when her fingertips found the neat embroidered mark of his monogram. "You make no sense to me, William Callaway."

"There's no sense to make," he said, as lightly as he could. "Leastwise nothing to be found in a handkerchief."

She shook her head, glancing from the white linen up at him. "You know that's not what I mean. You—you *perplex* me."

He tried to smile, to make a jest of it, but it was too late for that, and both of them knew it. Instead matters had come to this at last: the truth, the truth, ready to trip him in a thousand little ways, and remind him of the men who'd died, and what he owed them, and that he'd far more important things to do than loiter on the street with a pretty girl in his arms.

He plucked the handkerchief from her hands and stuffed it back in his pocket. "I'll call you a cab back to Penny House."

He turned away, heading into the street with his hand raised to signal a driver. Two passed him by, either already engaged or more likely put off by William's shabby appearance, but the third driver stopped, drawing his horse alongside the pavement. William opened the door just as Bethany joined him, her skirts already bunched to one side in her hand.

Automatically he took her arm to steady her as she stepped up. If he'd any scrap of conscience left, it would be the last time he'd ever touch her. Instead, he circled his arm around her waist and swept her close, and kissed her.

Hungrily he deepened the kiss, feasting on her mouth like a starving man desperate for more of her. He didn't notice that she'd knocked his hat from his head to the street, or that the driver was peering wide-eyed from the box, deciding whether or not to lash William with his whip.

Nothing else existed but Bethany. She tasted sweet as honey, sweet as hope, the kind of sweetness that could make a man forget everything else.

Everything, that is, until she shoved her hands hard against his chest, pushing him away.

"How dare you?" she demanded breathlessly. "How *dare* you?"

"Because I wanted to, Bethany," he said, his voice ragged. "Damnation, because I wanted *you.*"

"You can't," she said quickly. "Not me, not like this. You—you can't."

"But I can, lass," he said. "I can, and I do."

Her blue eyes were huge, her cheeks flushed, and her mouth was ripe with his kiss, her lips parted and silently begging for more, Without looking away, she slowly dropped back onto the seat, her hands limp in her lap. As

William latched the hackney's door, she said nothing, and neither did he.

"What place, mate?" the driver asked. "Where's the lady bound?"

"Penny House, in St. James's Street," William said, his gaze still locked with Bethany's. "Below the Square. Take her there safely, mind?"

He stepped back to watch the cab pull away and rattle down the street, Bethany's face a pale oval in the window. He watched even after he could see no more, nor imagine that he did. Then he retrieved his battered hat from the street, and began the long walk home.

"Miss Bethany!" Pratt hurried to greet her as soon as she entered the front hall, his brow furrowed with distress. "Praise God you have returned!"

"Of course I've returned," Bethany said, quickly untying the ribbons on her bonnet and handing it to a housemaid before Pratt noticed its battered condition. "Why else wouldn't I?"

"The length of your absence gave us cause to worry," he said, his sharp dark eyes noting her hat's broken brim as it was born away. "You have been missed."

Bethany paused at the looking glass, wishing she could smooth the guilt from her face as easily as she was brushing back her hair. How much could Pratt read in her expression—how William Callaway had saved her, spoken to her, kissed her?

"No one should have missed me," she said, praying her voice wouldn't betray her, either. "I sent word with the baskets from the market that I was going to visit Mrs. Barney at St. Andrew's before I returned home."

"As you say, Miss Bethany." Pratt bowed, the slightest bow from the waist that proved he didn't believe a word of what she said. "Your sister has asked that the moment you return, you are to join her with the others below stairs, in the kitchen."

"The kitchen?" The kitchens were Bethany's exclusive domain, almost never visited by Amariah, especially when Bethany wasn't there. "What others?"

"The gentlemen," Pratt answered with maddening, deliberate vagueness. He was not about to offer her any further information unless she confessed more of her own.

Which, of course, Bethany had no intention of doing. With a little *harumph* she marched across the hallway's checkerboard floor and down the winding stairs to the kitchen below.

But instead of the orderly preparations for the club's evening that she expected, she found the baskets from the market still unpacked and nothing begun. Her staff was standing in a nervous line along one wall, with some of the younger maids sniveling into the corners of their aprons.

"Here you are at last, Bethany!" All smiles, Amariah came toward her, arms outstretched and ready to embrace her.

"Pratt seemed ready to have the river dragged for me." Bethany presented her cheek to be kissed, looking past her sister to her agitated staff. "Amariah, what is happening here? I'm gone for one morning, and you've addled everything here."

"I've addled nothing, Bethany, only made certain improvements to benefit us all." Amariah's smile widened as she ushered a strange man forward. "This is Mr. Fewler, Bethany. He is a former Bow Street man, and an expert in prevention. He specializes in establishments such as our own."

Fewler bowed, his cropped black hair as oily-sleek as a seal's. He had a barrel-shaped chest exaggerated by the double row of polished buttons down the front of his waistcoat, mimicking some sort of military uniform, and he wore a pistol tucked into the wide sash at his waist. Behind him were two other men in lesser versions of the same dress, but every bit as officious.

"I am honored to serve Penny House, Miss Bethany," Fewler said, his thin-lipped smile showing no teeth. "A club with so brilliant a membership poses a special challenge to my resources."

"Doubtless it does." Bethany grabbed Amariah by the elbow. "Sister, we must talk. You will excuse us for a moment, Mr. Fewler?"

She hustled Amariah into the small dairy room where the butter and cream was stored, and closed the door. "Why is that man here, in my kitchen, interfering with my responsibilities and threatening my staff?"

Amariah smiled, the faintly patronizing older-sister smile that usually meant trouble for Bethany. "I told you, lamb. It's for your own good. I know how much you wish to continue your charitable works from the kitchen—and I agree with all my heart, because that is what Father would wish, too—but we cannot afford to have anyone poisoned at Penny House. Mr. Fewler and his men will see to it that everything and everyone is exactly as they should be."

"You mean they are here to *spy* on us!" Bethany exclaimed. "What do you think Father would say to that?"

"Be reasonable, Bethany," Amariah said, sounding all too reasonable herself. "It's not just the club. I don't want you being poisoned, either."

"But to have these men in my kitchen, upsetting my staff?" Bethany rubbed her hands along her arms to warm them; the dairy room was always kept chilly, almost cold—much like her sister's manner toward her. "And my poor flock—they have a natural fear of anyone smacking of the law. They'll disappear as fast as dew in the morning once they hear of Mr. Fewler and his men, and I cannot say I blame them."

"They're not 'the law,'" Amariah said. "They're more like special guards, watching over us all."

Bethany puffed out her cheeks with a dismissive little whistle. "That seems a precious fine distinction, Amariah, deciding who shall be watched for safety and who shall be watched to turn over to the constables as a dreadful danger."

"That is why we must rely on Mr. Fewler's experience, Bethany," Amariah said, "and why he comes with the highest of recommendations. He will perceive these fine distinctions at once."

"Oh, yes, *perceiving,*" Bethany said. "Exactly how is my staff supposed to work whilst they are being *perceived* over their shoulders?"

Amariah set her hands at her waist, determined not to give in. "I doubt very much that Mr. Fewler and his men will have any interest in your staff at all, Bethany. They've already decided that this morning. Nor will they be concerned with the poor widows or waifs that gather here for their suppers. No, they will be looking for more dangerous people, those who could commit such a dreadful crime, such as that man that Pratt says was causing you such bother the other day."

"William Callaway?" Bethany exclaimed, shocked. "I do not know what Pratt has told you, but I can assure you that there is nothing—nothing—about Mr. Callaway that would mark him as a criminal."

"So now you know the man's name," Amariah said with surprise. "You have seen him again, then?"

"I have learned his name, yes." Too late Bethany realized she'd blundered, her cheeks now hot with a guilty flush as the memory of William's kiss came rushing back to her. Amariah was accustomed to the titled, moneyed gentlemen who filled the gaming rooms upstairs; she'd never look twice at a man like William, nor would she try to understand him the way Bethany was. "But I do not see how that should mark him as a villain."

"I didn't say that it did." Amariah leaned back against the counter, her face now filled with concern. "Bethany, you know we cannot let ourselves be quite as trusting as we could be in Sussex, not when—"

"*No.*" That was, oddly, the same warning that William himself had given her. "As I recall, Father taught us to judge others by who they were, not how they dressed or how great a fortune they possessed."

Amariah's mouth tightened. "He also taught us to look after ourselves, Bethany, and to recognize when we might need the help of others to do so. I'll grant you that having Mr. Fewler and his men here will not be easy and I am most sorry for the disturbance they may cause in the kitchen, but as long as these poisonings continue to plague the city, they must remain."

She turned to open the dairy room door, determined to have the final word without further discussion.

But Bethany swiftly pressed her own hand over her sister's, stepping into the half-open door to block her path. "Why don't I have a say in this decision, Amariah?"

"Because you've let your passions overrule your senses, Bethany," Amariah said. "Cassia agrees with me. We both wish to do what's best for us, and for Penny House."

"I will not speak ill of any of my staff or my flock to those men, Amariah," she said fiercely, "and I won't tell any secrets that have been entrusted to me. And I will not—*I will not*—tell him one word about William Callaway simply because he did not meet Pratt's impossible standards."

Amariah's gaze searched her face, hunting for the truth.

"This Callaway man is only another of your vagabonds, isn't he? One with so sad a past that you wish to shelter him?"

"Amariah, please," Bethany said. "I desire to help all those who come to my door."

"I am serious, Bethany. It is one thing to do God's work with the poor, but it's quite another to confuse kindness with an infatuation. You know what a dangerous mistake it would be to entangle yourself with a man you know nothing about."

"I know he is one of my flock!" He wasn't, not really, and she remembered how he'd refused her soup that first afternoon. Besides, he seemed to have a flock of his own in the men who'd served with him, and the concern he'd showed for their welfare had been another odd sort of bond between them.

And he wanted her. She couldn't forget that, any more than she could forget that kiss. He wanted her, and God forgive her, she wanted him, too.

"A member of your flock?" Amariah repeated, the worry in her voice genuine. "That is all he is to you?"

"What else could he be, Amariah?" Bethany didn't know which made her feel worse: speaking with such deceitful care to her sister, or trying to ignore the impact that William's rescue—and his kiss—had had upon her. How could she, when she wasn't sure herself?

She swallowed, trying to keep any telltale emotion from her voice. "Mr. Callaway is a man who has suffered a great deal. He deserves better from life, and I have no intention of doing anything to hurt him further. And that is all, Amariah. That is *all*."

She lifted her hand from Amariah's and hurried through the door before her sister could ask more questions, and nearly straight into the brass-buttoned chest of Mr. Fewler.

"Miss Bethany," he said with an extra bow. "If you please, miss, I've been waiting to speak with—"

Bethany didn't stop, continuing down the hall and making him follow. "I'm sure you've already heard more than enough from Mr. Pratt and the others. I've nothing more to contribute."

"Beg pardon, miss, but I believe you do." He smiled at her side, so close that she could smell the scented oil he used to slick his short dark hair down over his forehead. "I could not help overhearing your conversation with Miss Penny, especially the part about—"

"If you were ill-mannered enough to listen to our private conversation, Mr. Fewler, then you surely heard that you are here against my wishes."

"I heard your sister explain that I am here to help, not hinder, Miss Bethany," he said without any shame or apology for his eavesdropping. "I understand how a lady like yourself must find such matters disturbing, Miss Bethany, but I can assure you that my operations here at Penny House will be conducted with the very height of discretion."

"I did not realize that listening at doorways had become discreet behavior." She jerked her apron from the wall peg, snapping the white linen through the air as she tied it around her waist. One of the guards was already posted at the back door with pistols in his belt, ready to seize any murderer who might come hoping for soup, while her poor staff tried to continue their tasks.

What would they do to William when he—if he—dared to return? Would they judge him as suspicious, and haul him off to who knew where? Or would he challenge them and fight back with that same ruthless efficiency he'd shown today in the street, with disastrous results for everyone?

"Miss Bethany," Fewler said, trying again to persuade her, "if you will only assist—"

"You will have no assistance from me, Mr. Fewler," she said firmly. "My sister has decided to take this path on behalf of Penny House, and though I cannot dissuade her, I do not agree that your presence here is right, or necessary. Now if you'll excuse me, I must try to recover the time *you* have stolen from my staff to prepare the meals for tonight."

But the man persisted, remaining at her elbow as she made her way into the kitchen. "Have you ever seen anyone die of poison, Miss Bethany? It's not a pretty sight, I can assure you."

With an impatient sigh she seized a knife from the nearby block—the same knife, she realized, that she brandished when she'd been alone with William. She turned to the nearest table and reached for an oversized purple-and-white turnip.

"And have you, Mr. Fewler, ever seen a man butchered like a goose for being an imprudent, interfering fool?"

With a single practiced stroke, she sliced the turnip into neat halves. She was gratified to see him step back, resting his hand lightly on the butt of his pistol.

"Such rash talk is surprising from one so young, Miss Bethany," he warned, striving to sound playful, and failing abysmally. "I urge you to consider before making such an idle threat."

"It's not idle, I assure you," she said. "Like any good country cook, I am capable of butchering every edible creature in England and preparing it for table. I doubt you'd present much of a challenge."

He narrowed his eyes, watching how deftly she chopped the turnip. "If you continue like that, Miss Penny, I'll be forced to add you to my list of suspects."

"Add away, Mr. Fewler," she said. "I'm not afraid of you, or your list."

"Then I will, Miss Bethany." Fewler wasn't smiling now. "Your sister ordered me to find the truth, and to report it to the magistrate, no matter who the villain may be. And I will, Miss Bethany. I will."

Chapter Six

There were few things that escaped William's eye as he walked through the dark London streets toward home. The barefoot waif of a girl on the corner could be the lure for the bully-boys in the shadows of the alley, waiting to prey on whomever might pause. The basket of old straw near the stable door might shelter a mad dog, and the weaving cluster of young swells on their way to a brothel could abruptly decide that setting fire to a beggar was the grandest sport imaginable. William had seen all these things and more, but the carriage with the liveried footmen and perfectly matched bays—the carriage he missed entirely.

He had just turned down Bowden Court. The crooked old house where he lived was now in sight, the lantern that his landlady hung by the door giving off its customary smoky glow into the street, and in her ground-floor window he could just make out the rounded silhouette of her ancient tiger cat, hunkered down on the sill. There were the familiar smells from cooking pots, onions and pork, mingled with the river's tide and the standing water puddled in the streets, and the end-of-day sounds of tired arguments and fretful babies.

Maybe it was this familiarity that lured William into

inattention, the sense that he was already home and could let his guard slip. More likely he'd been thinking again of Bethany Penny, for what little good or purpose that would accomplish. Once he'd seen her safely on her way home, he'd gone to visit two other charity kitchens, and resolutely kept away from Penny House, and from her. She might be innocent enough to believe that they could work together to solve this mystery, but he knew otherwise. There was too much danger involved to include a country parson's guileless daughter; he'd only to consider what had nearly happened to her this morning. Didn't he already have enough sorrow to burden his conscience without putting her at risk, too?

But far worse was realizing his own wretched weakness, knowing that he'd be willing to trade her safety for the pleasure of her company. It was wrong, it was selfish, and he loathed himself for it. Yet he could not forget how quickly Bethany's surprise had turned to passion, of how she'd kissed him, *him,* as he was and who he was, without recoiling from—

"Watch yourself there!" From instinct the man raised his arm just as William crashed into him.

Awkwardly William caught himself from falling, his leg twisting as he reeled away to the side of the other man. Gasping with the pain of the sudden motion, he reached at once for the knife under his coat. "Watch yourself, you clumsy bastard!"

"Begging pardon, m'lord." The man squared his shoulders and touched the front of his cocked hat, warily watching the knife in William's hand. "I didn't mean to startle you, m'lord."

"Who the devil told you to call me that?" he demanded, but he could already see the answer. The man was dressed in a footman's dark crimson livery and a powdered wig, and even here in the murky shadows the curlicues of braid on the deep cuffs of his coat were distinctive enough to identify his master's house.

"Her ladyship did, m'lord," the footman said, and from his placating tone William was sure he'd been warned to be patient. "The marchioness of Sperry, m'lord."

"Did she, now." Slowly William slipped the knife back into its sheath. While drawn knives would be perfectly appropriate for any gathering of his family, at least he could pretend to be civil. "Did my sister tell you anything else?"

"Yes, m'lord." The man touched the front of his hat again, then held his hand out to the side, motioning down to the end of the street. "If you please, m'lord, her ladyship would like you to join her directly in her carriage."

"She's *here?*" He couldn't believe Portia would deign to venture this far into dangerously unfashionable neighborhoods. But the waiting carriage was certainly hers, her husband's coat of arms on the door gleaming dully by the lamplight, just as this footman was her property as well.

"Yes, m'lord." The footman's extended hand became more insistent. "If you please, m'lord. Her ladyship has been waiting for some time for your return."

"Has she, now?" William looked again to the carriage. Waiting was not something Portia did with either grace or willingness, and he couldn't begin to guess what reason would be great enough for her to venture to Bowden Court to see him. After his convalescence, his family had purposefully distanced itself from him, as embarrassed by the changes war had made to his soul as by the wound that had made him less than the perfect English lord. In return for the first time he'd seen his family as self-absorbed, vain, and completely insufferable, and he'd obliged everyone by removing himself from their lives to a far more humble one of his own making.

At least until now.

"If you please, m'lord," the footman said softly, "her ladyship—"

"Her ladyship will have your head if you don't return with me in tow." William swore to himself, more resigned than angry, and more at his tangled life than at his sister. "I know my sister's ways, and I'm not about to make you suffer for them. Lead the way, lad, and I'll follow."

A second footman opened the carriage door and flipped down the small folding step, expecting William to climb inside.

But William knew better.

"Portia," he said from the pavement, his arms folded across his chest. "What devil has swept you into my path this night?"

"Stop skulking, William, and let me see you properly." His sister leaned forward on the leather seat, into the lantern's light so that William in turn could see her as well. Portia was as beautiful as ever, her face as flawless as the rubies that hung from her ears and around her throat, her golden hair styled into an elaborate crown of curls and red silk ribbons that must reflect the most current of fashions. His sister was ranked among the great beauties at Court; William would grant her that much.

But that would be all. Portia's perfect features might have been carved from chill alabaster for all the warmth they showed, and the Italian lace shawl that draped across her shoulders might as easily have been a spider's web.

Her pale eyes—the same near-colorless grey that William shared, though hers were more almond-shaped, tipping up at the corners—flicked across William's person.

"You look ghastly, brother," she said with undisguised satisfaction. "Quite the pauper, aren't you?"

"I should return the compliment, dear sister, and ruin

your day," William said. "I'll grant you three minutes of my time, no more."

"Three minutes should be sufficient." She turned her head a fraction, her gaze raking him up and down, appraising, as she waved her hand toward the other seat. "Pray do not tax me further, William. Sit."

"It's your time to squander, Portia." Carefully William pulled himself into the carriage.

Portia wrinkled her nose with distaste. "So you are a cripple, just as Father said you were!"

"How deuced generous of him to notice." William winced as he settled on the leather cushions. "Is that why he sent you here?"

"Who said Father sent me?"

"Because he's the only one who could make you do it," William said evenly. "But for what reason, I wonder?"

"There are two." She let herself slip back against the squabs, pointedly drawing a perfumed handkerchief from her beaded silk reticule. "First, Father has asked that you cease your street-brawling."

William's expression didn't change. He wasn't surprised that his father had heard of his recent scuffles. Given Father's money and his tentacles, he'd always been able to learn anything about anyone that he cared to find out.

Father's reasons, of course, would be another story entirely. "Since when does Father give a damn how I spend my time?"

"What else can he do, now that you've turned yourself into a virtual hermit, living by choice in this—this squalor?" Portia sighed, daubing the scented handkerchief to her nose for emphasis. "What recourse have you left him? As disgraceful as your behavior is now to the family, William, getting yourself killed in some sort of common squabble would be infinitely worse."

No wonder Bethany's kindness had warmed him so, when this was the sort of rank selfishness practiced in his own dear family. "Dying by any means is generally considered bad enough, Portia."

"Oh, be reasonable, William," she said irritably. "Nearly everyone believes you dead already. Consider what the papers would make of such a scandal—the youngest son of the Marquess of Beckham, murdered in the gutter! Why, everyone would be so full of troublesome questions about you that it would be quite, quite tedious for us all."

"Ah, Portia, you haven't changed a bit, have you?" William's smile was bitter. After the first of his men had been poisoned, William in his deepest grief had even wondered whether Father might have been behind it, plotting and preferring such an end for him instead of something more embarrassing or public.

"I'll leave you now," he said, beginning to rise, "to spare you from the tedium of my presence."

"No, William, you cannot go." Imperiously she pressed her gloved hand to his arm, keeping him on the seat across from hers. "I must tell you my second reason for coming here. You see, Father is willing to take you back."

"Take me *back?*" William laughed, not bothering to hide his contempt. "He never sent me away, Portia. I left by my own will."

"Well, then, he wishes to reconcile." She waved the handkerchief through the air, ready to brush aside his objections. "Don't play with words, William. This is serious. Father is willing to forgive your obstinacy, and welcome you back."

William snorted derisively. "Father has never welcomed anyone in his life, Portia, least of all his children. The only reason he had me brought back from the Peninsula was to keep the Spaniards from further defiling any of his sainted Callaway blood."

"If he'd known what you'd become, William," she said, looking pointedly at his threadbare coat, "he might well have left you there to rot among the Diegos."

He thought again about the poisonings, his suspicion leaving a hollowness in his chest. "Then maybe Father will just kill me now instead, and be rid of the inconvenience forever."

"Oh, he wouldn't do that," Portia said, her sudden smile far too knowing for William's comfort. "He has other plans for you. He's found you a bride."

"A *bride?*" This made no sense, even from his family. His two older brothers already had three strong, healthy sons between them to carry on the line, making William a very distant—and unnecessary—sixth in the succession to the title.

"Yes, yes," Portia said, almost purring. "It's quite a match. The lady's family is delighted, and we all wish the banns to be read as soon as possible."

"Have you all lost your wits?" he demanded, wishing he hadn't thought so instantly of Bethany Penny. "I've never heard anything more ludicrous!"

Portia clucked her tongue in mock disapproval. "What a sorry commentary, William. You can suggest that our father would wish you dead, but you cannot believe he'd want you to have the bliss and contentment of married life."

"What I believe is that he'll stand to profit from whatever alliance he proposes," William said, disgusted. Like most girls of their rank, Portia and his other two sisters had been bartered off in marriages made for mutual benefit, not love, but he'd never thought his father would sink so low as to do the same for one of his sons.

"What's my value to Father, then?" he demanded. "Is it land, gold or another vote in the House?"

Portia tipped back her head and laughed with relish, the

jewels in her ears sparkling in the half-light. "*So* cynical, William. To be true, I have heard of a small favor regarding adjoining land that Father wishes from the lady's family, a variance or some such, but when Lady Emma's prospects are considered as well, then—"

"Lady Emma? Not Lady Emma Dalembert?"

Portia shrugged, answer enough.

"If Father wasn't already bound for hell, than this would secure his place." William shook his head, aghast. "You've known Lady Emma as long as I, Portia. The poor creature has the mind of a child, and will never grow beyond it. She couldn't begin to comprehend the meaning of a marriage, to me or any other man."

"Well, yes, I'll grant that a Season in town for her is not possible," Portia admitted. "And the wedding will by needs be small, so as not to distress her pitiful sensibilities."

"Damnation, listen to what you're saying!"

Portia shrugged again, unconcerned. "It's not as if you're a prime catch yourself, William. Once, perhaps, but not now."

But Bethany Penny had kissed him, hadn't she, kissed him because she'd wanted to?

Swiftly he shoved the thought aside. "That's hardly the point, Portia. Even you must realize it."

"Oh, I know the little coney is quite mad," she said. "But once you're wed, you can settle her in the country where she can be looked after by some sort of keepers. You shall be doing her family a great favor, too, taking her away, and the settlement she'll bring along with what Father will add should more than—"

"I'm not going to listen to any more of this, Portia." William rose to his feet, unwilling to hear another pitiless word. It was bad enough that his family now considered him sunk so low that he'd actually consider such a scheme, worse still that they'd show no compassion for the sad little intended bride. The casual, unthinking cruelty of it was despicable, even for his family.

"I'd rather Father put a pistol to my temple with his own hand," he said, "than be a part of such a grotesque sham, and so you can tell the old bastard directly."

"Don't be such a self-righteous ass, William." Portia reached for William's arm once again, but this time he'd already shoved open the carriage door and lurched down to the pavement. "You're hardly a paragon yourself."

William turned back to face her. She was leaning out the carriage door, the light from a nearby lantern casting harsh shadows across her beautiful face. He'd always known they shared the same pale eyes, but this was the first time he'd seen the same emptiness in hers that he recognized in his own.

What had cursed his family like this? What had corrupted them, rotted them, stolen away their souls along with their consciences? What had made them so unworthy of anything good, anything loving?

"At least consider the money, William," his sister was saying. "I know you mean to squander nearly every last farthing you've received from Mama's legacy on your squalid beggars, and you're fortunate Father hasn't had you locked up in some distant asylum for that. But I still cannot believe you'd walk away from a fortune like Lady Emma's, not when you're living in a street as pitiful as this one."

"I'd rather live under the stars without a coin in my pocket than take a single shilling of a fortune earned like that, Portia," he said, latching the carriage door closed between them. "And you can tell that to Father, too. Good night, dear sister, and goodbye."

But at once she leaned her head through the open carriage window, unable to accept his dismissal even as he began walking away.

"You're a prig *and* an ungrateful fool, William!" she called after him, too angry to behave like the peeress she was. "And I wouldn't be surprised if Father did come shoot you dead!"

And neither would he, William thought grimly, his shoulders hunched with bleak fatalism inside his greatcoat. A pistol or poison, it would all be the same to Father, and likely to Portia and the rest of his siblings as well. Nothing had changed about that.

It never would.

Wearily Bethany climbed the kitchen stairs to the public rooms behind Pratt's straight back. Although it was well past midnight, the club was still crowded and noisy, with some late arrivals just beginning to settle in for their night of drinking and gaming.

But for Bethany the long day that had begun so early—and so dramatically—seemed to be dragging on without end, and the last thing she wished to do now was to be summoned to meet another gentleman who wished to compliment her cookery in person. This was terribly ungrateful, she knew, but she was so tired that if she had to endure one more portly, drunken, long-winded lord trying to ask for her hand on account of her enchanting way with a Madeira sauce, she might slip to the carpet and go to sleep at the man's feet. It wasn't even a matter of being as gracious and charming as the Penny sisters of Penny House were always supposed to be; it was simply being able to keep her eyes focussed and awake.

Though if it had been William waiting, you'd be running up these stairs, wouldn't you? The same way that you'd been at the kitchen door today with your soup half an hour early, watching, waiting, your foolish heart racing with the hope that he would be there with the same eagerness to see you.

And no matter how hard she'd wished it, he still hadn't come....

She smoothed her hair with her palms and followed Pratt through the crowd to the supper room, where Amariah was standing before one of the fireplaces. Beside her was a young gentleman in a magnificent green dress uniform glittering with gold lace and brass buttons as bright as his blond hair, with one hand resting with studied nonchalance on the hilt of his sword. Clearly his commission had bought him a place in one of the most fashionable of regiments.

A soldier, she thought, an officer, and at once she thought of William. She was so accustomed to him now in his worn greatcoat and uncocked hat that she couldn't picture him dressed in such gaudy resplendence. And as for the sword—William seemed so ready to use his fists that she could only imagine the kind of battlefield heroics he'd lead with a warrior's sword like that one in his hand. The quick temper and the efficient violence that came with it was the part of him that both frightened her, being so alien to her upbringing, yet fascinated her, too.

"Here is my sister now," Amariah was saying, her hand outstretched to welcome Bethany. "Bethany, lamb, I should like to present Lieutenant John Macallister. Lieutenant, my younger sister, Miss Bethany Penny. The lieutenant is a great admirer of your work, Bethany."

"You are too kind, sir." Bethany forced herself to smile through her weariness. At least the man did look as if he enjoyed dining enough to make his compliments genuine. His jovial face was round and rosy, and the brass buttons on that splendid green coat strained across the front over his belly. Clearly there'd been no hardships or deprivations wherever he'd served, and she thought again of William's sunken face and haunted eyes, and the suffering that had so obviously left its mark on his body and his soul.

"Kindness has nothing to do with it, Miss Bethany." The lieutenant beamed at her. "A lady as fair as yourself deserves whatever praise is given her. More than deserves it!"

"Thank you, sir." Letting the personal compliment slide by unanswered, Bethany thought back to what the kitchen had prepared for that evening's table. "We try to please every gentleman's taste as best we can. I hope you had a slice or two of the goose with the oyster Madeira dressing. That was a new dish for tonight."

"Oh, I didn't mean the cookery," the lieutenant said, "though that was deuced fine, too. I meant your charity work. Who would ever guess that lady as lovely as yourself would show so much concern for those below her? Your sister tells me that you feed not only us jolly fellows, but the poor wretches in the street, particularly the old war veterans."

"Some are not so old, sir." Bethany didn't bother to smile now. "Some are far younger than you, mere striplings when they went to fight the French. I suppose they are fortunate because they lived to see homeland again, but oh, lieutenant, how these poor men have suffered for a country that offers them so little solace!"

Macallister frowned, and his cherubic mouth puckered with concern. "It is a great disgrace, Miss Bethany. I cannot agree with you more. At least the magnitude of the unhappiness is born by the men of the lower classes, enlisted or pressed men who are accustomed to a hard lot in their lives."

Bethany could not believe he'd say such a thing. "You believe the poor feel no pain?"

"I do," he said, without the slightest bit of irony. "Because they are raised to it from birth, the suffering surely is not so great as it would be for another who had grown accustomed to every comfort and blessing."

Bethany gasped with indignation. "What, sir, you would

say that the man whom misfortune has condemned to sleep on the cobbles feels less pain and shame than his counterpart in a featherbed in St. James's Square?"

"I speak of an officer of the king, Miss Bethany, placed against the lowest foot soldier." Macallister chuckled indulgently. "To begin with, the two can not fairly be called counterparts, not enough to be judged, not when birth and rank are—"

"Are they both not men, created by God's hand?" Bethany demanded, her voice rising so that other guests turned to look. "Are they both not blessed with the same two legs and arms, a heart and a head? Can they not feel the same joy and pain, or show the same bravery and courage in battle?"

Swiftly Amariah placed her hand on Bethany's arm, restraining her from saying more.

"God's great plans are everywhere on this earth, my dear, and I'm sure Lieutenant Macallister would agree," she said, her voice firm, the warning behind it unspoken but clear. "But for now all he wishes to do is to praise our efforts to ease the suffering—*any* suffering—of the poor."

Bethany took a deep breath and nodded, all too aware of the sin she'd just committed. Penny House was supposed to be a pleasant refuge for its gentlemen members, a respite from the trials of the everyday world—particularly from the nagging women that all gentlemen seemed to claim as a personal affliction.

She lowered her eyes, striving for quiet modesty even as the apology stuck in her throat. "I am so sorry, Lieutenant Macallister. Please forgive me for questioning your—your beliefs. Of course a gentleman and an officer of your stature would only have the most—the most honorable of intentions."

"Quite right, quite right." Macallister's smile returned, mollified, and he puffed out his chest like a pigeon. "And just to show there's no ill will between us, Miss Bethany, I'll send round a contribution tomorrow for you to give out however you please. God knows the ragged bastards need it, eh?"

"You're most generous, sir," Bethany said. She wished she could refuse any contribution given in such a spirit— if in fact the lieutenant did actually send anything in the morning. How much more she respected William's true generosity, how he himself would go without so that he could slip a coin into the hands of another in worse straits.

No doubt that was where he was now, where he'd been this afternoon. For what could a single stolen kiss matter beside the noble mission he'd set for himself?

"Your gift will be much appreciated, Lieutenant Macallister," she said softly, her thoughts far from the smug man before her. She glanced at Amariah, silently begging to be excused to return to the kitchen. She hated being upstairs, forced to talk with odious men like this one. She'd take the poor men in her flock any day.

But Lieutenant Macallister wasn't done yet. He leaned closer to Bethany, lowering his voice in unwelcome confidence. "You take care now, Miss Bethany. Your sister told me she'd had to hire guards to keep you safe from the rabble."

"We've done nothing of the sort!" Bethany exclaimed. "Those guards downstairs are not to protect me, sir, but my little flock, to help keep them safe from the poisoner!"

"Your *flock?*" He brushed his hand over his mouth, only half-succeeding in masking his smirk. "Do you really believe beggars are in such a danger that they require guards?"

"It's wise to be careful," Amariah said, quick to answer before Bethany could. "They say the poor men who have been poisoned died in great pain and suffering."

Disdainfully the lieutenant flicked an invisible speck of lint from his sleeve, clearly losing interest in the topic. "More likely the only poison for those poor sots was a bad lot of gin."

But Bethany could think only of William's concern for each dead man, of his grief for each by name. "The poisoned men were all soldiers, Lieutenant. Perhaps they served under you, and you knew them. Tom Parker, Jemmy Reed—"

"I am sorry to disappoint you, Miss Bethany, but I have heard of these poisonings. All the dead men were from the lowest ranks, and our acquaintance would hardly have intersected." He gave her a condescending little half bow, his heels together. "Now if you'll please excuse me, ladies, I see a friend whose purse I promised to empty over the hazard table upstairs."

Amariah nodded, and he turned to join his friend, but Bethany persisted, unable to stop without one last question, and, perhaps, one final answer. "If you did not know them, then perhaps you knew their Major. William Callaway is his name. Major William Callaway."

Macallister stopped, and though his half smile remained in place, Bethany was sure she saw a flicker of surprise and recognition in his eyes, and perhaps something more.

"Callaway?" he said lightly. "I knew the name, yes— who didn't?—but not the man. Though I cannot see how he would be of interest to you, Miss Bethany. After all, he died by Spanish gunfire, not by poison in London almshouse."

Bethany shook her head, confused. "That cannot be, sir, considering—"

"Perhaps you mistook him for another gentleman, Miss Bethany." He bowed more curtly, and began through the crowded room. "Adieu, ladies."

Amariah slipped her arm around Bethany's waist. "What was that, sister? Why did you mention William Callaway?"

"He is a wounded officer, that is all," Bethany said.

She shook her head, unwilling to explain more even to Amariah until she'd sorted this out for herself. Macallister's response had made no sense: she knew that William had fought in Spain, because he'd told her so, but he was most certainly not dead. So why, then, did the other man seem so convinced he was? And why was William an officer that everyone would recognize? She would ask him to explain as soon as she saw him again.

If she saw him again...

"The lieutenant can be a taxing gentleman, I know," Amariah was saying, "but thanks to the mills his father owns in the north, he is also a gentleman with extraordinarily deep pockets that he's not afraid to empty at our gaming tables."

"How much better it is that I stay below stairs, and leave all this to you!" Bethany said, watching Macallister and his bright uniform make his way up the front stairs. "Do you believe he'll truly send us a contribution tomorrow?"

"It doesn't matter if he does or not," Amariah said. "According to Pratt, the lieutenant's luck is so poor at hazard that he'll make us a handsome contribution one way or another. You know, duck, you can't save the entire world, or make it right."

"I know." Bethany rested her head lightly against her sister's shoulder, and thought again of William's efforts to do exactly the same. In some ways they were so much alike, while in others—in others she could not begin to understand him. "But I cannot help myself from trying."

"Then don't," Amariah said softly. "Just know the challenges, and the trials. Father would never wish it otherwise for you, nor would I. Do what you must, and let the rest follow."

Chapter Seven

Damnation, where was she?

William stood diagonally across the street from Penny House, leaning against the wall with his hat pulled low over his face and his hands shoved into the pockets of his coat. For the past three days, he'd kept to this post, watching and waiting. From here he could see not only the club's white stone steps and front door, but also the passage that led to the back alley and the kitchen, as well as anyone who came or left Penny House, whether a high-born member of the club or the carter delivering the coal and wood for the big house's many fireplaces, stoves and grates.

But no Bethany Penny.

All he wanted was to make sure she was well, that the attack by that bastard near St. Andrew's hadn't left any lasting injury. That was what he told himself: that it was purely her health, her welfare, and not the ridiculous hope of another kiss, another chance to hold her in his arms and feel her warmth thaw the iciness within him.

He swore softly at his own foolishness, then stretched and bent his leg again, trying to ease the dull ache from standing so long.

She might not even be in the house. She could be staying with friends elsewhere in town, or maybe she'd even fled back to the safety of the country. She might have gone anywhere to avoid him, and then she—

Then she was *there,* so instantly that he thought at first she was a mirage, conjured up by wishful thinking and his weary imagination. He blinked, and she was real enough, walking with her usual brisk purpose from the alley and around to the street. He felt his blood quicken, his spirits come more alive just at the sight of her. She was wearing the same plain blue redingote and gown that she'd worn to St. Andrew's, but the rose-colored bonnet was different, replacing the one that had been crushed earlier in the week.

She waited for a carriage to pass, then crossed the street, coming toward him almost as if they'd arranged it. Without thinking, he stepped away from the shadows and the wall, and fell into step beside her.

"Bethany," he said softly, lifting his hat. "Good day to you, lass."

She started when he spoke and realized he was beside her, her cheeks turning pink inside the rosy-colored bonnet, but she didn't break her stride. "Good day, Major Callaway."

So no given names this day, not a good sign.

"You are well?" he asked, even though she looked fine—extraordinarily fine. "Unharmed?"

"Of course," she said, as if he'd just asked the most ridiculous of questions. "You should have realized that when you kissed me."

"You kissed me in return."

The flush returned to her cheeks: too much to hope from remembered pleasure. More likely from guilt, likelier still from anger.

"I suppose I should thank you for your concern," she said, "but I can't imagine why you'd fear me to be otherwise."

"Because I haven't seen you in days," he said, more gruff urgency in his voice than he'd intended. "Not since the morning near St. Andrew's."

She lifted her chin a defiant fraction. "I haven't seen you in the courtyard with the others, either."

"You have guards there now." He'd noticed them that first afternoon; they'd been hard to miss, their presence changing the entire atmosphere of her kitchen-door suppers. "I'm not the only one who's staying away."

To his surprise, she nodded in agreement.

"I know," she said unhappily. "There's only been half as many waiting as usual in my flock. Those men are supposed to be protecting everyone, poor and rich, from the poisoner, but the poor seem to fear the guards more than the poison."

"A man with a pistol, studying every face for the one that seems suspicious," he said. "That's bound to keep many poor folk to keep away. Not even your stew's worth the risk of being swept into gaol."

She glanced up at him from inside the curve of her bonnet's brim. "Is that why you stayed away, too?"

"Reason enough," he said, though the truth would be more complicated than that. He didn't want questions about himself, who he was or why he lived the way he did, and most of all he didn't want her to know who he was. That part of his life, when being the son of the Marquess or Beckham had been most important, was done.

"If you wished to avoid the guards," she said, "then you could have come to the front door."

He cocked a single skeptical brow. He knew she wasn't happy to see him, but he couldn't tell if that was because he'd kept away, or because he'd come now. "What, put my sorry feet on those pristine white steps?"

"Why not?" She was watching him closely, looking for

more than just what his words said. "The steps are the usual way one reaches the doorway."

"For legs that come dressed by Bond Street tailors," he scoffed. "I'll wager the butler and the footmen at that door are every bit as vigilant as those hired monkeys in your kitchen. Likely more. Do you truly believe they'd admit me if I'd offered my card?"

"They would if I told them to," she said promptly. "You forget that one-third of Penny House is mine, and if I say you are welcome, then you are."

He wasn't convinced. Not only could a good butler at the door rival the sternest of sentries, but he still wasn't certain she'd give the order to let him in.

And he had other reasons, too. Why should he risk going through the club's front door and risk meeting others from his past, gentlemen he'd no wish to see, full of questions he'd no desire to answer?

"Where are you going?" he asked instead as they crossed the next street. "Too late for the market, and too early for the shops."

"But not for St. James's Park," she said. "I often go walking there when I can spare the time. All the greenery clears my head, you know, and makes me think of where we used to live in Sussex."

"You go to the park alone?" he asked, appalled, even though it was clear that she did. "My God, after all that has happened to you?"

"Actually, very little has happened to me," she said evenly. "At least not enough to make me change how I live."

"But to go walking in the park without a suitable escort?" He could think of so many evils that could befall a single lady that he couldn't begin to enumerate them. "To go alone?"

"Absolutely alone," she agreed. "Except for all those scores of other people who will be there as well on this lovely morning, gentlemen on horseback and governesses with little girls and flower-sellers and apprentices pausing on their masters' errands to watch the puppet shows."

"But that's not the same," he protested. How in blazes could he make her understand the dangers of a London park? "You are a young lady, a clergyman's daughter, not some common flower-seller."

"I am a young woman who is responsible for my own support and welfare," she said, the slightest edge of irritation creeping into her voice, "which makes me rather more like the sturdy flower-seller than the delicate young lady that you have conjured from the air."

"I'd never forgive myself if anything more happened to you," he declared, and he meant it.

He expected—or rather, he wished—she'd smile then.

She didn't. "How *noble* of you, Major," she said. "Noble, but unnecessary."

"It's necessary," he said, frustration reducing his voice to a growl. "Damned necessary."

"I thought you didn't believe in guards."

"For you, I do," he said. "Given the circumstances, you shouldn't ever be left alone in London."

"But so long as you keep walking beside me like this, then I'm not alone, which is why you're continuing to do so," she said with maddening reason. "*Those* are the circumstances."

"You're deuced good at twisting words about, aren't you?" he said. "Right into a sailor's knot."

"You're rather good at it, too," she answered. "If you come with me and keep me away from the lions and wolves prowling St. James's Park, then you shall feel all gallant and heroic. That's what you want, isn't it?"

He stopped abruptly. "What the devil do you mean by that?"

"You know well enough." She took three more steps before she finally stopped, too, and turned back to face him, almost as if stopping were an afterthought. "Do you come with me, Major Callaway, or should I say my farewells here?"

He stared at her, standing with her hands in bright green gloves clasped before her and her reticule swinging gently from her bent wrists. The slight breeze made her skirts drift around her body, revealing, then hiding, the curves of her hips and waist. The pale morning sun lit her face inside the bonnet, turning her curls to red-gold and her eyes brilliant blue. He'd never seen a woman look more enchanting, or more ready for a challenge.

He didn't owe her a thing, let alone his protection or his company. He'd kissed her once, true, and he'd liked it, but that should be an end to matters then and there. Let her walk in the park alone; let her walk down the Strand stark naked at noon, for all he cared.

She smiled grimly, tipping her head to one side before she began to walk away from him. "Good day, then, Major."

"Oh, no, you don't." He joined her again, purposefully taking his time to make her wait, and so that his limp wouldn't be as noticeable. "If you insist on going to the park, then I go, too."

"I cannot stop you," she said. "You are an Englishman, free to do what you please."

Her walk turned into a march, quick and determined and without mercy. She kept her eyes straight ahead so that all he could see of her face inside the bonnet was the tip of her nose.

He set his chin, equally determined to keep up with her, no matter how much it tested his leg. He could already feel the scarred muscles begin to protest. Sweat prickled under his collar and beneath his hat.

Hell, who would have guessed a minister's daughter could set a pace that would rival a crack infantry?

"Set your guard now, Major," she warned as they passed through the gates to the park. "They say the tigers are most fierce at this time of the morning."

"Especially the females," he growled in return, feeling as ill-tempered as any hungry tiger himself. Certainly on this bright summer morning, St. James's Park didn't appear to be the nest of menace and threat that he'd cautioned her against. The early sunlight slanted through the trees, dappling the paths with ever-changing shadows, and the glitter of last night's dew still clung to the grass. The other visitors were exactly as Bethany had predicted, and exactly as benign: gentlemen on horseback, ladies with extravagant hats in their open carriages, nursemaids strolling with their well-bred charges and vendors selling everything from fruit to rolls to kites and penny-dolls.

Yet even on this cheery morning, William could not put aside his suspicion of unknown dangers hiding behind every bush and bench. It was so much a part of his life that he could not help it. The suspicions were so deep, so carved into him, that they felt more like some witch's premonition than anything founded in truth and logic. Two years ago, he would have laughed at it, but now, after everything else, he could not stop looking for danger, his gaze sweeping restlessly across the paths and fields for anything different, anything threatening, anything wrong.

The morning had been sunny on that other day, too, sunny and hot beneath the Spanish sky. Other armies had stripped the land around them clean, leaving no trees, no grass, in a landscape that was already harsh. The narrow road they followed toward the coast had been baked to rutted clay that twisted their feet and made their progress slow. Fine red dust drifted through the air and settled into their sweat, coating their skin and clothes and choking in their throats.

Yesterday they'd filled their canteens at a brackish stream, and there had been no more water to be found since then. Each man had eked out his supply as best he could, but William knew they would not be able to go much farther, not in this heat. His own eyes burned, his tongue felt three times too large for his parched mouth, and his legs swayed beneath his body. When he scanned the barren horizon, the image shimmered and shook and offered false promises of rivers and ponds.

But William didn't dare stop. Only twelve of them were left of the specially chosen force, all that had survived from his battalion after the skirmish. They'd come this far together, and they wouldn't falter now. Somewhere ahead was English territory, English troops and supplies and food, while behind them were the Spanish, eager to finish what they'd already begun.

And by all that was holy, William was determined not to let that happen.

But when they'd labored over the crest of that last hill and seen the blackened ruins of the farm with the stream snaking through it, his excitement had been as real as the rest of his men's. This was no mirage, no empty temptation, and he'd stumbled and lurched down the hillside with the others.

But then had come the brilliant flash, searing his eyes and his memory and everything else that followed except the certainty that his carelessness had brought disaster, and shame, and pain, and death.

Death—

"William?" she asked, her voice breaking his tortured reverie. "Look at me, and tell me. Are you well? Tell me, William. *Tell* me."

He blinked, and turned toward her voice. Her face was so taut with concern for him that he was unable to accept it and looked down. But there he saw his hand clasped in hers, his knuckles white and his fingers shaking as she placed her other hand over his. Her palm was warm, calming, offering a comfort and strength that he didn't deserve, yet was impossible to resist.

"Would you like to sit, William?" she asked, more softly now that she had his attention. "Here I've been racing along at my usual clip, without any thought for you or your—"

"I'm fine," he said, and even to his own ears his voice sounded like a dry, damaged croak. His throat and his head still seemed clogged with that damned Spanish dust, filtering everything he saw and heard through a ruddy haze. "Thank you, but I—I'm fine."

"Yes," she said, accepting his answer even though they both knew it wasn't true, that he wasn't fine, and likely never would be again. She lowered their joined hands to her side, turning his desperate clutch into the link between friends or lovers, and slowly led him along with her.

"Here's an orange seller, William," she said. "There's nothing quite like an orange for refreshment, I think."

He nodded, wishing desperately that he could find himself and focus, *focus,* and find the words that belonged in the mouth of Major William Callaway.

She drew two coins from her reticule and gave them to the orange seller, an old woman in a gaudy plaid apron who was watching him with the same scornful curiosity that people reserved for madmen and halfwits.

"I love oranges, William, especially eaten out-of-doors." She leaned over the orange-seller's wares and plucked one of the bright fruit from the nearest basket, tossing the orange lightly in her palm like a ball. "Would you like to choose one for yourself, William, or shall I find one for you?"

She leaned closer, her whisper confidential. "Stay clear of those on the top, the ones with the smooth, shiny skin.

That's an old seller's trick, you know, to boil the fruit that's begun to shrivel and rot inside until the skin plumps up and freshens again."

"'Ere now, you've no right saying that," the seller protested. "Me oranges is all fresh an' fine."

Bethany smiled serenely, her face so beautiful in the morning sun that William could have wept from the sight.

"There's no sin to taking care with a purchase," she said to the seller. "Everyone at market knows that fruits and vegetables are often not what they appear."

"Don't tell me, miss." Wounded, the woman sniffed and folded her arms over her chest. "I know all about how what be 'andsome and right on the outside be rotten on the inside. Not that 'e would know the difference, now, would 'e?"

Right on the outside, rotten inside: was there any better description of how he'd become to the world?

"There's none of us so without flaw as to judge another," Bethany said mildly to the woman, choosing another orange to hand to William. "Come now, William, let's sit on this bench, under the elms."

He felt like a child, letting her lead him about like this, yet still he obeyed, sitting beside her on the slatted wood bench. They were sheltered from the others on the path by bushes, as much privacy as anyone could ask in a park.

He took a deep breath, then another, and forced himself to release her hand. She smiled and pulled off her gloves to peel the oranges, and to his shame he saw how the force of his grip had left her fingers blotched red and white.

"I'm sorry, lass," he muttered with genuine misery. "To hurt you like that—I'm sorry."

She didn't look up, concentrating instead on working the peel free from the fruit. "I told you, I'm not fragile. Here you are."

With fingers wet with juice, she held the segment out

to him, and he took it. So damned obedient, he thought as he slipped it into his mouth, like every good soldier: follow orders, no matter what misery they bring.

But this wasn't misery: this was as sweet and complicated as this day, the juice squeezing onto his tongue as he bit into the segment. Sweet and wet and nothing like the dry dust of Spain, nothing like the madness that was colored the same as dried blood.

Now he could see the green grass and two boys trying to get a kite to fly, running across the open field, just as he could hear the hurdy-gurdy player not far away, and smell the moist, musty scent of the dirt—good, rich English dirt—at their feet.

The knot between his shoulders faded and his heartbeat slowed, and now, when he turned to look at Bethany beside him, she might have been under a naturalist's glass, he could see her that sharply: the loose wisps of red-gold hair escaping from inside her bonnet, the freckles scattered over her nose and the orange juice glistening on her lips, the sunlight making her puffed linen sleeve translucent around her arm.

She realized it, too, and now her smile was relieved and happy, as if welcoming him back from a perilous journey.

And in a way, that was exactly what she'd done.

"There now, I told you oranges were the most refreshing fruit in God's entire creation," she said. "That one little piece has restored you famously."

"Why—why do you care?" he asked, his mouth still slow to form the words. "I—I never asked you to."

"I know you didn't." She smiled again. "It's my way, that's all."

He tried to harden himself against her, and what she offered. "Don't pity me."

"I don't," she said. "Pity serves no useful purpose. But

caring for another's welfare, helping them along when they need it most—that is useful indeed. You know that yourself, from caring for your men."

Caring: so that was what she called this, so much a part of her that he doubted she could put it aside, even if she wished to. He took a deep breath, daring to trust and tell her more.

"Sometimes I-I'm afflicted by the past," he said, trying to explain what he couldn't understand himself. "I know no other way to say it."

"That says it well enough." She shrugged, using her thumb to free another piece of the orange. "We've all us parts of our past that bring us sorrow. I've heard midwives say that even the most innocent new babe weeps and wails from the pain of his birth and guilt of his mother's suffering. Why should the rest of us be any different?"

"You are…kind." He looked down at his hands, resting on his knees. The memories that haunted him *were* different because they were such fragments, with no resolution, no tidy ending. Ah, there was so much she'd never know of him, so many secrets that would send her running from his side if she only knew!

"I told you before that your past is yours to keep as you please," she said, lowering her voice to a soft whisper. "But this I must ask of you. Has there been another poisoning?"

He looked up sharply. "What have you heard?"

"Nothing," she said, just as quick. "Nothing at all. But I thought you might have heard first."

"No." He realized he'd been holding his breath, dreading what might come next, and now it hadn't. He reached for the second orange and began peeling it, glad for the distraction that occupied his hands. "To the best of my knowledge, there's not been another for over a week now."

"Please God that there are no more." She glanced at him

sideways, clearly trying to decide whether to say more or not. "I was guessing, and wrongly, too, it seems. When you were—were afflicted, you spoke of death. I thought you meant the poisonings."

"I am—was—a soldier," he said. "I've seen so much of death that it's never far from me."

She nodded, her expression thoughtful. "I suppose you must grow accustomed to seeing awful, tragic things in a war."

"Never," he said without hesitation. "Even Wellington himself would tell you that. Each death makes you value life more, not less."

"Which is why you care so very much for the men who were poisoned."

"How could it be otherwise?" He bit another orange slice, trying not to let his thoughts travel back on that same dark path. "The army makes brothers of the men who serve it. To risk all for a cause together, whether win or lose— that bond will always be there, and every man of every rank will respect and understand it."

"Not quite all," she said, watching the boys with the kite instead of meeting his eye. "There was an officer at the club this week—a guest, not a member in his own right—who seemed at first to recognize your name, then pretended otherwise. It was most peculiar."

William frowned. Like every officer, he had had his share of superiors that he'd rubbed the wrong way, but he couldn't imagine any of them refusing to acknowledge his acquaintance.

"Do you recall the man's name?" he asked. "His regiment?"

"I didn't recognize his uniform," she said, apologizing, "except that it was very gaudy with gold lacing. But I do recall his name. John Macallister. Lieutenant John Macallister. Do you know him, even if he doesn't wish to know you?"

"Macallister." He thought back before the army, before the wild days in London. "I knew a boy by that name at school. A plump little rabbit of a boy, two years below me, and much tormented by his peers. His father was in trade."

"My sister says his father owns mills, and is vastly wealthy from them," she said. "Or so it would be if this is the same Macallister. I suppose it must, for now as a man he is still rather plump and pink. He was also quite full of himself, for no reason that I could see."

That made William laugh. "Surely the same. Well, it's his right not to recognize my name. He never was one to make much sense."

"But it was worse than that, William," she said. "He claimed you were dead."

"Did he, now?" He tried to smile, to make light of this for her sake. "He must have confused me with another."

She shook her head. "That's what Lieutenant Macallister told me, too, that I was somehow mistaken. But I think he did know you, and wished otherwise, though to claim you were dead seemed unnecessary."

"Oh, I'd venture that to most of the world I am as good as dead," he said, striving to sound as if none of it mattered to him. "Once my father sold back my commission—a decision he claimed I could not and would not make for myself—I did cease to exist as far as the army was concerned. Everyone else abandoned me long ago."

Her eyes widened with a gratifying outrage on his behalf. "That is monstrous cruel, to say you no longer exist!"

"Oh, I exist, just not where I did before." He held his hand out before him and waggled his fingers. "There I am, real enough in this life for now, not the next."

She reached out and pushed his hand down. "Don't say that," she ordered with such vehemence her voice trembled. "To make such a jest, about such matters—don't. *Don't*."

"Why?" he asked, surprised by her reaction. "It's true enough."

"Because *I* am glad you're not dead." She raised her chin, the small mark of defiance that he was coming to recognize, and expect. "Because I do not believe you should tempt fate like that. Because I've seen death, too, even though I'm not a soldier, and I don't wish to see it again so soon. Especially not you."

"Why, Miss Penny, I'd no notion I'd such a champion." He meant it as another jest, a way to tease away her seriousness, but the seriousness won for them both. It wasn't a jest; it was the truth. For the first time in months, he realized he *did* want to live, and much of that realization came because she wanted it, too.

He looked back at the last segment of his orange in his hand. The color was as vibrant, as alive, as Bethany Penny herself, and he'd never be able to think of one without the other again.

He held the orange segment out to her. "Here," he said. "You gave me the first from your orange. This will make us even. Here now, open your mouth."

She didn't answer, and her gaze stayed locked with his. Slowly she leaned forward, the white skin of her throat so transparent that he could see the pulse beating within. Finally she opened her mouth, and he slipped the fruit between her lips. For a long moment she held it in her mouth, then bit it so hard that the juice dribbled from her lower lip.

She swallowed, and didn't laugh, and neither did he. With his fingertips, he wiped the juice from her lips, and as he did she opened her mouth just far enough to be able to taste the juice on his fingers.

Even though he could not make himself look away from her mouth, he still found a way to untie the ribbon bow beneath her chin, to push the bonnet back from her head, to tangle his fingers in the rich silk of her hair and pull her head closer to his, close enough so he could kiss and savor the orange on her lips.

She reached up and rested her hands on his shoulders, steadying herself as she turned her head just enough for him to deepen the kiss. The pins were slipping from her hair, the heavy waves falling around their faces. He groaned with the sensual pleasure of kissing her and tasting her, the sound vibrating between them like another connection, and he felt her own wordless answering shiver of joy.

She broke away to look at him, her breathing filled with rapid little catches as she twisted to ease herself closer to him, craving the contact as much as he did. "You're the first man I've ever kissed like that."

"You're the first woman I've ever wanted to," he said, and tipped her back into the crook of his arm to kiss her again. Blindly his fingers unfastened the tiny row of buttons on her redingote, and he slipped his hand inside. She wore some sort of corset—he brushed against the unyielding buckram and boning—but the summer-weight linen of her gown was no barrier at all, and he quickly tugged it lower to free the soft, full curve of her breast. Her nipple tightened at once against his palm, and in response she arched against him with a whimper of pure impatience.

She was so full of life and fire that he'd never tire of discovering more. He wanted this; no, he *needed* this. There was nothing shy about her, no show of maidenly reluctance; she wanted to be here with him as much as he wished to be with her, and he sensed it would take precious little coaxing to take her the rest of the way, with the two of the sprawled half-dressed and gasping on this bench like any other pair of lovers in the park.

She shifted beneath him, her legs tangled around his. He

knew he shouldn't be going this far this fast, just as he'd known he shouldn't have kissed her that first time by the hackney. But he still didn't want to think about her kissing anyone but him, and he didn't want her thinking about any other man, either, not now or ever, no matter what more happened between them.

"This is why you cannot die," she whispered fiercely against his cheek as she brushed tiny, orange-scented kisses along his jaw. "You are too good a man, William, too worthy, too much a hero by ten, and ten times more after that!"

He froze, each of her words hitting him like a thrown rock. Didn't she realize that he wasn't good, and he wasn't worthy? The devil knew he wasn't a hero, not by any reckoning at all. The hero that Bethany wanted would have done anything to save his men. That hero would never have let them suffer, either on the dusty Spanish road or here in London.

And a true hero would not be here now, taking advantage of the kindness he did not deserve, and never would.

"That's enough," he said, and before his resolve faltered again, he pulled away from her on the bench.

"What do you mean, William?" Her eyes were heavy-lidded and confused with unfinished desire as she pulled her gown back over her bare breast. "What—what are you doing?"

He rose, scattering scraps of orange peel over the grass, and held his hand out to her.

"I'm taking you home. I said I'd look after you, Bethany, and keep you safe," he said wearily, his voice hollow. "I never meant to take advantage of you like this, and I'm sorry for it."

"Well, perhaps *I* am not." She scrambled to her feet, shoving her skirts down, and began rebuttoning her redingote with short, angry jerks. "Perhaps my father educated me so that I might determine and decide my own actions, without waiting for an officer of the king to order me about."

"Damnation, Bethany, I—"

"No oaths, if you please," she said. "Perhaps I wrongly believed that we could be friends and share what we felt, and not fall into this conventional situation with you as lord and master of—of *everything!*"

"You're distraught," he began, his own anger beginning to match hers. "When you're more calm, you'll—"

"When I'm more calm, I'll *be* more calm." She snatched her bonnet from the bench. "You said you did not want my pity. Well, I *do* pity you, William, if you believe that this is the proper, honorable way for a gentleman to behave with a lady!"

He stared at her, stunned, not sure where he'd misstepped. "How in blazes am I supposed to behave, if not like this?"

"If you do not know, sir, then I cannot begin to tell you." She reached out with one hand and gave his chest an impatient shove. "Now if you'll excuse me, I mean to return home."

"Now who's giving orders?" He reached for her arm, but she shook him away. "I'll see you back to Penny House."

"No, you won't." She'd already stalked away from him, and now was determined to leave him behind as she headed back toward the main path. "Not when you—"

"Miss Bethany! Hold there, Miss Bethany!"

William turned toward the man's voice, recognizing him as one of the hired guards from the back door. Hell, this was all he needed, this idiot interfering before he could sort things out properly with Bethany and make her understand that he'd only meant the best for both of them.

She'd stopped, her arms folded at her waist while she

waited for the man to come to her. While she did, William joined her first, standing to one side.

At least she didn't shove him away again.

"Who sent you here after me?" she demanded imperiously as soon as the guard reached her. "You've no right to follow me, you know."

"Forgive me, miss." The man gulped for air, his chest heaving from having run through the park. "Mr. Pratt sent me, and Miss Penny, too. They say you must come directly."

At once concern flooded her face and her back tensed, and without thinking William slipped his arm around her shoulders. "What has happened? What is wrong? Oh, if my sister—"

"Miss Penny's fine, miss," the guard said, glancing past her and up at William. "But she said to fetch you quick. She's had word that another poor bloke's been poisoned from charity food."

Chapter Eight

"**O**h, not again!" Bethany cried. She'd dared to hope that the murders were done, yet here was another, and in an instant all her irritation with William on the bench seemed to puff away as insubstantial nonsense and wounded pride. "When did this happen? You must tell me!"

"This morning, they say, miss," the guard said. "Now come back to Penny House with me, miss, so your sister can tell you the rest."

"What was the dead man's name?" William's voice rumbled with urgency behind her, demanding to be obeyed. "Tell me, man. Tell me!"

The guard shook his head as he looked up at William, his uneasiness palpable. "Don't know. They didn't tell me."

"Blast." He turned to Bethany, his face an impassive mask, yet still she remembered what he'd said about never becoming immured to death, how each one struck him fresh with its sense of loss. "Come, lass, hurry. I want to hear what your sister has to say."

He took her arm, ready to go, but she hung back. "Wait, William, please. You can't go with me, not to Penny House."

She saw something—surprise? pain?—flicker through

his pale eyes. "Are you that ashamed of me, Bethany? Is that it?"

"No!" She glanced at the guard, not even pretending he wasn't listening. She pulled William to one side, and turned their backs so the guard couldn't hear more. "It's not that at all, William. It's just that with these foolish guards cluttering the house, I don't want you to be—"

"To be seen," he said, finishing her sentence in a way that she'd never intended. His expression hardened against her. "I thought you were different, Bethany. All that nonsense about how I'd be welcome to come through the front door of Penny House—"

"No, William, please!" She'd never thought that way about William, not from the first time she'd known him, and she couldn't understand why he'd think she'd judge him so callously now. "It's Mr. Fewler and his infernal guards. He's already asked about you, suspecting you, and for your own sake I wished to spare you—"

"But I prefer to determine my own actions, lass." He smiled as he tossed her own words back at her, a smile so grim and cold that her heart sank. "I'm not going to waste any more time standing here quarreling with you. Go back to Penny House. I'll go to that almshouse."

"We're not quarreling," she said defensively, trying to remind herself that this poor man's death mattered so much more than any of her own petty problems. But half an hour ago, William had been kissing her with such tenderness and passion that she'd felt as if she were the only woman in the world, or at least in his world, and now—now somehow they'd come to *this*. "And if you're going to the almshouse, then I'm coming with you."

"No, you're not," he said brusquely, also making it perfectly clear that they were in fact quarreling. "You're going to Penny House with this man, and try to be useful."

"I would be useful at the almshouse, too," she said quickly. "Usefulness is something I'm very good at."

He paused just long enough to show he didn't agree. "I'm still going alone. You send me word if you learn anything important."

She sighed, accepting, though she didn't like it. "And where exactly would I send that important word?"

"To my quarters, of course," he said, as if she should already magically know where he lived. "Mrs. Ketch's house, in Bowden Court. I must go now."

Yet the sight of his familiar broad shoulders—wide enough to accept every burden placed on them—as he turned away to leave struck her more deeply than she'd expected.

"Wait," she said softly, reaching to rest her hand on his arm. "Please take care, William. Whatever you find at the almshouse, watch yourself, and take care."

Surprised by her concern, he looked back over his shoulder, and for the first time since they'd left the bench, he smiled.

"No one's going to harm me, lass," he said in a gruff whisper meant only for her. "God knows they've tried before this, but I'm not about to let them."

She didn't answer then, but let him go, turning away herself before she said more than she intended. Yet as she hurried back to Penny House with the guard at her side, the tears of frustration and worry that threatened to spill from her eyes were all too real.

John Macallister leaned over the jeweler's case, his hands clasped behind his back as he studied the shop's offerings.

"This bracelet is most appropriate for a lady, sir." The jeweler draped the strand of cut rubies set in sterling across his gloved hand, turning it gently to make it sparkle. "For day, sir, or for evening. The color shows especially well with the current fashion for white muslins."

Macallister frowned at the bracelet. He wanted something to catch Bethany Penny's eye and make her think fondly of him, but he didn't want her to think he was trying too hard. A sensible woman like her might see a wristful of rubies that way, and besides, they were awfully dear for a first gift.

"This lady don't wear white," he said. "She favors blue, to match her eyes."

"Ahh." The jeweler nodded sagely, meeting Macallister's gaze over the tops of his spectacles as he set the rubies back onto the velvet display. "You are a wise gentleman, sir, to notice such a nicety for the lady. Ladies do appreciate that. Might I dare to recommend these pearls, sir? Pearls always show so well against a lady's delicate complexion."

"True, true." The pearls seemed at once modest enough for Miss Penny's taste, but still showy enough to prove he was a man of his word. Besides, having the bracelet sent from this particular shop would prove to her that he didn't mind digging deep into his pockets. "I'll take that one, then."

"A most excellent choice, sir." The jeweler lifted the pearls from the case. "I am certain the lady will be most delighted by your choice."

"She should be, shouldn't she?" Macallister grinned and winked, and hiked his trousers with his thumb in the waistband. He liked to think of himself as a man of action, one who took charge. That's what all that gold braid on his uniform meant, didn't it? He'd admired the lady, made her acquaintance, and now he meant to claim her by whatever means he needed—to carry her off and make her his prize, as it were.

"Would you like us to send it, sir?" the jeweler asked, and Macallister nodded.

Better that than to call unannounced, where, in his far-too-large experience, ladies were just as likely to pretend they weren't at home and leave him standing like an idiot on the steps. Amariah Penny had been a bit more welcoming than her sister, but he wanted to be sure she was his ally. He'd write something witty on his card, and let the pearls do his talking. Then when he did call, that door would open for him, posthaste.

He rubbed his palms together, imagining the warmth of Miss Penny's gratitude. She would be perfection for him. He'd had no luck with the high-bred fillies at Almack's who cared only for a fancy title, but Miss Penny wasn't like that. He'd be the one who was the catch, not the other way around. Oh, she was beautiful, yes, but she was also cared more about tending her kitchen than dithering about in expensive shops. She was sensible and thrifty and her sister said she was a good manager, which meant she could keep to a housekeeping allowance. Even Mother would approve.

The only part that gave him pause was that she'd mentioned Callaway. How in blazes had she pulled that name out of the air, anyway? She'd only come to London in the last year. She couldn't possibly have known him; she *couldn't*, and yet there she'd been, singing his praises as if they were the dearest of friends.

He swore to himself. It had to have been coincidence. Perhaps she'd read about Callaway, or heard of him from one of the other gentlemen in the club. Besides, the man was dead, no matter what she believed. What could a dead man do to him?

He looked down at the next case, to the display of wedding and betrothal rings. Once he'd settled that other affair, he could direct a concentrated campaign of wooing, and, with luck, he could ask for Miss Penny's hand by Christmas. Christmas: by then his troubles would all be over. He could forever forget his unsavory past and his shameful fear of its discovery, and look forward to a delicious future with Miss Penny at his side and in his bed.

Ah, yes, a glorious shared future instead of his wretched, cowardly past. The prospect was deliriously appealing. Was it any wonder, then, that Macallister was whistling as he left the shop?

Bethany and Amariah sat side by side in straight-backed armchairs before the fireplace in the front room, while the three men—Pratt, Fewler, and, slightly back, the guard who'd come for Bethany in the park—stood in front of them to give their reports. Everyone was so solemn, so serious, that Bethany felt as if she and her sister were magistrates sitting in judgment. In an awful way, she supposed they were.

"Clearly the man died by the same hand as the others," Fewler was saying. "The distance between his last meal and his death, plus the witnesses' descriptions of his convulsions and delirium—oh, yes, it cannot be otherwise."

Amariah tapped her fingers on the arm of her chair, and leaned forward. "But you say no one else who'd eaten the same food was stricken? Not even those who were served directly before and after?"

Fewler shook his head. "No, Miss Penny. Not his wife nor his children, who were there with him."

Pratt sniffed with disdain. "Then perhaps the wife should be considered as the culprit. She wouldn't be the first woman who'd wish to shed an inconvenient spouse."

"Don't be so cynical, Pratt," Amariah said, her voice for once testy. "I'm certain the constables are considering all the sensible possibilities, even one so dreadful as a wife wishing ill to her husband."

"Oh, it's been considered, all right, Miss Penny," Fewler

said easily, knowing better than to offend his employer. "But the wife was such a sorry little drab with nothing to gain, and with no access to the poison, that she was quickly dismissed."

"We should be offering a new widow comfort in her loss, not dismissing her for her deficiencies," Bethany said indignantly. "What is her name? Where does she live?"

Amariah rested a restraining hand on Bethany's arm, something she seemed to be doing far too often lately for Bethany's tastes.

"Of course we'll see to it, Bethany. But what must concern us now is how this latest tragedy affects Penny House."

"Surely I might ask the dead man's name," Bethany said, for that would be what William would wish to know, too. "And can't I ask if he were known to us here—if he were part of my flock? There's no sin in that, is there?"

"No, miss." Fewler referred to a folded sheet with scribbled notes. "His name was plain as his life, miss…. Smith, George Smith."

"Was he in the army, too?" she asked. "Another who'd served his country in the French wars?"

Clearly surprised that she'd asked, Fewler glanced back at the sheet. "Aye, he was in the army, until a cannonball took his leg and sent him back home here in London for good. But that is why there's great suspicion that the poisonings are a French plot, murdering our gallant warriors one by one to depress the country's spirits here at home. The vermin aren't clever enough to strike the generals or lords, but the common soldier's fair game."

"How awful." She searched her memory of those who'd come for her soup and bread. There'd been at least a dozen who'd lost a leg, but none who'd come with families, or with that most common of names, and she hoped for William's sake that he could say the same. But this *was* exactly the sort of information that he'd asked her to learn, and at once she began planning how to send it to him, as she'd promised. "Though I don't believe this last poor man ever visited us here."

"At least that is a scrap of good news amongst the bad," Amariah said with more satisfaction than Bethany thought proper. "Though I find it hard to accept that even Buonaparte would conceive of such an evil plot."

Fewler smiled. "You have the tender sensibilities of a gentle lady, Miss Penny. But I can assure you that there is more evil in our world than any of us can imagine."

"There is also more good, Mr. Fewler, if you but care to look," Amariah said firmly. "You have nothing else of merit to report to us, then?"

Fewler made a brisk bow. "There is no other news at present, though I shall be sure to continue our vigilance here."

"I'm sure you will." Amariah sighed. "I would venture that your services are in part responsible for our safety, and why there can be no way to link Penny House to this particular poisoning."

"No, Miss Penny," Fewler said. "Leastways not this time. But if you please, I should like to ask Miss Bethany a question in return. Was the man you met in the park one of your, ah, your 'flock' as well? Is he a regular visitor?"

Amariah twisted around in her chair. "What man is this, Bethany? Is it someone I've met?"

Bethany flushed, but that wasn't enough to keep her from answering. She'd told William that she made her own decisions, even if she'd decided to behave like a shameless doxy on a park bench. Now she had to accept the consequences, too, as part of the bargain.

"No, Amariah, you haven't met him," she said evenly, striving not to sound defensive. "But yes, he has been part of my flock. For a fact he did wish to discuss these same poisonings with me, but he didn't feel at ease coming here with because of you, Mr. Fewler, and your men."

Fewler snorted, skeptical. "He should only fear us if he has something to hide, Miss Bethany."

"He is a very private man, Mr. Fewler," she said. She was working hard to keep her temper, knowing she'd accomplish nothing if she lost it. "He is not obligated to share any parts of his life with you."

"What is this private man's name, Bethany?" her sister asked quietly.

"William Callaway," she said. To her, William's name represented so much that was good and fine in the man that she couldn't keep the pride from her voice, nor did she want to.

But her sister heard something altogether different.

"Major William Callaway?" she repeated with a small frown of confusion. "Wasn't that the name of the gentleman that Lieutenant Macallister told you had been killed in the war in Spain?"

"But he wasn't killed," Bethany answered quickly. "The lieutenant was mistaken about that. How could I have met Major Callaway—spoken with him!—if he were dead?"

Fewler smiled indulgently. "It could be your man that's confused, Miss Bethany. Rascals like this one often steal the name and rank of another for their own use, just as easy as if they'd steal a purse."

"But he's not a rascal," she protested. "He's the most honorable gentleman I've ever met."

Fewler shook his head, while the other guard's brows arched with doubt. "Forgive me, miss, but from my experience, I do not believe this rogue's a gentleman at all, let alone an officer of the king. Henry here saw this Callaway when he came to fetch you in the park, and he reported to me that the man appeared to be the basest kind of vagabond, with a furtive look about his person. A young lady like yourself must take great care with a rogue like this so-called Callaway, miss. Indeed you must."

She would not jump to Fewler's bait. She would *not*.

"You may judge a man however you please, Mr. Fewler," she said, standing. "But I prefer to decide my acquaintance not by how a person dresses, but what qualities he possesses in his heart and in his soul. Now if you have no further information for us, I must ask you to excuse me, for I've many tasks waiting for me below stairs."

"Yes, yes, there's always so much to do each day at Penny House, isn't there?" Amariah rose, too, not bothering to hide her relief that the interview was over. "Good day to you all."

Recognizing their dismissal, the three men nodded and filed from the room, but as Bethany began to follow them, her sister caught her hand, gently linking their fingers together for a small, fond squeeze.

"One moment, Betts, if you please," she said softly, closing the front room's door after the men. "Something came for you while you were out."

"Truly?" Bethany smiled with anticipation, and relief, too. She'd been certain her sister would want to ask more about William, for Amariah seldom missed an opportunity to be the ever-protective older sister.

"Is it a package from Mrs. Cosgrove?" she asked as her sister crossed the room to retrieve a small wrapped package from the mantel. "Her shop was completely out of the narrow blue silk ribbon I prefer, and Mrs. Cosgrove thought she might be receiving more in a shipment this week."

"It's not from Mrs. Cosgrove's shop." Amariah handed the package to her. "I thought it such a great coincidence to be speaking of Lieutenant Macallister just now when he'd sent this to you earlier. Aren't you curious?"

"Not really, no." Her anticipation gone, Bethany looked down at the narrow package wrapped in brown paper in her hands. If the gift had come from William, her heart would have been thumping with eagerness over such a surprise, but from the lieutenant, it would only follow the same fate as every other such gift delivered by a servant to the front door of Penny House. Reluctantly she finally opened the paper, and then the lid of the narrow leather box, turning and tipping the box to display the contents to her sister.

"Pearls," she said, unfolding the note tucked beside the bracelet with a contemptuous sniff. "'For a beautiful pearl beyond price, forever your servant, Macallister.' How stunningly unoriginal."

"I wouldn't have expected anything more from him, Betts." Amariah studied the bracelet, lifting it from the padded box. "Very generous, if unimaginative. Recall the handsome donation he made to our charity work earlier this week, exactly as he promised."

"A donation that I have already acknowledged in the nicest letter possible. No doubt that was what gave him enough foolish hope to send this." She took the bracelet from her sister and stuffed it haphazardly back into the box, crumpling the paper back around it. "I'll have Pratt send one of the footman to return this directly, just so he's not encouraged any more than any of the others."

With a discontented sigh, she returned the bracelet to the mantel. "Why is it, Amariah, that so many of our fine guests mistake our hospitality for availability? It's not as if we were parading about like the actresses at Covent Garden, displaying ourselves to attract a new protector and apartments to match."

"I suppose it's a sign that we're succeeding." Amariah plucked a brown-petaled lily from the bouquet on one of the tables, then shifted the other flowers in the vase to fill the empty spot. "If we weren't making this the most agreeable respite for them, then they wouldn't wish to spend even more time with us."

"Still and all, it's hardly flattering," Bethany said, remembering how condescending Lieutenant Macallister had been toward her. "Why do they think because they have more money than we do, that we'll hop onto their laps in exchange for a foolish bracelet like that one?"

"Meaning that you find it much easier to be agreeable to a poor man than a rich one?" Amariah glanced up from the vase of flowers. "Perhaps you should like to invite this Major Callaway to take tea with us one afternoon, so that I might make his acquaintance, too."

"Here?" Bethany's voice squeaked as she thought of how disagreeably—and under what circumstances—she and William had parted. She couldn't imagine asking him here, not now. "You would invite him inside Penny House?"

"Of course," Amariah said, smiling. "If he's even half the paragon you claim, then he'd be most welcome company, and a pleasant antidote to all the Lieutenant Macallisters we must entertain."

"He won't come," Bethany said quickly. "On account of Mr. Fewler and his guards. He doesn't like them, or what they represent."

"Then he can come in through the front door, like every other gentleman." Amariah's smile widened, coaxing. "From how you've described him, Betts, I doubt he's a shy little violet. I should think he'd be pleased to join us here."

Most likely he would, thought Bethany miserably, or at least he would have before today.

"Not yet, Amariah," she said softly, looking down. "Perhaps we shall come to that, but not yet."

"I can wait, duck," her sister said, and reached out to draw her close in a hug. "It must be your decision, not mine. Recall how long it took for Cassia to bring her Richard to us, and he was already one of our guests."

"William—that is, Major Callaway—isn't at all like Richard," Bethany said, desperately not wanting either of her sisters to be disappointed by him in comparison to Cassia's husband. It wasn't just that Richard Blackley was a very rich man, he was a man with enormous power and position both in England and abroad, while William's life was on a far smaller, more humble scale. "Major Callaway's much more concerned with others than with amassing a worldly fortune, and he doesn't care a fig about how he dresses."

"Then he should be a most admirable fit at our tea table." But despite her cheery assurance, Amariah drew back from their embrace, her expression filling with worry as she searched Bethany's face.

"You know I trust you, Betts, just as you must know I'd do anything for your happiness," she said. "But promise me you'll take care with this man, and not let your impulsiveness lead you into any danger. I should feel much more at ease if you'd have him visit you here at Penny House than skulking about together in the park."

Bethany's cheeks flamed. "William's not the way Mr. Fewler says. He's not some low rascal. His honor's worth more than any of the so-called honorable gentlemen who belong to the club, and we were not—not *skulking!*"

"I know, I know." Amariah's smile was still filled with concern, though there was wistfulness there now, too. "Father always said that no one could tell you what to do, and how right he was! But for this once, Bethany, with this man, I beg you to follow your head instead of your heart."

William blinked, letting his eyes grow accustomed to the murky shadows. As dim as the unlit stairwell had been, this room at the back of the house was darker still, the air made thicker by the stench of so many people working and eating and sleeping together.

There were no fires in the empty hearths, no candles or oil-lit lanterns, for all of those were too costly for this place. Instead smoky makeshift lamps punctuated the dark with a pinprick of light, a twisted rag for a wick floating in a sea of tallow or slush in a battered bowl. The lamps sat on the floor, reducing the people around them to dark wavering shadows with distorted faces, but at least tonight the lamps were there, not only to guide William, but as a way to mourn the dead.

"A gentleman t'see you, Sarry," whispered the woman who'd guided him this far. She crouched down beside a smaller woman, huddled against the wall with a fretful baby in her arms. "He says he knew your George in the war. He says he's come out o' respect, Sarry, t' tell you so."

William bent as far as his leg would let him. "Your husband was a good man, ma'am, a brave soldier who deserved better. I am sorry for your loss."

The woman turned toward him. Even in this half-light, he could see that her face was swollen from weeping, her disheveled hair pasted across her cheeks by her tears, her eyes glassy with sorrow and shock. She was young, too, very young, with a fading glimmer of prettiness that would not last another winter.

"He was with me this morning, sir, my Georgie, sleeping beside me." She pointed to the bundled pallet in the corner of the floor. "He died worse'n a mad dog, twisting and writhing and begging to be freed of th' torment. He din't deserve that, sir, he din't!"

She buried her head in her hand and sobbed, and the baby in her lap wailed in mournful sympathy. Gently William rested his hand on her shoulder, his anger at whoever had done this growing with her sorrow. He remembered George Smith as small and quick in a foot race, popular with the other men because he knew an unending string of bawdy songs. He'd been on the dusty Spanish road, too, and he lived only to suffer and die here, begging for release, exactly the same as the others had before him.

One more gone, lost, one more struck from the dwindling number that he hadn't been able to help before it was too late....

"I'm sorry, ma'am," he said, wishing he didn't feel so damned helpless. "I'm sorry."

"They—they din't even give him t' me for burying proper," she said, her shoulders shuddering as she rocked gently back and forth. "They—they said my Georgie must belong to th' surgeons, on 'count of being poisoned. But I loved him so, sir. I did love him!"

"What would make it better, ma'am?" William asked urgently, appalled that she hadn't even been permitted to keep her husband's body. If the surgeons had him, then it would be too late to retrieve his remains, but he was determined to do whatever else he could. "What can I do for you and the child?"

Somehow she opened her eyes. "I want—I want t' go home to my mam," she whispered raggedly. "In Lancaster. I want t' leave this wicked city, and—and go home."

"Then you shall, you and the child both." He took her hand and pressed the coins she needed into it, hoping the others around her wouldn't notice. "Tomorrow I'll have a wagon here for your belongings, to take you back to your mother's home."

She stared at him, uncomprehending. "Why, sir? Why?"

"For your George," he said, feeling the weight of his own sorrow for the lost young soldier. "He served beside me in Spain, with honor and courage. He was one of my men, ma'am, one of my own. Whatever I can do for you now won't begin to be enough."

Still sobbing, she turned to grope beneath the pallet, and pulled out a grimy cloth bag that she pushed toward William's hand.

"Georgie would never sell this," she said. "He—he said it was special, an' not for sale at any price. He—he'd want you t' have it, sir, for what you're doing now."

With the care reserved for the holiest of relics, William unwrapped the ragged strip of cloth to find a worn brass square: a shoulder belt plate, the ones worn by every rank-and-file infantryman, still kept polished as bright as a golden mirror. All that remained of George Smith's once-glorious uniform, the immediacy of such a familiar object struck William hard.

With trembling fingers, he turned the brass over, tipping it toward the nearest little lamp to see the engraving. There was the crown and cross, topping the circular insignia with *Lancaster Regiment* curved inside, around the regiment's number: 52. William caught his breath, and rubbed his thumb over the name and number to make sure he'd read it right.

The Lancaster Fifty-Second. Not his regiment, and not his George Smith.

"He'd want it t' go t' you, sir," the new widow was saying. "He did love his soldiering, my poor George did. He'd want you t' have this, being his mate."

"Thank you, ma'am. I'll treasure it." Slowly William wrapped the rag back around the brass plate. There was nothing to be gained by telling her the truth, that her George Smith had been mistaken for another and paid the highest price for having such a common name. Of course William would still send her home to her mother in Lancaster, still make sure there was an extra purse full of guineas to help see her through her sorrows.

But if William had wanted more proof that someone was using a list of names to choose the next victim, then this was it.

Bethany looked up at the driver on the box of the cab. "Wait for me, if you please," she said, determined not to make the same mistake twice. She'd slipped away from the kitchen in the middle of the evening preparations, and while her staff was perfectly capable of continuing without her, she still did not want to stay away for long. "I'll only be inside for a minute or two."

The old home before her had long ago been made over into a rooming house, but though the neighborhood might have slipped from its former pretensions, it remained respectable, and bustling with noise and activity, even this late in the day. Bowden Court might not be St. James's Square, not at all, but it was still far from the worst neighborhood that Bethany had seen so far in London, and certainly better than William's own ragged coat had led her to expect.

A plump cat sat in the open window, watching with wary orange eyes as Bethany climbed the steps to knock on the door. The older woman who answered her knock was much like the cat, plump and wary, her worn linen apron blotched with a patchwork of whatever she'd been cooking.

"Mrs. Ketch?" Bethany's smile was as winning as she could make it. "Good day to you. Please tell Major Callaway that Miss Bethany Penny is here to see him."

Mrs. Ketch was not won. "Major's not here."

"Do you know when he'll return?" Bethany said, stepping forward to keep the door from closing.

"Nay." Mrs. Ketch looked her up and down. "You can wait in his rooms, if you must."

"In his own rooms?" She hadn't expected that, and she wasn't sure William would want her there.

Hands on hips, Mrs. Ketch glared at her. "I can't very well have you cluttering up my stairwell, can I?"

Bethany took a deep breath. "Thank you, Mrs. Ketch. Perhaps I will wait, for a short time." She followed the landlady inside and up the stairs, imagining William here in this same place. "If Major Callaway doesn't return, I trust I can leave a message for him with you?"

"Trust as you please." The woman stopped at a door, and sorted through the keys that hung in a jingling mass from her waist. "Major's a quiet man. Keeps to himself. Months and months he has no callers, and now this."

She unlocked the door. "I'll tell him you're here directly he returns. You, and the other."

"The other?" Bethany asked, frowning.

The landlady nodded, and pushed the door open for her before she headed back down the stairs.

But Bethany stopped, too startled to enter. Sprawled across William's bed was one of the most beautiful women she'd ever seen, exquisitely dressed in a gown of embroidered white Indian muslin, an oversized Kashmiri shawl draped over her bare arms and patterned silk stockings on her languidly crossed ankles. She wore enough jewels to stock a shop, and her golden hair was so artfully braided and curled and dressed that it must have taken her servants hours to arrange.

"Well now," the woman said, her laugh deep and throaty as she curled her legs beneath herself and plumped the pillows behind her head. "Dear William does have his secrets, doesn't he?"

Chapter Nine

❦

Bethany stepped forward, her hand extended to the woman on the bed. Father had always taught them to be prepared to meet every kind of person that might cross their path, no matter how different from themselves—though in his parish in Woodbury, he'd likely never come across one exactly like this.

"Good day, ma'am," she said as pleasantly as she could. "I am Miss Bethany Penny."

The woman smiled, but more with her own amusement than in any sort of greeting.

"Of course you are," she said, studying at Bethany's out-stretched hand as if it were some great curiosity at the fair, and not a nice one, either. "Miss Penny, or Farthing, or Half-Crown. How you must appeal to William's egalitarian nature!"

Acutely aware of her plain linen kitchen clothes, Bethany drew back her hand, clasping it with its mate at her waist. At least she'd taken off her apron before she'd left Penny House. But although this woman was being barbarous rude to her, there was no excuse for her to be rude in return. Besides, what new jest to her name could the woman possibly invent that Bethany hadn't already heard years before?

"You are also an acquaintance of Major Callaway's?" Bethany asked instead, working to make polite conversation. "You must be, if you are here."

"I've known William for simply *forever*." The woman laughed again, clearly relishing her position. She waved her hand at Bethany, her bracelets slipping and clinking together down her wrist. "I give you leave to take your ease, and sit."

Somehow Bethany kept her smile, trying hard not to consider too closely what William's relationship to this dreadful woman might be. "I am sorry, miss, but I do not believe I require your leave to sit."

"Oh, but you do, Miss Ha'Penny," the woman replied, gently stroking the tassels on her shawl with her fingertips. "You see, I am the Marchioness of Sperry, while you are quite…quite *nothing*. Now sit, pray, before you weary my neck by forcing me to look up at you. That is, if you can find a chair in this dismal male den."

"Forgive me, my lady." Bethany turned, not so much to find a chair, as so she wouldn't have to meet Lady Sperry's eye.

She knew she had no choice but to do as the countess ordered—if Father had taught her to be agreeable to all, then Penny House and its members had instilled the necessity of respecting the titled—but she still didn't have to like it. A marchioness: so this was the female counterpart of all those arrogant, demanding lords who believed the world was theirs by birth?

But how did a man as kind and generous as William have anything to do with a lady like this? How would they even have met, let alone share the great intimacy that the countess implied by lying so comfortably upon William's bed?

And a darker, more unworthy thought crept into her mind as well. As sheltered as Bethany had been, she could tell that this was the kind of alluring, sensuous beauty that gentlemen found hard to resist. What if this woman, draped with silk and jewels, was already William's lover, his mistress, leaving no place in his heart or life for Bethany?

It was all more of the same incongruous puzzle that was William himself. Pieced together, none of it made sense—not the monogrammed linen handkerchief inside his shabby coat's pocket, nor the stacks of scholarly leather-bound books she was now moving from the chair, nor even the Italian painting of a Venetian canal in the gilt frame on the wall in hired rooms in Bowden Court. Not even the way he spoke like a gentleman, with a gentleman's accent and vocabulary. And the more pieces that she discovered, the more confusing the whole became.

"So what is your business with William this day, Miss Ha'Penny?" the marchioness asked. "Or is it only pleasure that has brought you here?"

"I am here at the major's invitation, my lady," Bethany said, perched on the very edge of the leather-covered chair. "I have certain information that he has requested, and that will be of use to him."

The marchioness twisted around in a sinuous curve to sit upright, her eyes alert with new interest.

"You could tell me," she said, "and then I could tell him."

Bethany forced her hands to keep still, and not betray her true irritation at such a suggestion. "Thank you, my lady, but I would rather tell him myself."

Lady Sperry tipped her head to one side, the cut stones in her earring swinging gently against her neck.

"It could be hours before William returns," she said, coaxing with the practiced ease of someone who usually got her way. "Are you willing to wait for him?"

"If I must leave today without seeing him, my lady," Bethany said, "then I know he'll come to me tomorrow."

"I absolutely hate to have secrets kept from me." The marchioness pouted like a spoiled child—which, to Bethany's mind, the lady was in every way but age. "William has told you that about me, hasn't he? That the one sure path to tease and torment my very soul was to hide something from me?"

Bethany shook her head. Of course William hadn't told her that; he hadn't even told her of the marchioness's existence. If anyone were keeping secrets, it was William himself.

Lady Sperry sighed with exasperation. "Oh, you can pretend otherwise, impudent Miss Ha'Penny, but I can guess the truth. Of course William's told you. He may even have sent you here after me, as a trial, and expressly to plague me."

"He has not, my lady," Bethany said. "Not one word against you."

Lady Sperry scowled, furiously twisting one of her curls around and around her finger. "What if I tell you my reason for coming here? Will you confess yours to me in return?"

Even if she were willing to bargain, Bethany wasn't sure she really wanted to know the woman's reasons for anything. "I'm sorry, my lady, but I don't believe that I wish to—"

"Oh, but you do! You know you do!" The marchioness slid to the edge of the bed, leaning forward so her face with its artfully painted cheeks and lips came closer to Bethany's. "I've come here with a special invitation for William, for him to join me at a grand entertainment that could be— *should* be—in his honor if only he agrees, and accepts."

Again Bethany shook her head, not only because she wanted to hear no more confidences from Lady Sperry, but also because she could not imagine her William as the guest of honor at any grand entertainment that the marchioness would sponsor.

But Lady Sperry was quick, and read the reluctance in Bethany's expression as easily as if she'd spoken aloud.

"You don't know William at all, do you?" she asked, suddenly lowering her voice to a husky purr of triumph. "If you did, you wouldn't be treating me like this."

Bethany raised her chin, concentrating on her experience with William as a good and noble man and trying to ignore the malicious doubt that the marchioness was trying to plant. "I have my own opinions and judgment of Major Callaway, based on our acquaintance."

"Oh, your *acquaintance*," the countess said, slathering the word with sarcasm. "Whatever little game William is playing with you, Miss Ha'Penny, recall that to him it *is* a game, and nothing more. He may pretend that he is the holiest of saints, replete with a vow of poverty and oaths to do only good, and other ridiculous palaver."

She swept her hand through the air between them, dismissing everything.

"But I know William," she continued, "and I know his past, and I know that this all must be a ruse, Miss Ha'Penny, all false and cheap as tin, and not worth the value of your name, and if you—"

"Good day, my lady," Bethany said sharply, nearly jumping to her feet in her haste to leave. She'd heard more than she needed, and far, far more than she'd wanted. "I can wait no longer for Major Callaway."

The marchioness's eyes glittered with the same hard edge as her jewels.

"You cannot go, because I didn't grant you leave," she said smugly. "And we've only begun to speak of dear, dear William."

"Perhaps you've only begun to speak, my lady," Beth-

OFFICIAL OPINION POLL

ANSWER 3 QUESTIONS AND WE'LL SEND YOU
2 FREE BOOKS AND A FREE GIFT!

0074823 ‖‖█‖‖█‖‖ ‖‖█‖‖ ‖‖█‖‖   **FREE GIFT CLAIM #** 3953

YOUR OPINION COUNTS!

Please tick TRUE or FALSE below to express your opinion about the following statements:

Q1 Do you believe in "true love"?

"TRUE LOVE HAPPENS ONLY ONCE IN A LIFETIME."
○ TRUE
○ FALSE

Q2 Do you think marriage has any value in today's world?

"YOU CAN BE TOTALLY COMMITTED TO SOMEONE WITHOUT BEING MARRIED."
○ TRUE
○ FALSE

Q3 What kind of books do you enjoy?

"A GREAT NOVEL MUST HAVE A HAPPY ENDING."
○ TRUE
○ FALSE

YES, I have scratched the area below.

Please send me the 2 FREE BOOKS and FREE GIFT for which I qualify. I understand I am under no obligation to purchase any books, as explained on the back of this card.

2 FREE BOOKS AND A FREE GIFT

H7II

Mrs/Miss/Ms/Mr _____ Initials _____

BLOCK CAPITALS PLEASE

Surname _____

Address _____

_____

_____

Postcode _____

Visit us online at www.millsandboon.co.uk

THE READER SERVICE™
FREE BOOK OFFER
FREEPOST CN81
CROYDON
CR9 3WZ

NO STAMP
NECESSARY
IF POSTED IN
THE U.K. OR N.I.

any said, her hand on the door, "but I find I'm finished listening. Good *day*."

She left with her head high and she didn't look back, and she'd never imagined that slamming a door in the face of a marchioness could ever be so satisfying.

Or, ultimately, so very dangerous.

Slowly William climbed the steps to the front door. It was not so much the weariness in his body that weighed upon him, but the exhaustion of his spirit from all he'd seen and heard today. He could not put the memory of the new little widow from his mind, her tear-swollen face and the keening cry that had come straight from her broken heart. He'd done what he could to ease her suffering, but it would never be enough, and he knew it.

"There you are, Major." Mrs. Ketch stood in her open door, her cat twitching possessively around her ankles. "A lady's waiting for you upstairs."

"A lady, Mrs. Ketch?" he asked, immediately picturing Bethany Penny. "By what name?"

Mrs. Ketch shrugged, as if to say such a detail was too meaningless for her to consider. "*Says* she's your sister."

"My sister is here?" He glanced up the stairway, half-expecting to see Portia tapping her toe on the landing. How had he missed her carriage in the street? "Here. My God."

"There was another," Mrs. Ketch said. "She left."

"Another what? Another lady?" His hope rose again.

"Copper hair, in a cab," the landlady said. "Said she couldn't wait."

That must have been Bethany: it couldn't be anyone else. He wondered what news she had, what she'd learned, but most of all he wished he'd been here to see her when she'd come. His weariness forgotten, he turned back toward the door, intending to go to Penny House.

"Here now, what of the other upstairs?" Mrs. Ketch said, her normal suspicions growing. "That sister of yours? Can't keep her in my house."

William sighed. "I cannot say I blame you. And Mrs. Ketch, for good or ill, she truly *is* my sister."

But the landlady's *harrumph* as she closed the door showed she didn't believe it, and with another sigh of recognition, William headed up the stairs to his rooms.

And to Portia.

He turned the key as quietly as he could, and was rewarded by the sight of his sister on her hands and knees, searching through the lowest drawer of his chest.

"Have you found any state secrets, Portia?" he asked as he entered. "Maps plotting a French invasion, or a cache of Russian gold?"

"Don't be cruel, William," she said, closing the drawer and turning to face him without the least pretense of guilt. "You have been away for eons, and I was bored to distraction."

"Apparently you found it, too, searching my rooms." He didn't sit, intending to leave again as soon as he could move his sister along. "What is it you want, Portia? Surely you had a better reason for appearing here than to inventory my stockings."

She scrambled to her feet, standing before him. "I did," she said. "I've come with an invitation from Father."

"Then you can take it back to him directly," William said. "Didn't you tell him I've no interest in participating in his schemes, or his life?"

She rearranged the shawl over her shoulders. "Father won't accept your refusal from me. He insists on hearing it from you yourself."

"He can insist until an apoplexy takes him," William said, feeling as if they'd already had this conversation.

"I'm not going back to his house for any reason, and you can tell him that."

Portia scowled, making her face determinedly unpleasant. "Father will not be pleased."

"He shouldn't be, Portia. I'm not, either."

She sighed dramatically, a preposterous stage groan. "That wasn't all, William, though I swore not to tell you. Father had heard that another one of those old soldiers was poisoned this morning, and he wanted me to make sure it wasn't you, his son."

"Don't try my intelligence," he said. "At least the man who died today left a family who are grieving for him with all their hearts, which would hardly be the case with our charming group."

"Father is willing to attempt a reconciliation," she said, though without much conviction. "It's you who are being difficult."

"Father doesn't want a reconciliation. He wants a body guaranteed to carry his bloodlines that he can barter for his own gain."

"Father says that the Dalembert girl is quite lovely," Portia said. "Most gentlemen would be delighted to have a wife who was not only rich and beautiful, but also as obliging as an obedient child."

"I am not most gentlemen, and I find the thought of a wife who's no better than an obedient child sickening." He'd forgotten how much his sister represented everything that was so wrong with his family, and everything he wanted to escape. Pointedly he took her arm to guide her to the door. "Now off with you, Portia. I have another engagement."

"What, with that ill-mannered Miss Ha'Penny?" she asked, digging in her heels. "As damaged as you are, William, I'd have thought you could do better than a common little chit like that. You cannot begin to fathom how rudely she treated me."

"Damnation, Portia, what did you say to her?" William demanded. "Which of your lies did you spread?"

Her eyes brightened, and too late William realized he'd tipped his cards. "No lies, dear brother. But it did seem she knew precious little of you and your past, especially the gaudy legion of her predecessors."

"Is that why she left?" he asked, his dread growing. His past before the army *had* been lurid, replete with all-night drunken debaucheries with actresses and demireps. But though he wouldn't pretend otherwise, he still didn't necessarily want Portia telling every last lascivious detail to his country-bred minister's daughter. "My God, Portia, I cannot believe even you would do this for your amusement!"

"So she means something to you, does she?" Portia teased. "How *common* you've become in your tastes!"

"Answer me now," he ordered. "What the devil did you tell Miss Penny, Portia?"

"Oh, nothing of great interest," she said with a careless shrug. "She left before I could tell her the worst."

"There's a small blessing in that," William said, not entirely believing her.

Portia sighed. "She was in a great tearing hurry to return to—well, to return to whatever low place she's from. Why, she didn't even give me time to explain that I was your sister!"

"Why the devil didn't you tell her, Portia?" he asked, aghast.

He'd no doubt that his sister had purposefully misled Bethany into believing she was his mistress. It was exactly the kind of twisted, malicious mischief that Portia most enjoyed, and because there was so little resemblance between brother and sister, it was also a confusion that might actually succeed.

But how much of Portia's nonsense had Bethany believed? She'd only known William as he was now; would she accept that he'd somehow keep a woman as frivolous and obviously expensive as Portia as his mistress?

And if she had, would she be willing to listen to him long enough to hear the truth?

"You're leaving now, Portia," he said, grabbing her arm to lead her across the room. "You've done enough here."

"Oh, William, please, you're hurting my arm!"

"Don't be ridiculous," he snapped, pulling her through the door with him. "I've known you all your vain and empty life, Portia, and none of your drama works with me."

She twisted around to face him, once again trying her best to coax him into obliging. "But what shall I tell Father?"

"Tell him to go to hell," he said, not bothering to hide his bitterness. "And you, Portia, may lead the way."

"You go on upstairs, Letty," Bethany said, sitting at the big oak kitchen table with a cup of tea and a cookbook open before her. "I'll bank the last fire when I'm done here."

The cook shook her head, her ruddy face concerned. "Are you sure, miss? It's nearly four in the morning as it is, with you bound for the market by six. Even you must sleep some time, miss."

Bethany smiled at that. She *was* tired, exhausted, and her head ached as well. But her mind was still racing on and on with everything that had happened this day, and she knew if she tried to sleep, she'd never succeed, not yet.

"I'm almost done, Letty," she said, looking down at the market list she was making. "I've only to finish the menus for tomorrow, and then I'll be going upstairs myself."

"Even those infernal guards have gone to bed by now, miss. You'll be all alone here, and that's not right, not these days." Letty frowned, clucking her tongue with concern.

"Miss Penny will come hunting below stairs for you, see if she don't."

"More likely Miss Penny's already blissfully asleep, and not noticing whether I'm in my bed or not." Bethany had often envied her older sister's ability to put the day behind her and fall instantly, deeply, asleep as soon as she put her head to her pillow. "Another few minutes for me here will make no difference to her."

"What'll make a difference to her is if you topple head-first into a kettle tomorrow because you're that weary."

"I won't, Letty, I promise." Bethany sat back in her chair, rubbing her forehead. "And I promise I'll be in bed myself soon. Good night."

"Good night, miss." Letty dipped a quick curtsey and headed on up the stairs, her footsteps slow and heavy on the treads.

Bethany turned back to the cookbook, trying to make herself concentrate on the long line of ingredients for a savory game pie. Usually deciding the next night's offerings for the dining room was one of her favorite occupations, and one of her most absorbing.

But tonight instead of imagining how this herb would complement that vegetable, all she could picture was the grace of Lady Sperry's voluptuous figure as she'd sprawled across William's bed, her golden curls catching the last of the evening light through the window. Not even Eve in the Garden could have been more tempting, more alluring, and Bethany wrestled with her own jealousy and disappointment. No matter how much she reminded herself that William had made her no promises, she still couldn't stop thinking of how his eyes had lit when they'd met, how he'd smiled at her and how right it had felt when they'd kissed. No wonder she kept trying to fight the feeling that she'd already lost before she'd won.

She shoved aside the cookbook and buried her face in folded arms on the table. She couldn't fault William. He'd done nothing wrong. This was all her own foolish fault. She wasn't exactly sure where she'd erred, where she'd let herself misunderstand, or what she might have done to make things other than what they were, but she did know that she hurt inside, and that somehow, in some way, she must have brought it on herself.

Lost in her own misery, she didn't hear the tapping at first. Little taps, like water dripping from a newly scrubbed dish into the wash bucket, taps that didn't register. But finally the sound was persistent enough that it roused her, and she looked up.

And saw William's face at the window beside the door.

She pressed her hands over her mouth, convinced her imagination had conjured him there, not reality. But she blinked, and he remained, and now that he'd realized she'd seen him, he waved as well.

He *had* come back to her, but her excitement was immediately tempered by realizing that he'd caught her moping and feeling sorry for herself. She smoothed back her hair and patted her cheeks, trying to compose herself, and hurried to open the door.

"You're here," she said, and felt foolish as soon as she'd said it.

"And you're awake." He entered quickly, waiting for her to shut the door after him. With an efficiency that gave her chills, his gaze shot around the kitchen, checking to see if they were truly alone. "I hoped you would be. I had to wait for those damned nursemaid guards of yours to leave."

"I hope that wasn't too long." Unsure of what else to do, she went to stand by the table, her hands on the back rung of the chair. He was acting as if nothing had happened, nothing had changed. "Did you learn anything from the almshouse kitchen?"

"Not from there, no," he said. The lines on his face were marked deep with weariness. "They've been locked down tight as a drum, with every shutter latched and not a soul to be seen. But I did manage to learn the name and address of the new widow from a gossipy old woman with long ears. I almost wished I hadn't."

He dropped into the chair at the far end of the table, and automatically Bethany set a cup before him and filled it with tea.

"Did you go to her?" she asked softly, watching him sip the tea, steam curling around his face. It hadn't even been a day since she'd seen him last, yet she'd missed him.

He sighed, and nodded. "She was scarce more than a child herself. Her heart broken with grief, a baby in her arms, and not a farthing to her name. I did what I could to help her."

Without thinking she reached out to rest her hand on his arm. "I'm sure you did, just as I'm sure she appreciated it."

"She might someday," he said. "Now she's too distraught to notice much of anything. But the worst was knowing there was no need for her suffering."

"What wife ever expects to lose her husband so young?"

"It wasn't that, Bethany." His voice rumbled with unhappiness. "George Smith was chosen and ruthlessly poisoned, when no others around him were harmed. The murderer's only mistake was to choose the wrong George Smith, from the wrong regiment. All the men who've been killed have been innocent, but this one—this one was doubly so."

"Oh, William, I am sorry," she said, her hand pressing his arm in sympathy. He was right, this death did seem doubly wrong.

"So am I," he said, his pale eyes bleak. "Now tell me, Bethany. Do you still trust me?"

She nodded, shoving aside those faint whispers of doubt that Portia had planted in her head earlier. It was only because she was tired that she'd let her mind again peek down that path.

"I'm glad you have such faith in me," he said, which made her hate those doubts even more. "You might not if you'd seen that poor grieving girl today. And the sad truth is that I'm still not one step closer to learning who's doing it, Bethany. Not one single blasted *step*."

She drew her chair close beside his, slipping her fingers into his. "But maybe you are, William. Mr. Fewler—he's in charge of the guards here—he'd heard that the authorities now believe the French are behind the poisonings. They think that the French hope to demoralize us English by murdering our common soldiers."

"How in blazes can you trust your safety to a man who'd believe in such drivel?" William asked with disgust.

"I didn't hire him, nor did I say I believed him," Bethany protested, wishing that her information was so easily and lightly dismissed. "Mr. Pratt and my sister did. And I never did—"

"Then listen to me." He began counting the reasons why not by thumping his finger on table. "The French don't need to demoralize us at home, because they're already doing a damned fine job of it abroad. Murdering a pauper's not their style, not from a country that lopped off the heads of its king and queen."

"Oh," she said, feeling sheepish and ignorant. "That does sound more plausible."

"Of course I'm right," he said, and the thumb counted out another reason. "And even if they were to try such a stunt, they wouldn't bother to select one man at a time, from the same small group of soldiers. They'd poison the whole lot at a single almshouse, and toss a grenade into the crowded yard just to be sure."

"A grenade?"

"A kind of small bomb with a timing device," he explained, brusque and businesslike, "thrown by the hand, that can cause every kind of bloody destruction and mayhem when it explodes."

She didn't want to linger on that picture any longer than she must, or be reminded that he was too familiar with such nightmarish details of war. "Then if it's not the French, who is it? What reason could there possibly be for such a crime?"

"I do not know." He sighed deeply, and hung his head, his dark hair falling over his forehead. "I do not know. Someone has made a list of these men, and is finding and killing them each in turn. He doesn't know them personally, else he wouldn't have erred with George Smith."

"But how can you blame yourself?"

"Because I'm the only connection to them all, Bethany." He pushed the tea away. "I can't predict the next death before it happens, but afterward, the link is clear as day. It's me. It's *me*. As hard as I try to deny it, or seek another possibility, it always comes back to me."

"But a regiment has dozens and dozens of men in it, doesn't it? Even with you as their major, I cannot understand how you can fault yourself for—"

"I don't wish to discuss it," he said, his voice a muffled growl of finality as his face, too, shut her out, warning her to ask no more. It was the same thing that happened yesterday in the park, when he'd claimed to be fine and so obviously wasn't.

What was crossing before his mind's eye that could cause such a response? What old horror from the war came back to haunt him like this?

"Very well," she said evenly, hoping she could catch him before he sank too low. "Would you care for more tea?"

He looked up with her from beneath his brows, not bothering to lift his chin, his pale eyes haunted. "Lady Sperry. What did she say to you?"

"Her ladyship the marchioness?" At once Bethany pulled her hand back from his arm, where it had no business being. "She spoke of many things, none of any consequence."

"She let you think she was my mistress, didn't she?"

Bethany flushed. "I told you she said many things, William, things that could perhaps have been construed one way or another."

"She's not my mistress, Bethany, nor ever has been," he said. "She's my sister."

"That lady is your *sister?*" Bethany said, thrown off balance. She'd been more willing to believe they were lovers than siblings, and the incestuous overtones, even in jest, shocked her. "Forgive me, but I do not see how—that is, there is so little real resemblance between you that I never would have thought you related."

"Thank you," he said, reaching out to reclaim her hand. "That's a far greater compliment than you can realize, not knowing my family. My sister has strange ways of amusing herself at my expense."

"But—but she said she was a marchioness, the Marchioness of Sperry!"

"So she is," he said. "I know that may be hard to swallow, but Portia has made the most of her beauty and her gifts, and married well. Very, very well. Now what else did she tell you?"

"Nothing of consequence." She was still stumbling over William being brother-in-law to a marquess. It was possible, of course—just as he might have turned to the army to improve his lot, she could well have used her obvious beauty to marry a wealthy, titled husband. But as close as Bethany was to Amariah and Cassia, she found it impossible to imagine any sister willing to hint at such scandalous behavior with her brother simply for her own amusement.

"She said I didn't know you at all," she continued. "She implied that you had led a frivolous life at one time, and she tried to make you sound like a rake, instead of who you are."

"But I *was* a rake," he said without any surprise. "That was no invention. I was also very young, very foolish and very easily led by bad companions."

"You're not like that now." His sister was right; she didn't know him well at all.

"No." He looked down at their clasped hands. "Not now, and not for a long time past. I couldn't be like that again even if I wished to."

"That is what I told your sister." Yet none of this explained the contradictions in his dress, his speech or the rich man's amusements in Mrs. Ketch's rooming house. "I told her that no matter what she said, I would judge you as the man I knew, and not the gossip she was repeating."

"Such rare trust from you, Bethany," he said in a hoarse whisper. He glanced down at her mouth, as if marveling that such words could have come from it. "God knows the mess I've made of my life until now, even without Portia to remind the world of my sins. What makes you see otherwise in me, I wonder?"

She'd never seen his smile so sad. Why, she wondered, when it was so clear he was going to kiss her?

"I told you I'd judge you for yourself, William Callaway," she whispered in return. "For what you are, not what your sister or anyone else says."

"Then judge me, Miss Penny," he said, reaching out to

cradle the back of her head in his large hand, drawing her into him. "Judge me now for what I am."

He kissed her, and she closed her eyes, and realized that she'd already judged him. His tongue parted her lips and met hers, hot and passionate and possessive, and she knew she'd long ago made up her mind—and her heart—about him. He was a good man, an honorable man, a man she could trust. The doubts and the rumors and the secrets would not change that, not while they kissed like this. He was William, her William for now, and that would be enough.

Yet as blissful as this was, she still heard the familiar creak of the stairs above her, and her eyes flew open.

"You must go," she said, breaking their kiss with a frantic little gasp. "I'm sorry, I'm sorry, but that's the first of the scullery maids come to light the kitchen fires, and she can't find you here."

At once he was on his feet, grabbing his hat and shoving his chair back into place.

"I'll go now, but I'll come back to you," he said with that familiar raspy urgency that she found so exciting. "I won't leave you for long. Good night, sweetheart."

He bent down and kissed her again, so quickly it was like touching her hand to a hot kettle and pulling away before she was burned.

And then, like that, he was gone, his shadow fading through the glass into the dawn and Bethany slipping his tea cup and saucer into the wash bucket before the sleepy girl came down the steps.

Macallister scowled down at the pearl bracelet on his desk. He couldn't believe that Bethany Penny had returned it to him; he'd never heard of any woman returning an expensive piece of jewelry like that, without any real reason or provocation. Weren't all women by nature greedy, conniving? The accompanying note said only that Miss Penny regretted that she was unable to accept any personal gifts from club members.

"Club members be damned." He wasn't any ordinary club member, was he? His intentions were the most honorable in the world. She should be damned grateful he'd pay any attention to her at all, being who and what she was. Look at her sister: everyone in London had made a fuss over her wedding, and the best match she could make for herself had been to some mysterious dark bastard straight out of the West Indies sugar-fields. Surely Lieutenant John Macallister, serving his king and country with honor and distinction, was a sight more creditable than that!

She'd taken his contribution to her charities fast enough, though. That kind of gift she'd take. Maybe that was the key to her good graces: putting the money in the Penny House poor box instead of into the jewelers' tills. Once it had come out of his pockets, he didn't care where it ended up. If feeding a pack of rascally beggars was what made her smile at him, well, then, he'd do it. He'd do it in a heartbeat.

Because the more *Miss* Bethany Penny refused him, the more determined he was to have her. He hated being denied anything—he always had—and thanks to Father's money, he almost never was. He'd set his sights on this woman, and by God, one way or another, he'd make her his.

He'd picked up the scorned bracelet when his servant appeared with a letter for him. The coarse paper looked incongruous on the silver charger that the man held, but Macallister recognized it at once, his pulse quickening with anticipation.

He tore the seal open even before the servant had left, hurrying to the window for more light to make out the spidery handwriting. There were two sheets this time, each addressing different questions and written at different times, but neither included his name, or the sender's, as Macallister had arranged. In matters as sensitive as these, there was never a possibility of being too cautious.

The first sheet crowed with success. The next impediment on the list had been removed as planned. There had been no trouble, no mistakes. The constables were in a righteous funk, without any clues or suspects. Macallister chuckled as he read, especially the part where the letter-writer described how, in disguise, he'd made concerned inquiries of the very constable who'd been called to view the body.

Oh, the whole thing was rich, very rich. Even if he hadn't been forced into this unpleasant little arrangement to preserve his honor, he might still have done it, just for the amusement.

He was still smiling when he turned to the next sheet, and all his amusement vanished.

Sir,
In the other matter, I must inform you that your information is correct. Callaway is alive. Although his wounds were most grave & left him a mockery of his former self, he did survive the attack. However, where he is living is not known. He is no longer in contact with his family & friends, & they regard him as good as dead. He is commonly believed to be contained in a private hospital or an asylum somewhere to the north or on the Continent.
It must be your decision as to whether he shall be added to the list with the others.
Yr. ob't. s'vt. in All Things,
X.

Macallister read both letters a second time, the sheets shaking in his hands, before he tossed them into the fire. He stirred the ashes with the poker to make sure every scrap was obliterated, then poured himself a full tumbler of brandy.

Hell. William Callaway was alive. A lord in his own right, the son of a peer, a highly ranked and decorated officer, not some barely human refuse that would not be missed.

William Callaway, who would know everything that had happened, and be believed if he told it.

Hell, hell, *hell.*

Chapter Ten

Bethany smiled at the undersized boy peering from beneath the heavy shock of black hair. She'd seen him at her door many times before, and the name he went by—Twig—was one of the most perfectly descriptive nicknames she'd ever heard.

"Take an apple, too, Twig," she said as she ladled the soup into his bowl. "They're particularly fine today."

"Thank'ee, ma'am." The boy ducked his head, but didn't move along to the basket of apples. "You're kind as they come, ma'am."

"Thank you, Twig." She smiled, wondering why he stayed before her, shuffling from one bare foot to the other. She didn't want to rush him—she never liked to rush any of her flock—but the others behind him in the line were growing impatient, muttering and craning their necks to see what the delay could be. "Is there something else I might do for you?"

He nodded, quick jerks of his pointed little chin. Carefully he set his bowl on the ground between his feet, and dug his hand around inside his coat. He glanced from side to side, then beckoned for her to come closer.

Bethany leaned forward, and was surprised to feel him stuffing a folded paper into her hand, furtively, so no one else would see.

"It's from the guv'nor, Miss Penny," he whispered. "The tall one what has the limp. He said no one else was to see or know."

"I'll make sure they don't," she whispered back, tucking the paper into the pocket of her apron. A tall man with a limp: of course the note must be from William, and her day brightened immeasurably. She'd known she'd hear from him, because he'd given his word that he'd come back to her, but the past two days without him had been very hard to bear.

She reached out to ruffle the boy's hair, raising her voice at the same time. "You come back tomorrow morning, Twig, and I'll be happy to trim your hair for you. The way it is now, you can scarcely peep out."

"You don't have to do *that,* Miss Penny," the boy said, scuffling so quickly out of her reach—and that of her scissors—that Bethany laughed.

"Whatever you decide, Twig, take your apple," she said. "And take another, too, if you wish, for a friend or for yourself tonight."

She turned back to filling the bowl of the next person in line, trying to concentrate on the face before her. But she was as aware of the note in her pocket as if it had been a hot coal against her skin, and the line had never moved as slowly. When the final person took away his bowl and the kettle was empty, she hurried back inside, hoping to slip away to the pantry or the wine cellar to read the note in private.

"Forgive me, Miss Penny," the guard said, stepping in front of her to block her path. "But that boy outside—what did he say to you?"

"What he said is of no concern of yours," she said indignantly, hating the fact that she'd been watched. Twig had been wise to be so careful. "He spoke to me in confidence."

The guard nodded, but didn't move aside to let her pass, and Bethany was acutely aware of how her staff was watching her as they worked, waiting for her response. This was the first time she'd been so openly challenged in her own kitchen, and her temper simmered from the indignity of it, combined with the guilt of the note in her pocket.

"Mr. Fewler said to report everything that didn't seem right, Miss Penny," the guard said doggedly. "And that boy didn't seem right."

"You can tell Mr. Fewler whatever you please," she said warmly. "That boy has been a regular visitor to this house, and there is nothing wicked or suspicious about him. I will vouch for him however Mr. Fewler requires."

"Thank you, miss," the guard said, clearly unconvinced. "But I mean to tell Mr. Fewler. You can never be too careful with boys like that one, miss. Boys bring more trouble than the plague, and that's the honest truth."

Bethany made an impatient little *huff* to show what she thought of the trouble brought by boys and guards, and left the guard behind. To her relief, he didn't come after her, and she swiftly made her way to the privy in the corner of the yard. At least *that* would be one place Fewler's men wouldn't dare follow, and as soon as she latched the door shut so she couldn't be disturbed, she pulled William's note from its hiding place.

Strange to think that this was the first she'd seen of his handwriting, the words slashed boldly over the page from a broad-nibbed pen and heavy hand, yet somehow even from these few lines, she would have known it was his anywhere.

*Come to me at five o'clock, where yr. alley meets St.
James's. Do not let yourself be seen, nor shall I. I
count the minutes.
Yours like no other,
C.*

She traced her finger along the written words, imagining his pen scrawling across the page. These were dashing, exciting words, written not with care or consideration,
but in haste and honesty. And that closing "Yours like no
other," could there be any finer sentiment?

The note was so much like *him* that she couldn't keep
the silly smile from her face, as giddy as any green girl
fresh from the schoolroom. In two hours, he was coming
to see her, and no matter how difficult it would be to leave
the kitchen at the height of the preparations for the evening,
she would find a way to go to him.

He was counting the minutes until then, and so would
she, with every beat of her heart, and—

"Bethany, duck, are you unwell?" Amariah asked from
the other side of the privy door. "I do not mean to pry, but
in the kitchen, they said you bolted through the door as if
demons were after you. Letty in particular was most worried over you."

"I'm fine." She shoved William's note back into her
pocket, giving it a fond pat for good measure, then swung
open the door and stepped out to join her sister. "They
needn't have worried."

But Amariah wasn't as easily convinced. "You look
flushed," she said, laying the back of her hand across
Bethany's forehead. "Have you a fever?"

Bethany wriggled free, beginning back across the yard
to the kitchen door. She didn't like deceiving Amariah,
even in such a little thing as this. "If I feel warm, it's from

the kitchen fires. You know how warm they can be in the summer."

"I'm not so sure that's it." Amariah caught her arm, stopping her. "Letty said the guard was questioning you about one of your flock, and none too gently, either."

"It was one of the pack of orphaned children, a boy called Twig," Bethany said. "He wanted to whisper something to me alone, that the others wouldn't hear, and that great ninny of a guard thought I was hearing a plot to assassinate His Majesty himself."

"Bethany, don't say such things aloud, even in jest." Troubled, her sister searched Bethany's face. "I'm sorry Mr. Fewler and his men have been so vexing to you. You've had to cope with them underfoot much more than the rest of us above stairs. I wish they weren't necessary, truly I do, but especially now that the authorities believe that the French are behind these dreadful poisonings, why, I'm afraid I must—"

"The authorities are wrong, Amariah," Bethany said with conviction, automatically repeating William's argument that had made such sense to her. "Consider the facts. The French murder their royalty, not poor scarred English soldiers. And why would they be so selective, choosing one man at a time? If the French wish to terrorize the English here at home, they'd be more likely to try to kill a great many people at once, in a public place, with some sort of bomb or—or a grenade, thrown by hand."

"A *grenade?*" Amariah frowned, perplexed, and too late Bethany realized she'd perhaps quoted William more closely than was necessary.

"Well, yes," she said, hoping she sounded merely informed. "Something to cause a more public disturbance. *That's* what the French would do."

"I see," Amariah said slowly. Her mouth twisted to one

side as she thought, taking a good long moment before she spoke again. "I've been wrong here, duck, haven't I? When Cassia left Penny House, you and I believed we'd have no problem taking on her work as well as our own, but I see now I've expected too much from you."

"Oh, Amariah, that's not—"

"Oh, yes, it is, and don't pretend otherwise," she said wistfully, slipping her arm around Bethany's shoulders. "I'm sorry, duck. Truly. I should have known better."

"Oh, just hush, Amariah," Bethany said softly, curling her arm around her sister's waist. Ever since their mother had died when they'd been little girls, Amariah had tried to take her place, tried to act older and more protective wherever Bethany and Cassia were concerned. Sometimes it was irksome, but other times—like this, when so much else in her life seemed uncertain—Bethany was glad she had Amariah watching out for her. "Before we came to London, we decided that together we could make a go of Penny House, and we have."

"But I've let you do more than your share," Amariah said. "Running this kitchen, overseeing the staff and the provisioning and each night's preparations, coaxing the most fastidious palates in London, and then your charity work as well—that's more than enough for all three of us Pennys together."

Bethany smiled with proud determination. "And I've done it, Amariah, just as you've taken care of the upstairs. I'm not complaining, you know."

"Hush, hush, I never said you were," her sister said, soothing. "I'm only saying that perhaps we both need a small holiday. We're nearly to the end of the Season. We could close our doors for a fortnight or so, and go stay with Cassia and Richard at Greenwood, or even Bath. Away from the city, and away from these guards and the poisonings."

"But we can't close!" Bethany protested, stunned by the suggestion. "Our members will forget us, and go elsewhere!"

"Not when they've worked so hard and invested so much to *become* Penny House members," Amariah said, unperturbed. "They've all gone to the country, too."

"Not my flock!"

And not William, either…

"We can leave Letty in charge of that," she said, clearly eager herself to get away. "Oh, please say yes, Bethany! I want this to be special!"

With growing frustration, Bethany swept her hand through the air, encompassing the big stone house before her. "But to leave everything behind so soon after we've begun!"

Everything meaning William. *William, the first man who'd ever counted the minutes before he saw her again, the first she'd ever wanted to…*

Amariah's happy smile of anticipation faded, and with belated guilt Bethany noticed the weariness in her sister's face, the lines around her eyes that Bethany had been too busy herself to see.

"We've never had a real holiday away from home, you know," Amariah said softly, " and after this last year with Father's death and all that's changed in our own lives, I do believe we've earned one."

"But to go away from town now—oh, it doesn't feel proper." Bethany turned away, not trusting her face before her sister.

She wished she could confess her real reasons to Amariah. She wished she could show her William's note, and explain his suspicions about the murders and her own, too. Most of all she wished she could tell Amariah about the way she felt when William kissed her and held her and counted those minutes that kept them apart. But these weren't just her secrets: they were William's as well, and as much as she wanted to confide in Amariah, she knew to do so would betray William, and she could not do that.

But maybe it was time to think not only of him, but of herself, too. As much as she respected William and the past that cast so dark a shadow on the present, she needed to know more if they were to share any kind of future. She wasn't going to let herself be one of those women responsible for her own downfall at the hands of a man. She'd learned that by watching her sister Cassia find her way with Richard, whose own secrets had very nearly torn them apart before their marriage.

And all the kisses in the world would mean nothing if William couldn't begin trusting her.

"I know you intend only the best, Amariah," she said instead, "but this just doesn't seem like the right time for us to leave London."

Amariah reached out to brush her fingers against Bethany's cheek, her voice full of disappointment. "I won't force you to do anything against your will, of course. But I want you to consider it. Please, Bethany. For me, but mostly for yourself."

"I will," Bethany said softly. This much she could offer to Amariah without compromising William, or herself. "Though I'll make no promises, I will consider it."

William had told himself he wouldn't return.

No matter what he'd so impulsively promised, he knew he'd no business going back to Bethany. If he truly cared for her, then he'd do whatever he must to keep her from becoming tangled in his sorry, uncertain confusion of a life. What did he have to offer her? With each question he asked about his murdered comrades, he knew the risks grew more hazardous, more perilous, and he'd no right asking her to share those risks. A true gentleman with any sense of honor would have walked through that kitchen door, leaving her safely behind, and never turned once to look back.

But he wasn't a gentleman anymore, and he'd long ago put aside honor as having no place in the reality of his life. Instead he'd sent his scrawled invitation, and now he walked toward St. James's Square, toward Penny House, toward Bethany.

It wasn't just that he wanted to see her: he *needed* to see her, to touch her, to feel the warmth of her smile and her skin and her soft body against his and the vibrancy of *life* that she carried within her.

He shook his head, cursing his weakness as he walked with his eyes downcast. He and death were such old, grimly familiar companions: why should he balk now? Yesterday, after he'd made sure that George Smith's widow and child were safely on their way to the country, he'd gone to Surgeon's Hall to try to wrest Smith's body from the grips of the quacks and butchers for a proper burial. What he'd seen there was as bad as any battlefield, mangled corpses with their hair cut away and their teeth pulled out to be sold, severed limbs tossed together with a cackling disrespect for what the dead had been in life. He'd left empty-handed and sickened, his stomach for such sights gone and his hope of discovering any fresh clues or details still a taunting, empty failure.

He'd found no more peace in his bed last night, his conscience too full of what he'd seen. He'd lain awake and through the open curtains at his window watched the stars travel over the chimney pots. Finally in desperation he'd turned to the bleak solace of a tawny port, his thoughts turning ever-blacker as he emptied first one glass, then another, and another, waiting for the golden liquor to do its work and numb the twin pains of his leg and of his spirit enough for him to slide into sleep.

And yet, no matter how dark his thoughts had become, no matter how much he loathed himself, the memory of Bethany had been there, too, a copper-haired angel guiding him through the gloom.

And to her.

He'd scarcely turned the corner when he saw her hurrying to meet him. She'd come straight from the kitchen, with moist little tendrils of her hair peeking out from her plain linen cap, an apron still tied around her waist and her cheeks flushed and glowing from the heat of the fires.

Or, if he dare to delude himself, perhaps from the joy of seeing him.

"You came," he said as soon as she was in hearing.

"Of course I came." She stopped just short of where he stood, suddenly shy, as if she should ever be unsure of herself with him. She curled her fingers around her ear, smoothing back a stray wisp. "Is there any news?"

"No news," he said, feeling as if he'd drawn her here on a false pretense. He wanted her to help him forget the poisonings and his inability to stop them, to forget, not remember. "Nothing more than yesterday."

"I'm sorry." She shifted her feet back and forth, a little dance of nervousness, and glanced back at the alley behind her. "I thought that was why you sent for me."

He already felt like the biggest fool in the world; how much worse could he make it? "I wanted to see you, lass. You. That was all."

"That is...*lovely.*" Her sudden smile, relieved and delighted at the same time, nearly stole his breath away. "How could you guess that I wanted to see you as well?"

"I didn't." He smiled, too, risking so much that he felt his whole face tighten with the effort. "I wanted to see you, and try to make things up to you. I thought we could take a boat on the river, and I'd buy you supper, and we could talk."

"Oh, William, how grand!" She reached up and rested the palm of her hand on his cheek, her fingers smelling faintly of apples and rosemary. Automatically he slipped his arm around her waist, drawing her closer, and her smile widened. "I cannot think of anything I'd rather do, and besides, we do need to talk."

"Then let us go, ma'am," he said, turning around her as gallantly as he could, as if they were together on the dance floor. "Away, away!"

She laughed, but her face had no gaiety, and she gracefully pulled away from his arm. "I wish I could, William, but I cannot."

"Why the devil not?" he asked, disappointment turning his voice gruff. "You just said you wished to more than anything."

"And I still do. But these are the busiest hours for the kitchen, preparing all the dishes for the gentlemen tonight, and I must—"

"Hang the other gentlemen," he said, taking her hand back. "They can get along without you well enough for one night. Better than I will, anyway."

"We're very busy," she protested, but he could hear her wavering, her fingers twisting around his. "The club kitchen's my responsibility, you know, and all the staff below stairs. There's so much to do."

But now he knew the flushed cheeks were for him, and his confidence rose.

"Please, Bethany," he said, his voice low, coaxing. "Now. Come with me."

She took a deep breath, then nodded, a quick little jerk of decision. "Very well," she said. "This once, William. Let me tell them, and I'll be back directly."

She didn't wait for his answer, but darted back to the house, her footsteps echoing against the alley walls. She'd be back; he didn't doubt it for a second. He grinned, and now his mouth curved easily. She'd chosen him over the kitchen and all those damned noble *members* upstairs, and he intended to make the most of it.

"Letty will watch over the meal for me," she said, hurrying up to him. She'd left off her apron and tossed a lemon-yellow shawl around her shoulders, and looped over one wrist was a small bundle wrapped in a knotted napkin. "I told her I'd be gone for a bit, and that she could make any decisions that needed making. Not that any will."

She laughed, a giddy trill, as if she were some low scullery maid who'd escaped from the head cook, rather than the head cook herself.

"I told you so." He took her hand and slipped it into the crook of his arm, feeling as if he'd escaped himself, too. "What's the point of being queen of the kitchen if you can't grant yourself a bit of time away from it?"

"You sound exactly like my sister," she said, falling into step beside him. "She says I need to take a fortnight away from Penny House. She wants us to close everything up and go to the seashore, or down to Hampshire to visit our other sister. But too many people depend upon me, and I don't see how I can simply shutter my kitchen for the sake of a holiday."

He thought of her ladling out soup from her kitchen step, a kind word and genuine interest for each one who shuffled before her, and how she'd been the first—perhaps the only—caller at St. Andrew's parish house after the poisoning there. He remembered how she seemed to be the first one in the kitchen in the morning, and the last to leave it at night, and how she was as concerned about the lowest scullery maid chopping carrots as the greatest duke nibbling at a slice of goose while he dropped another hundred guineas at faro. Even Twig had known that she'd put feeding her "flock" before her own sister's wedding party.

"Your sister may be right," he said, searching her face for signs of overwork. "Perhaps you do need a rest."

"Which is why I am here with you tonight," she said promptly. "But any more than that—I take my responsibilities too seriously to abandon them for such a frivolous reason."

"It's not frivolous, lass," he said. "Even soldiers are permitted leave away from the front. Responsibility can be a sword with two edges. The more one worries about others, then the less one has to worry about one's own welfare."

She tipped her head to one side as she gazed up at him. "Like you?"

He shook his head, not following. "We're discussing your situation, Bethany, not mine."

"But it could be yours as well, I think," she answered. "Turn the looking glass at yourself, William. Even though you've long left the army, you still concern yourself so much for the fate of the men who served with you that you scarce spare a moment or a farthing on yourself."

"Damnation, Bethany," he grumbled, bristling at what she was suggesting. He had come to her wanting to forget his flaws, his failures, not be reminded of all that he could not accomplish. "Now you sound like my own sister. Would you like me better if I squandered my time fussing over the perfect knot in my neckcloth like every other blueblood halfwit instead of returning the loyalty of those who most deserve it?"

"Oh, hush," she said, unperturbed. "I'm not finding fault. However could I?"

"It damned well sounds like finding fault to me."

"The truth often does," she said, "and I don't like hearing it any more than you do."

"Then why say it—even if it were the truth, which it's not—and spoil this evening?"

"I'm only saying that perhaps we're more alike than either would care to admit."

"If that *were* true," he said, still feeling defensive, "then I should carry you off to Brighton to a house by the sea for at least a month and keep you there with me until you forgot every last responsibility you've ever had. We'd both be helping each other, you see, and we'd let the rest of the world go straight to hell."

"I never said that," she answered quickly, her cheeks turning bright pink. "Especially not the part about—about the house."

The house, ha. She was thinking of him loving her into mindless, ecstatic oblivion. And so, God help him, was he.

"All I meant, William," she continued, "was that because we share the same goals, we'd make better allies than foes."

So she could imagine what would happen in a house in Brighton, too: good for her, good for him, good for them both. Could there be any better way to remind him of life, and to make him forget death?

He knew his smile was teasing, hinting at all manner of wickedness. "Allies don't kiss, Bethany."

Her flush deepened. "Neither do foes."

"It's far more interesting when they do." He'd wager she was imagining that, too.

"I wouldn't know." They'd reached the stone wall near the river's embankment. She stopped, and looked at him, fidgeting with the knotted bundled on her wrist. "You haven't asked what I brought you."

"If I do, then I'm showing too much concern for you," he said. "But if I don't, then I'm letting you show too much concern for me, having brought me a gift when I didn't."

"But it's not a gift," she protested, untying the napkin, "not really, so neither of us is too concerned about anyone else. Here. This came from the oven just as I was leaving."

Swathed in the napkin was an oval-shaped meat pie, the golden-brown pastry glazed with a glossy egg wash and trimmed with a curlicue of pastry leaves and vines. He broke off a quarter, releasing a heady, fragrant rush of steam and spiced meat, onions and juices, and popped it into his mouth. Had she any notion of how sensual and personal such an offering was to him?

"Now that is fine," he said with a happy groan, his words muddled by the pastry in his mouth. "Perhaps the finest pie I've ever been honored to taste."

"Thank you," she said, clearly still thinking too much of that house in Brighton. "Though it's not a gift."

It *was* a gift, especially coming from her, but he was enjoying the pastry—and her company—too much to argue with her now. "Then you must be fattening me up for the kill."

"Don't talk like that," she scolded halfheartedly, the breeze from the water tossing the fringe on her yellow shawl and making the loose copper tendrils dance around her cheeks and the creamy nape of her neck. She was too busy watching him eat to be truly cross, taking such obvious delight in his pleasure that he thought once again of that house in Brighton.

He slipped another piece of the pastry into his mouth, aware of her watching him lick the sauce from his fingers. "Where did a country parson's daughter like you learn to cook like the French king's chef, eh?"

She smiled, clearly both pleased by his question, and relieved by the ease with which it could be answered. "It's all Father's fault, actually. Before he wed, he'd accompanied the son of our local squire on his grand tour across the Continent. He acquired a gourmet's tastes quite beyond his means, and also beyond the skills of my poor mother and any of the housekeepers we could afford. I cannot tell you how many we had that departed in haste and in tears, but when the last one left, when I was ten, I decided to keep the peace in our house, and try my hand deciphering the French and Italian cookery books. I did well enough that Father sent me to learn what I could from Sir Allen's French cook, and that—that's how it began."

"But it's more than that," he said through the last bite. He could imagine her as a girl, bustling around an old-fashioned hearth in an oversized apron. "You have talent. You have a gift, and the passion to see it through."

"I've also made my share of burnt offerings in the process." She laughed, and leaned over the wall, watching the boats on the river. "Father always said that every one of us is blessed with a talent, and I suppose that cookery is mine. But what of you, William? Were you a military kind of boy, lining your friends into neat ranks while you plotted battles through the orchard?"

"Hardly." His own smile faded. He'd been a spoiled, selfish boy, always in trouble of one kind or another, too rich, too indulged, too handsome, for his own good. When he'd finally been sent down from school, the list of his sins had been impressive: gaming, drinking, bullying, whoring, fighting, petty theft to break the boredom. He would never have found favor in the Reverend Penny's household; more likely he would not have been let inside the gate.

"I doubt you were so very bad," she scoffed, clearly imagining a variation of her genteel little family. "A rascal, perhaps, but not bad. Did you have a dog, a favorite pet? Were you good at games? What was your family like? You already know a great deal about me, you see, but I know next to nothing about you."

"You'd be disappointed." He *had* been bad, badder than she could ever imagine, and he didn't want her to know it, any more than he wished her to know how disreputable and dissolute the family of a peer could be.

"How could I be disappointed by anything to do with

you?" Her smile was so warm, so winning, that he felt even more unworthy of her blind, sunny trust.

"You would. Believe me," he said, more sharply than he'd intended, and he turned away from her to look out at the river.

She didn't say anything at first, standing so quietly that he feared he'd finally driven her away. That would serve him right, and serve her better, too, to be rid of him.

But soon he felt her hand on his arm, light as the proverbial feather. "You're tired, aren't you?" she asked softly. "Here I've made you traipse all across London, without any regard for your leg. Does it pain you greatly?"

"My leg is fine," he muttered, unable to accept the excuse she was offering, or maybe, in her generosity, she believed it so. "And it won't get stronger if I don't push it."

"I'm sorry," she said without any reason to apologize, or maybe more reasons than he knew. "I should be going back to Penny House anyway."

"Not yet." He didn't want her to go and he didn't want to be left alone, especially not on such a note. He glanced down at the water, desperate for a reason to make her stay with him, and found it. "Have you ever traveled the river by boat?"

"In one of those little boats?" She leaned over the wall beside him, not wary, but curious. "No, I haven't."

"Then you shall now." He seized her hand and led her down the nearest steps to the water's edge. Several of the long, narrow skiffs were tied up at the bottom, the men sitting at their shipped oars and smoking their pipes while they waited for a fare. William motioned to the nearest boat, and the oarsman held the boat steady for William and Bethany to climb aboard.

"What place, guv'nor?" the oarsman asked as he pushed away from the landing. "Where are you an' the lady bound on this fine summer's eve?"

"Upstream and down," William said, settling his arm protectively around Bethany's shoulders as they sat side by side. "The lady's never seen the river firsthand."

"Ah, a pleasure voyage, is it?" The man flashed them a tobacco-stained grin as he bent his back to the oars. "Well, then, you've chosen the proper man."

"And you shall be our Captain Cook," Bethany said as she settled into her place in the rocking boat with William. "I expect a proper voyage of discovery."

The man's pipe stem twitched between his clenched teeth. "You'll have it, ma'am, you'll have it and more."

And for the next hour, William decided the oarsman was exactly as promised. He rowed them expertly through the river's currents and under the bridges and around larger craft, all the while keeping a cheerful commentary about the sights they passed along the shore. Free of the need for conversation, William could concentrate on simply being with Bethany, holding her close and feeling her relax beside him. He could feel her happiness, too, a kind of glow that matched the sunset flickering across the river's surface and the swinging lantern in the little boat's prow. There was no responsibility here, no families, no guilt over what had been done or not done. All they had was each other, and for the first time in years—maybe in his entire life—William realized he was happy, too.

"Another bit upstream, gov'nor?" the oarsman asked as they neared the steps where they'd first started. "It's your coin."

"I should go back to Penny House, William," Bethany said with obvious reluctance. "I don't want this to end, but I must go back."

"You are certain?" He didn't want it to end, either.

"I must." She twisted gracefully to face him, her hand

resting on his chest. "It wasn't quite Brighton, but I won't forget it."

"This was fine," he said, his voice deep and low, "but Brighton will be better. Much, much better."

She laughed softly, and kissed him before he could answer, a quick promise of a kiss for the future just as the boat bumped against the landing. Although the boatman looked discreetly at the water, William wished a more private place to kiss her as she deserved. He helped her from the boat, paid the man and led her up the shadowy steps, glistening faintly with moisture and lit only by a single lantern at the top.

She laughed, a conspirator's laugh, her arm looped familiarly around his waist. "I feel as if we're on some mysterious adventure, William," she whispered. "It's as if we were in Venice, creeping up from a gondola to our palazzo, and—"

The explosion came without warning, drowning her words. Fiery white stars blinded him, and instinctively he reached for Bethany, desperate to shield her with his body and protect her any way he could. But then came another explosion, and another after that, the same as it had been on that dusty Spanish road, and with sick horror at the unfairness of it, he knew in his heart—he *knew*—that he could no more save her than he'd saved the others.

Chapter Eleven

"Fireworks!"

At the top of the steps, Bethany gasped with delight and surprise as she stared up at the brilliant starbursts, like flowers spreading over the night sky. They'd be in honor of the Duke of Richmond's birthday: now she remembered hearing of the display earlier in the day.

"Oh, William," she said, clapping her hands together in appreciation of another burst, "could there be a more perfect ending to this day than this?"

But in the crush of other people hurrying to the side of the bridge to watch the fireworks, William had vanished. She pushed back through the crowd, searching for him among the faces lit by the sudden flashes of fireworks.

"William?" she called. He couldn't have simply abandoned her like this, not now, and not after what they'd just shared. He wouldn't have just *left* her without saying goodbye. "William, I'm here! Here!"

She made her way back across the bridge, back toward the steps to the water. Perhaps for some reason he'd returned to the oarsman. Perhaps he'd forgotten something in the boat. Perhaps—

Another flash of fireworks, followed by the excited exclamations and squeals and applause from the spectators gathered on the bridge. And in that staccato flash of light, she found William.

He was crouched down on one of the steps, pressed against the wall with his face buried in his folded arms. He was doing all he could to shut out the world, every muscle tensed. He couldn't see the fireworks: he couldn't see anything beyond his own demons, and she rushed to his side.

"William, love, William," she murmured, slipping her arm around his shoulders. She wasn't sure she could reach him, not when he'd retreated so far into himself this way, but she had to try. "It's all right, William. I'm with you, and you're safe. Can you hear me, sweet? No one can harm you here."

He didn't answer or move, and her worry grew. She couldn't leave him here, but she didn't dare force him to move, either. Not five minutes before they'd been kissing in the boat—the sweetest of kisses, full of passion and promise—and now it was if he'd vanished from her entirely.

"Listen to me, William," she whispered, bending down beside him. She brushed his heavy dark hair away from his ear, leaning close so he could hear her. "Trust me, sweet. You're safe. I'm here, and I won't leave you."

The fireworks exploded and shot high into the sky, flashing as they crested. But this time William's head jerked up, his face slicked with sweat and his expression rigid with terror as he stared blindly up at the cascading shower of sparks.

Gently Bethany took his face in her hands, trying to make him see her instead of the fireworks. "Look at me, William. I'm Bethany, and I'm here, and I won't let anything or anyone hurt you. *Look at me.*"

He shuddered, his breath growing more rapid. The fireworks rose and flashed and fell, and this time she could see him beginning to focus on her face, the blank fear slowly fading from his eyes as he made his way back from wherever he had been.

"There now, sweet," she said, smiling her encouragement and relief, too. "I told you everything would be all right, didn't I?"

But instead of smiling in return, he jerked away from her and stood, wiping his hands over his face like a man newly wakened from deep sleep. He shoved his hair back from his face, and grabbed his hat from where it had fallen to the step, doing anything to avoid meeting Bethany's eye.

"William," she said softly, rising to her own feet, too. "How do you feel, sweet?"

"I feel like a damned fool," he said, his voice a furious rasp. He squinted up as the next round of bright flashes lit the sky. "Fireworks, for God's sake. *Fireworks.*"

"They're to celebrate the Duke of Richmond's birthday. They startled you, William, because you did not expect them," she said, keeping her voice purposefully calm, soothing. "That's all. No one saw. No one else knows."

"And you believe that's any damned comfort to me?" he demanded, shaking her away as she reached for his hand. "*I* know what happened. I know what a puling, worthless coward I am, ready to run like a coney from blasted *fireworks.*"

"That's not true, William, not at all," she insisted, following after him as he lurched up the steps. "No one would call you worthless, or a coward!"

"I would," he said without bothering to turn back toward her. He headed for the nearest street, his hand raised to summon a hackney. "And I would be the one in the position to know."

"And I say you're not," she cried, the fireworks still thundering overhead, "and I would know, too! William, stop, please! This isn't like you, not at all!"

He wheeled around to face her. "How would *you* know?

You said this very night that you didn't know me at all, and you don't. No one does. Not one bloody person in this whole bloody world does."

"You're not being fair, William!"

"Nothing in this life is fair." A hackney slowed and stopped, and William flung open the door for her. "Why should I be any different?"

"Because you *are!*" She pulled her shawl more tightly about her shoulders, refusing to let him cast her off like this. "Or am I not permitted to hold any opinions of my own? Am I only supposed to obey and accept whatever you tell me, like the lowest soldier in your command?"

It wasn't just her own pride that made her determined to stay: she'd never seen him in so black a humor, and she feared what he might do to himself if left alone.

But William ignored her. "Take this lady to Penny House, driver," he called up to the man on the hackney's box. "St. James's Street, off the Square."

"I'm not going to let you dismiss me like this," she said, backing away from him and the cab, her arms folded over her chest. "Not until you can give me a better reason for leaving you."

"Then I'll make it easier for us both," he said, "and leave you instead."

He climbed into the cab, but the awkwardness in his leg slowed him just enough for her to be able to slip in beside him.

"I won't let you leave, William," she said, her own determination a match for his, "any more than I'd leave you. Not until you give me reasons, good reasons, for doing so."

His face seemed to grow even darker as he slammed the door shut after her. "Very well. Stay. Though never say I didn't give you the chance to go."

He leaned through the window to speak to the driver, and the cab rolled forward.

"Where are we going, William?" Bethany asked, squeezed into the corner of the seat so their legs wouldn't accidentally touch. "Where are you taking me? Back to Penny House?"

"To Bowden Court," he said curtly. "You want reasons, and by God, I mean to show them to you."

She knew better than to answer now, not when he was like this. Instead she stared straight ahead, bracing her back against the hackney's rocking, and tried not to consider that she'd chosen the wrong path. When she'd been a child in Woodbury, there had been a strange old man who wandered about the village talking to himself and lashing out at imaginary enemies with a willow-whip. He'd lost most of his fingers to frostbite while fighting in the American War, and while Father had explained that the shock of what some soldiers experienced could be so bad that it addled their wits forever, she'd secretly thought then that the old man would have been peculiar even if he'd been a shepherd.

But now, sitting in grim silence here with William, she wasn't nearly as sure.

The carriage had barely stopped before he'd shoved open the door. Without a word he grabbed her arm and hauled her from the hackney, pulling her up the steps after him. She twisted around to look for Mrs. Ketch and her cat, hoping for the landlady's attention in case she might— *might*—need it. But on this night, Mrs. Ketch's windows were dark and her door closed tight, and the rest of the house seemed empty, too, with no witnesses to—to what?

"What do you—do you want, William?" she asked breathlessly, striving to keep the fear from her voice as he drew her up the stairs to his rooms. "What do you want from me?"

"Only what you wanted for yourself, *Miss* Penny." He unlocked the door and pulled her inside, then finally released her.

At once she stepped back, rubbing her wrist where he'd held it so tightly, watching him as he lit the lamp on the desk, his head bowed as he concentrated on finding the spark. His fingers were shaking, making the little flame bobble and his shadow waver across the wall.

She swallowed, not sure of what to expect. He'd been right: she didn't really know him at all. She glanced back at the door. She could leave now, flee, and even if he tried to chase her, she was sure she could outrun him. But if she left, she also knew somehow she'd never see him again, not in this life.

And so, fool or not, she stayed.

"William," she said softly, twisting her hands in the edges of her shawl. "William, I—"

"Don't." He jerked his arms from the sleeves of his coat and flung it to the floor behind him. "This is what you wanted, Bethany, isn't it? To know why I am the way I am?"

His breath was coming in short, agitated gulps as he tore open the buttons at the throat of his shirt, then yanked it over his head. With a shuddering gasp, he finally turned to face her.

"There," he said, squaring his shoulders by the lamp's light. "There is your answer, Bethany, your proof."

She caught her breath, her hand hovering before her mouth to stifle her reaction. His chest was broad, his stomach flat and lean with not an ounce to spare, his skin pale and patched with whorls of dark curling hair that thickened and trailed down into the waistband of his breeches: a fine figure of a man in his prime, worthy of any woman's admiration.

But that she saw later. What she saw first were the scars, just as William had intended.

Innumerable white nicks and slashes crisscrossed his chest and his arms, some shallow, some gouges through puckered flesh. The paler scars were peppered with black gunpowder seared into the skin, some no more than a speckle, others an ebony blot drilled deep, and every one a silent testimony to William's suffering. All the scars, black and white, were centered on his chest, growing more sparse on his sides, with none on his neck or shoulders: some sort of explosion, then, some catastrophe that he had confronted head-on, and for which he'd paid this awful price.

"Oh, William, look at you," she said gently. She'd guessed at the scar that twisted his leg, but she'd never dreamed he carried this as well. How long must it have taken to recover from so many wounds? How much agony had he been forced to endure? "Look at you."

His jaw rose, defiant. "Look your fill, Bethany. This sorry body will be mine until I die, always there to remind me of my weakness, my shame."

She shook her head. "There's no shame or weakness in being wounded in battle. I've always believed such scars were more a sign of sacrifice and honor than any mere ribbons or medals could—"

"*Honor.*" He practically spat the word at her, and flung out his arms, holding them away from his body as if daring her to inspect the scars more closely. "There's no honor in this, Bethany. This came from selfishness, from betraying my men, from my own pathetic lack of judgment!"

"I don't believe you, William," she said fiercely. "I don't believe any of it. I may not be familiar with the—the details of your past, but I know in my heart that you are a good, unselfish and honorable man!"

"Then your heart is a fool." He laughed, bleak and without humor. "After the last battle, I'd been chosen to go with a small force for reinforcements from the coast. Only a handful of us, but each man worthy of the greatest trust. Except for me, the devil take my worthless soul straight to hell now."

"Don't say that," she said swiftly. "It's wrong, and it's not true."

"But it is," he said hoarsely. "The truth, Bethany. We'd been set upon twice by thieves and snipers, yet still we pressed on, because we had no choice. The sun was hot, the dust like red fire, our water nearly gone. If I'd been strong, I would never have led them into those ruins, no matter if there'd been a hundred wells. I would have seen it for the ambush that it was, and I would have kept them away."

He let his hands drop down to his sides, his shoulders sagging with their weight. "If I'd been worthy, not one of my men would have died. Not then, not now."

She'd never heard such despair in another's voice, yet she knew better than to pity him. "How were you to know the ruins were a trap? Did you have some sort of warning about the enemy that you ignored?"

He shook his head. "In that country, there never were warnings. Everything changed too quickly for that, and none who knew the land could be trusted."

She wondered if he was listening to himself, and hearing what he said. "Was there any other time before that that you'd failed your men as their leader?"

Again he shook his head. "I always tried to put them first. No officer who wishes to keep the loyalty of his men would do otherwise."

"But that was what you were doing, wasn't it?" she asked, praying she wasn't going too far. "The day was hot, and the march was long. Your men were thirsty, and you wanted to find them water."

"I was sure I had, Bethany," he said, his voice suddenly shifting away from defensiveness to bewilderment. "I could see the water myself there from the hill, real water, no mirage."

"How do you know it wasn't real?"

His sigh dragged from deep in his chest. "I don't," he said. "I never will."

"But did the others see it, too? Didn't you ask them?"

"When?" he asked, the single word so bleak that he could have been asking himself instead of her. "I came over the hill, and called the others that I'd seen the water. As we ran over the hill, I saw the first of the Spaniards, their guns and the small artillery piece they'd hidden behind the rocks, but by then it was too late. There wasn't even time to shout for retreat. All I could do was try to save the man nearest to me."

"The powder scars," she said, beginning to understand what happened that day, but also understanding far, far more about him. "That was from the explosion."

"I tried to save him, to put myself first," he said, his voice a hoarse whisper, his pale eyes blank as his mind replayed those last horrific minutes. "I saw the flash, felt the impact, and then—then nothing more."

"But afterward, when you awoke—"

"I was in England," he said, so quietly she could barely hear him. "Because of my father, I was in England, and everything else in my life with any meaning—with any *worth*—was done."

She let her shawl slip from her shoulders to the bed, and came to stand before him. Her hair had come unpinned, flopping loose over her shoulders, and impatiently she tucked it behind her ears. She could sense the tension in his body, in his soul, that had come with his explanation. No, his *confession,* for that was how he clearly thought of it: an admission of his faults, and his endless remorse over them.

"And I say your life isn't done." She'd stake her own life that this was the first time he'd told any of this to anyone, and she was poignantly aware of the responsibility that came with such a confidence. "Not by half, William."

He was trusting her with his greatest, darkest secret, trusting her to do the right thing in return. But what if she chose wrongly? What if she inadvertently did or said the one thing that would make him withdraw from her and the rest of the world? If he drew back from her, then he'd be lost to her forever, and maybe even to himself as well.

"Look at me and say that, Bethany," he said. "Nothing I do can make up for what I did. Nothing I will do can ever make me good enough to be with you."

"No, William, please, I—"

"No, Bethany, I'm right," he said, his shadow of a smile filled with bitterness. "With all you know now, look at me, and tell me I'm worth anything to anyone."

"I'll look." She stepped closer again, and he didn't move away, so close that now she could feel the warmth of his ragged breathing on her cheek. "And what I see is a man."

The muscles in his throat tensed, and without looking down, she knew his fingers had clenched into fists as he fought with himself. "Bethany, don't."

"You asked me to look, and I am," she whispered. She'd dared to come this far: she wouldn't dare stop now. "And what I see is a man who has flaws like any other man, but who also is good, and honorable, and worthy of whatever he wishes."

With infinite care she reached up and slipped her hand around the back of his neck. His skin was so warm as to feel feverish beneath her fingers, yet she didn't pause or hesitate.

How could he believe that she'd recoil from the scars, when they were so much a part of him? How could he think that the black splotches and puckered skin represented his unworthiness, when she could see so much more that was good?

"Bethany, please," he said, closing his eyes in one last attempt to shut her out. *"Bethany."*

"William," she answered, making his name a heady

breath as she arched against his chest. "*My* William. You asked me to look, and what I see is you. *Only* you."

Before he could answer, she pressed her lips to the hollow of his throat, there where the pulse of his heartbeat showed the life he wanted to forget. But she was determined to show him the power and the beauty of life, of *his* life.

She slipped her hands beneath his arms and around his waist, relishing his warmth and the feel of his skin as she held him close. She trailed feathery kisses lower along his chest, over the black gunpowder and the white scars, and slid her hands up and down along his back, lightly, so lightly. She'd never touched a man like this before, and she marveled at the play of his muscles beneath his skin, the hard lines of bone where she was soft, the purely male scent of him that was also purely William.

She wanted to forget the words that could trip her, and instead touch him so he knew she cared. She wanted to prove to him that the scars didn't matter, and neither did his past. She wanted to touch him so he knew that what she'd said was true.

But above all she wanted him to know that she loved him more than she'd ever loved anyone else.

She was trembling as she kissed his belly, her unruly red curls brushing against his scattering of dark hair. Her palms were damp as she touched him, her heart quickening with excitement, and with a small shuddering sigh she closed her eyes and turned her cheek against his skin.

"*Enough.*" His hands were firm on her shoulders, lifting her up, holding her face so she could not look away from his eyes.

"You are certain, lass?" His voice was the low rasp of a desperate man, his breathing ragged and his dark hair wild around his face. "You can bear such a wreck of a man? Truly?"

She tried to nod, her face imprisoned by his hands. "I would never tell you otherwise, William."

"But why tell me any of this, Bethany? Why now?"

She felt her eyes fill with hot tears of emotion. "Because of what you told me."

He lowered his head a fraction, preparing himself for what she might say. "Because you pitied me."

"Because I believed in you, William," she said, one tear easing free to slide down her cheek. "Because—because I love you."

"Because you love me," he repeated, his eyes full of wonder. He wiped away her tear with his thumb, and then before either of them spoke again he was kissing her, so deep and hard that she thought she'd willingly drown in the sensation.

Blindly she circled her arms around the back of his neck, losing herself in his kiss, her body pressed close to his. She shared the fever in his blood, burning so hot that she felt light-headed with it, needing him for support.

Because I love you...

She was scarcely aware of him working at the buttons of her gown, tugging at them one by one until the dress fell loose over her shoulders. He shoved it lower and she helped, freeing first one arm and then the other so the soft gown could drop with a gentle *shush* around her ankles.

Yet standing there in only her shift she still felt the heat through the sheer linen, and when he unfastened the tiny bow of the drawstring, she only sighed, and then gasped as he found her bare breast beneath, her nipple tightening at once against his palm. The more he caressed her, the more restless and willful her body became, wriggling against William and craving more. This was further than they'd gone before, and her scattered conscience tried to remind her of where all this would inevitably lead.

But then he kissed her again and her hands eased lower on his body, along the lean muscles of his hips and back, and he answered by pressing against her, easing her legs apart so she could feel the hard proof of his need in his breeches. He shifted again, letting that hardness rub gently between her legs, letting her choose how much she wished, and she gasped as the unfamiliar pleasure bolted through her eager body.

Because I love you...

He paused for a moment, holding her in his arms, and by the single lamp his face was taut, almost harsh, with desire, defined with shadow and light.

"You are—you are sure, Bethany?" he asked, searching her face. "You are certain?"

"Yes," she whispered fiercely. He had trusted her with his truth, and she would trust him now with hers. "Oh, yes, William, I am, and I—"

But his mouth had already found hers again, and as she reached up to steady herself on his shoulders she realized she was rocking backward, falling, falling, onto the center of his bed. Still he kissed her, but now the power of that kiss was magnified a hundredfold with his body on top of hers, touching her in new ways and new places. Although he kept most of his weight on his elbows, the featherbed gave beneath them, fluffing up on either side of her face, and the bed's rope springs creaked and groaned as they moved together.

And they were moving, that same rhythm that he'd begun while they were standing, and now she could answer it, following him and her instincts to roll her hips forward against his. The hem of her shift had worked high over her hips, leaving her bare to the top of her garters and stockings, and yet she did not care. She was past caring now, too lost in the pleasure, and besides, this was William. She was gasping for breath, all her energy coiling in a tight knot low in her belly.

He groaned, and pulled back off the bed.

"A moment, lass, that's all," he said, yanking at the fall of his breeches. Suddenly a coward, she squeezed her eyes shut until she felt the bed sink and he was kissing her again.

But this time when he lay beside her, it was different. This time, there was only his leg against hers, his skin against her skin, her shift pushed so high as to be no barrier at all. This time when he touched her, he did not stop at her thigh, but crept higher between her legs. She gasped, startled, and he hushed her, kissing her to calm her, to let her grow accustomed to his fingers. He touched her, stroked her, knowing exactly what to do to make that tension build faster and higher until she clung to him, whimpering his name.

Because I love you...

But then his fingers were gone, replaced by something hotter, larger, more blunt, pressing against her, parting her, driving deeper inside her than she'd dreamed possible. She cried out, tensing more with surprise than pain, and wondered what had become of the pleasure that had seemed so irresistible.

"I'm sorry, sweetheart," he whispered hoarsely over her, smoothing her damp, loose hair back from her face. "But it will be better, I promise."

She nodded, not trusting her voice. She must trust him again, even if she'd no real choice. Tentatively she rocked her hips again, trying to ease the pressure, and was startled to feel a quick rush of the earlier, elusive pleasure returning. She moved again, and William groaned, and began to move with her. The pleasure came rushing back, and as she discovered how to meet and match William's thrusts, curling her legs around his waist, she felt that pleasure build to such an intensity that she cried out again, and again, and then with the same kind of glory that she'd seen in the skyrockets over the river, the pleasure exploded for them both in a burst of boundless joy.

"You were right," he murmured afterward, gently tracing circles over her shoulder with his thumb. They still lay together with their bodies tangled intimately together, the bed's coverlet pulled haphazardly over them. "You understood."

Her smile was tremulous, and she was still too overwhelmed by emotion to trust herself to speak. She guessed he meant he loved her, just as she'd told him, and in her heart she knew he did, but she would have liked to hear him say so anyway.

Because I love you...

"There's no other woman like you, Bethany," he said, and his smile made her want to cry again. "What could I have done in my life to deserve you now?"

"I suppose we deserve each other," she said, her voice squeaking upward. She wouldn't beg him to say he loved her; perhaps this was as close as he'd come, being a man.

"Then I must be the most fortunate man alive." He leaned forward and kissed her again with rare tenderness. She'd no right to feel sorry for herself when he kissed her like that, not with everything else that was good in her life, and abruptly she thought of Penny House.

"What time is it, William?" She twisted around, trying to see the sky or the moon through the window and judge the hour. "How late?"

"We still have most of the night, if that's what you mean." He leaned over the edge of the bed, searching through his discarded clothes on the floor until he found his pocket watch, tipping it toward the lamp to read the face. "Half-past one."

"Half-past one!" She shoved free of him and the coverlet and rolled off the bed to hunt for her clothes. "Oh, William, I should have been back hours ago!"

"What, back to Penny House?" He propped his head on his arm, watching her as she turned her clothes right-side out. "I'll wager they haven't even noticed you're gone. I appreciate you far more, you know. Stay here with me, and learn for yourself."

"You know perfectly well I can't do that." She pushed her head through her gown, plucking the sleeves into place over her shoulders. "Amariah will have my *head!*"

"Then she can't be any more angry if you stay with me until dawn." He leaned forward and snaked his arm around her waist, pulling her back down onto the bed. "Please, sweetheart. Don't leave just yet."

She sat very still beside him, her breath quickening as he traced his fingers along the underside of her breast, a lazy, seductive caress that made her nipple instantly stiffen into a jutting point through her gown.

"Stay for me, Bethany," he said softly, a hint of the old insecurity showing in his eyes. "For us."

"Oh, William, you know I can't, no matter how much I might wish it." She sighed with regret, and forced herself to stand, reaching around to fasten the buttons on her gown. "Not this night, anyway."

"Then swear to me you'll stay tomorrow."

"Tomorrow, though you'll never make my father's daughter swear to anything." She leaned forward just long enough to kiss him. "I can't begin to guess how I'll do it, but I will."

"You will, and so shall I." He smiled, more handsome than any mortal man had a right to be, and she moved away quickly before her resolve faltered. He threw aside the coverlet and stood, stretching his arms over his head before he reached for his breeches.

But she stared. Shocked, she couldn't help herself. As shocking as the scars on his body might be, none of them had prepared her for the twisted, mottled deformity of his leg. No wonder he limped. Seeing it now, she was amazed that he could walk at all, and she thought with considerable guilt of all the times when she'd thoughtlessly charged ahead, expecting him to keep pace with her.

But that guilt was nothing compared to realizing that he'd caught her staring.

"So now you've seen the leg," he said. The flirtatious banter had vanished, replaced by the old wary bitterness that had served him so long. "'The' leg, mind, as opposed to 'my' leg. The cripple's leg."

He turned away from her, pulling up his breeches and buttoning the fall with quick, angry jerks, and too late she realized how badly she'd erred.

"It's still part of you, William, whatever you call it," she said as carefully as she could. "And I wasn't pitying you. I was thinking of how vastly brave you must have been. No, how vastly brave you *are*."

"No." He pulled on his shirt, then his coat, the distance yawning between them like a chasm. "Not at all. Now come, and I'll see you home."

"And I say no to you as well!" she cried, forgetting care entirely. "William, you have trusted me and I have trusted you with—with *everything,* and there's no sin at all in my believing or saying that you are brave, because you *are!*"

He kept his back to her, and didn't answer.

She grabbed her shawl from the floor and wrapped it over her shoulders, willing herself not to cry from frustration and disappointment.

"I thought there was more between us, William," she said. "I thought we—we meant more to one another than to end like this, before we'd fair begun."

Still he did not answer. She would *not* beg, no matter how stubborn he was, and with her head high but her eyes filling with tears, she began toward the door.

Yet before she reached it, he turned abruptly and caught her by the arm. He drew her close, circling his arm around her waist, and with a groan torn from deep inside, he buried his face in the tangle of her hair and held her, just held her.

No words, no promises, no apologies: but for Bethany, it was more than enough.

Macallister slapped his cards facedown on the green baize and pushed his chair away from the table without even waiting to see the others' hands. He knew he'd lost again, just as he'd lost every other hand he'd held tonight.

But now, it seemed, his luck was about to change.

He smoothed the embroidered front of his waistcoat and shot his sleeves from the cuffs of his coat. Amariah Penny was standing in the doorway, the white plumes in her hair nodding gracefully as she scanned the room full of gentlemen. Macallister smiled, and began to make his way over to her. He knew that Amariah was regarded as the most beautiful and elegant of the three sisters, but to him she seemed too stiff, too formal when compared to Bethany. Bethany was the true prize for any gentleman of discernment, which was precisely why he was so determined to have her.

But of course Amariah must be looking for him. Why else would she be here?

"Miss Penny," he said, bowing as he greeted her. "You have news for me, yes?"

She seemed surprised to see him, not what he expected, and though she smiled, she also opened her painted fan to flutter between them.

"I fear not the news you would hope, Lieutenant," she

said. "I have sent your invitation to my sister to join the company upstairs, but as yet she has not appeared. I told you before that she is a busy woman, with many responsibilities in the kitchen, but I am sure she will come the very second she is free."

He scowled, disappointed. What in blazes was keeping Bethany, anyway? He didn't like to be kept waiting, especially not by a woman.

"I could go fetch her myself," he offered. "She'd come if I went to her."

"I told you before, Lieutenant," she said, the fan's fluttering slowing to a more ominous pace, "that no members are permitted below stairs. I am sorry to disappoint you, but those are the club's rules, to be obeyed by every member."

There was a practiced steeliness to Miss Penny's words now, reminding Macallister of the consequences of going where one didn't belong at Penny House, of the burly-armed guards lurking in the corners of every room, of the lifetime banishment from Penny House, of how misbehavior of any sort was not to be tolerated.

He tried to smile to hide his irritation. "But I'm not just any member, am I? I'm a good deal more to your sister, aren't I?"

"Then you should not worry while she is delayed by her responsibilities in the kitchen." She smiled in return, but he didn't miss how her glance had flicked past him to one of the guards.

"She knows you are here, Lieutenant," she said, "and I am sure she will not keep you waiting any longer than she must. Ahh, my Lord Harleigh, good evening to you! However did you slip past me at the door?"

Infuriated, Macallister turned away without greeting the other gentleman. He knew when he'd been dismissed, just as he knew he'd been insulted, and if Miss Penny had been a man, she would have been meeting him at dawn with pistols in some distant corner of Green Park.

He plucked a glass of claret from one of the waiter's trays and went to stand alone beside the window. There should be more respect for an officer of the king, he fumed, more deference to the medals for courage and honor on his chest. He'd been willing—more than willing—to take Bethany Penny, to make her his wife with a handsome allowance, but not now. They'd ruined that for themselves. He was done with having these damned Penny women order him about.

He pushed the heavy curtains aside, hoping for a breath of cooler air to penetrate the closed heat of the card room. He glimpsed a woman hurrying down the alley outside, her yellow shawl pulled over her head, and he smirked. Some knowing slut on her way from one poor wretch to another, he thought, wishing she'd look up so he could see her face.

She stopped short of the gate to the Penny House yard, and a tall man in a plain, worn coat joined her. From the look of him, he'd squandered his last farthing on the slattern, and Macallister watched with growing interest as they embraced and kissed passionately. The man's hat hid his face just as the shawl hid the woman's, but Macallister was more entertained by how her skirts were pulling across her rounded bottom. Hell, if he'd been there in that scarecrow's place, he'd have turned the strumpet around and given her a fine flourish of his officer's sword there against the wall.

They kissed again, apparently in farewell, and as they separated, the woman's shawl slipped to her shoulders. Her coppery hair gleamed in the lantern's light, her face so familiar that Macallister felt it like a kick to his gut:

Bethany Penny, *his* Bethany, not in the kitchen, but whoring in the street with one of her beggars.

But then the man swept his hat from his head in a grand salute, his face bare as he laughed with Bethany Penny.

No beggar, no madman, but William Callaway.

Macallister's fingers tightened around the stem of his glass, and it took all his willpower not to dash it to the floor. There was the proof he'd refused to believe, standing with the woman he'd thought would one day be his wife. Callaway could destroy him whenever he pleased. With his entire blasted noble family behind him, Callaway could choose his time to tell what he knew about Macallister. He could say whatever he pleased, swear to whatever version of the facts he wished, and no one would doubt his word.

And Macallister—Macallister knew he'd be lucky to escape the court martial with his life.

He had to struggle to keep his face impassive and not show his fear to the others in the room. But he could handle this: yes, yes, he could do this as well as he'd done everything else. He'd have to make sure that court martial never happened, that Callaway never testified against him. It would have to be more subtle than poison, more ingenious. No one noticed when a pauper died, but the son of a peer was another matter entirely. He'd have to be sure the suspicion went as far from him as possible.

The key would be the girl. Of course there was no question of marrying her now; he'd never sully his family's name by linking it to a whore. But he still wanted her, wanted her even more after he'd seen her like this. What a delight it would be to tell the world that the genteel minister's daughter fouled her own nest! He could use what he'd seen to blackmail her into servicing him as well, and then he'd use her again to betray Callaway. He'd have the power, and she'd know it.

The power, and the woman with it.

And Callaway—ah, at last Callaway would be gone from his life and his conscience forever.

Chapter Twelve

"Oh, miss, how happy I am to see you!" Letty grabbed Bethany's arm as soon as she came through the door, pulling her to a corner of the kitchen where no one would dare to eavesdrop. "I've done my best, miss, indeed I have, but I don't like telling lies, not for anyone."

"What has happened?" Bethany asked, swiftly trading her shawl for her apron. "What did I miss?"

"Only your sister sending for you over and over," Letty said. "First there was some gentleman who wished you to come upstairs so he could pay you compliments, and I sent the footman off, saying you'd come when you were free. Then old Pratty himself came down, and I had to stop him on the stairs, saying you were too busy with the sauces. *Then* word came from Miss Penny herself, ordering you to come the very minute you returned."

"When was that?" Bethany asked, pinning a cap over her hair. "How long ago?"

"A good quarter hour," Amariah said as she swept into the kitchen and up behind Bethany. "Perhaps more. Bethany, why didn't you come when I sent for you?"

Quickly Bethany turned to face her sister, her face hot

with guilt. "I'm sorry, Amariah, but we've been so busy that I—"

"We haven't been busy at all," her sister said. "There is some sort of great secret boxing match being held in a barn tonight, and all the sporting gentlemen are tossing away their money there instead of with us. Surely you should know by how much is left on the platters coming back."

Bethany glanced at Letty, who nodded just enough to confirm what Amariah said.

Amariah shook her head, clearly agitated, and tapped her folded fan in the palm of her hand. "I know you don't like coming up among the company, Betts, and I certainly cannot blame you for wishing to avoid that dreadful Lieutenant Macallister. But to ignore me outright, especially with this news from Greenwood—"

"From Greenwood?" she asked with surprise. "You didn't tell me you'd heard from Cassia."

"I didn't." She sighed, and motioned for Bethany to follow her into the kitchen's office, where she shut and latched the door before she continued. "Richard sent a special message from the country to me tonight, asking me to come down at once. He says Cassia's ailing but won't admit it, and he wants my opinion."

"Cassia can't be ill," Bethany said, dropping into the little spindle-back chair behind her desk. "None of us ever are."

"I know that," Amariah said, leaning her hips against the edge of the desk, "which is why I am not overly concerned. My guess is that she's with child."

"Cassia?" It made perfect sense, of course, considering that Cassia and Richard had been sharing the same bed even before they'd wed. But now Bethany's thoughts made the very short leap from a baby for Cassia to one of her own. In the heat of passion, she'd conveniently forgotten that lying with Richard could well result in a child, too.

Now she could think of little else: a beautiful, charming baby, with his grey eyes and thick black hair.

A beautiful baby, yes, whose parents were not wed, nor likely to be...

"Yes, Cassia," Amariah said, fortunately unable to read Bethany's thoughts. "But I must go to her, which will likely make her furious since Richard has invited me without telling her. I'll be gone only a few days—I wish to help, not intrude—and you, duckie, shall be in charge here while I'm away."

"Are you sure, Amariah?" Bethany asked, stunned by the notion of so much responsibility thrust upon her shoulders. "The members come to see you, not me. I'm not witty or clever. I know none of the gentlemen's names or their titles, and I'm dreadful at chatter."

"They come here to escape their homes, and to drink and to gamble," Amariah said firmly. "We could dress an ape in a silk gown, and by the middle of the evening they'd all be drinking toasts to her beauty. Not that I'm saying that either of us are apes, only that my role is not as taxing as it might seem. Pratt will be there to help you with the names and titles, and Letty can handle the kitchen. The gentlemen will like the change. You'll do famously, I'm sure."

Bethany thought again of William and her promise to return to Bowden Court to stay the night through. "When must you leave?"

"In the morning," Amariah said. "Richard is sending his own carriage up to town for me, as if that shall not raise Cassia's suspicions. I expect I'll return by week's end."

"That's five nights." Five nights of dressing for evening instead of in her familiar apron, five nights of charming gentlemen instead of chopping vegetables, and hardest of all, five nights of not being able to see William. "Oh, Amariah, I do not know."

"I do," she said, "and I know you'll have no trouble at all. Didn't you tell me yesterday how you considered yourself old and wise enough to cope with anything?"

But that had been yesterday, and how many things had changed in Bethany's life since then!

"I'll wear that gaudy paste necklace of yours," she said, avoiding the question. "Perhaps that will make the gentlemen think I'm you."

"Be yourself instead. They'll be enchanted." Amariah reached out to touch Bethany's cheek. "Is there something you haven't told me, Betts? Something with your staff, or with your flock? Anything, anything at all that I should know before I leave you in charge?"

Bethany hesitated. William's loving had marked her with unforgettable intensity, changing her forever. Yet even as she was still aware of his scent and his touch lingering on her body, it was the confusion he'd left in her heart that ached the most, and she longed desparately to confide in her sister.

But as soon as she considered it, she imagined Amariah's horrified reaction, too. She'd be dismayed that Bethany hadn't come to her sooner, concerned for her happiness with a man like William, and the possibility of an unexpected child. Most of all, Amariah would try her best to make everything *right*, because she'd want Bethany to be happy. But right now Bethany wasn't sure what she wanted herself, and until she did, it didn't seem fair to William— or to herself—to introduce Amariah into their complicated affairs. Besides, Cassia did need Amariah now, and Bethany would be selfish indeed to steal Amariah's attentions away at such a time. There'd be plenty of time once Amariah returned.

"Nothing, Amariah." Bethany shook her head, striving to keep her features as noncommittal as possible even as her secret weighed heavily on her conscience. "You've thought of everything."

But her sister was still watching her closely. "What of that Mr. Callaway of whom you seemed so fond? Is he ever—"

"He is not a risk to Penny House, Amariah," Bethany said, which *was* true. "You need not worry about him."

"I worry about you, duck, not him." She sighed, tapping the blades of her folded fan on the edge of the desk. "Recall that if anything seems amiss, you'll have the guards about the house, too, the ones that Pratt has trained for upstairs along with Mr. Fewler's men."

"I'll be fine," Bethany insisted, "and so shall Penny House."

"Which is exactly what I believed from the first." Amariah slipped down from the edge of the desk, smoothing her skirts around her legs before she returned upstairs. She began to open the door, then turned back, her smile rueful.

"Strange to think how yesterday I wanted you to go to the country, Betts, to forget your work for a bit," she said. "Now here I'm the one who's going down to Hampshire, while I leave you behind with double the toil."

"Nothing stays the same, Amariah, and nothing is ever what we expect it to be." Bethany rose, retying the apron strings around her waist as she thought again of William, and how much she already missed him. She'd have to send word to him in the morning that she wouldn't be able to leave Penny House for the next few days.

"In a way this all reminds me of Father." Amariah's smile was tinged with sadness. "Remember how he always said that God has His reasons for everything, no matter what we lowly folk might wish otherwise."

Bethany nodded, her mind racing on. She could not go to Bowden Court, true, but there was no reason why William couldn't come here to Penny House. Hadn't Amariah already suggested it herself?

"You know, Bethany," she was saying now, "I hadn't planned on journeying to Greenwood this week, but if I return with joyful news from Cassia, then I'll forget every bit of the inconvenience. Perhaps in some way, your time here at Penny House will prove enjoyable as well."

But Bethany was already sure that it would.

It was nearly dawn before William returned to Bowden Court. Once he had left Bethany at Penny House, he had kept walking, hoping to sort out the jumbled mess of his thoughts about her. Yet by the time the eastern sky had turned pale pink and ache in his weary leg had turned to outright pain, he still had grown no closer to any real conclusions.

He dragged himself up the steps to his rooms, stripped off his coat, and fell onto the unmade bed with a groan as at last he took the weight from his leg. But as exhausted as he was, he found no real relief. The tangled sheets were full of the scent of their lovemaking, and he closed his eyes to savor the lingering fragrance she'd left behind.

He needed her, wanted her, with a desire he'd never felt with any other woman. It wasn't only that he found her surpassing beautiful, full of life and fire and kindness, or that she was independent and accomplished in ways that highborn ladies like his sister couldn't begin to comprehend. It went far beyond that. He felt a bond with Bethany that he found impossible to explain, almost as if she were the half of him he hadn't realized was missing. He'd trusted her with his darkest past, and she hadn't flinched. In turn she'd given him her maidenhead, a gift he'd never expected. She'd seen him when he'd been little better than a babbling Bedlamite, and she hadn't turned away. Always she had been there, finding good, seeing worth when he doubted any could be found.

He swore with frustration, his arm flung over his eyes as he lay on the bed. What in turn did he have to offer her? A title he didn't want or use, an estate he did his best to give away, a vile, self-centered family, a past that haunted him with unpredictable, shameful fits of madness, a future that was no real future at all?

And now, God help them both, when she'd finally told him she loved him, he'd been incapable of answering.

No wonder that when sleep at last did claim him, it brought no peace.

The dream was as familiar as an old enemy, and as impossible to shake off. The empty road, the blasted, barren land on either side, the hot sun and the red dust: all were the same, and always would be in his memory.

But this time he trudged along the rutted road alone. There were no others at his side, no one to command or be responsible for, no one to live for. If he gave in to the heat and let his legs give way, no one would know, and no one would care. He could die here, and all he would have for mourners would be the long-winged birds wheeling in the sky overhead, waiting for the moment that they could feast on his dust-covered flesh.

Here was the last turn in the road, and here was the same hill, the slight rise in the heat enough to make him huff with the strain. As he climbed to the top, he knew the ruins and the water would come next, the way they always did.

But not today, not in this dream. This time when he reached the crest, the land before him was empty and bleak beneath the unrelenting sun, without so much as a glimpse of the sparkling water that had proved his downfall. He blinked, unwilling to accept what his eyes told him, and now when he looked, he saw Bethany Penny.

She was standing in the same place as the well had

been, her hair burnished bright by the sun and her yellow
shawl draped in the crooks of her elbows. She shaded her
eyes with her hand to look up at him, then smiled and
waved for him to join her.

He stopped, swaying from the heat and thirst, yet not
trusting his eyes. Magically she was holding a crystal
pitcher of water, and as he watched, she poured it into the
goblet in her other hand.

"Here, William," she said, smiling. "As much as you
want, as much as you need, forever and ever."

"Bethany," he said, making her name no more than a
parched croak. He took one staggering step toward her,
then another. "Bethany!"

She laughed merrily, and held the water out to him.
"It's yours, dear, sweet William, yours alone. All you must
do to have it is love me."

He nodded, and smiled at the simplicity of her request.
Of course he loved her. Of course he could tell her so. Yet
when he tried to speak, the words stayed in his mouth,
scorched and silent. He held his hand out to her, desperate to make her understand, and as he did she faded and
crumbled away, disappearing into the red dust as if she'd
never existed, abandoning him, banishing him to always,
always, be alone—

"Major?" Hands tucked into the sides of her apron, Mrs.
Ketch squinted down at him as if he were some cabinet curiosity. "Are you unwell, Major?"

He blinked at her face and the bright morning sunshine
behind her, dragging himself back to the waking world. His
heart was pounding as if he'd run a footrace, his hands
shaking.

"Of course I am well," he mumbled, sitting upright on
the bed. "A bad dream, a nightmare, that is all."

Mrs. Ketch's mouth remained pressed in a tight line of suspicion. "Nightmares come at night. Most folk don't lie abed in the day unless they be ill."

"Well, I'm not." He shoved his hair back from his face, wishing he could do the same with the memory of the dream. "Why exactly are you here in my room, Mrs. Ketch?"

"The boy." She stepped aside, and now William could see Twig, wide-eyed, standing beside her, clutching a covered basket in his hands. "He knocked. You didn't answer."

"Damnation, because I was *asleep,*" he growled, rubbing the back of his neck. "That will be all, Mrs. Ketch. Twig, what have you there?"

The boy waited for the landlady to leave them before he handed William the basket. "It's from Miss Bethany, guv'nor. She said to give it to you an' no other."

"Did she, now." Strange that the boy would be standing here with this gift from Bethany exactly as the dream-Bethany was disappearing with the offered water. He could already smell the food beneath the checkered napkin—some sort of cinnamon-laced breads, a roasted fowl—and he smiled, thinking of how everything that mattered to her must come with food. "Did you sample a bite for yourself?"

"Oh, no, guv'nor!" Twig exclaimed righteously. "She made me eat my fill first at Penny House, so's I wouldn't be tempted."

"Miss Bethany is a wise woman." He lifted a corner of the napkin, and found the folded note tucked inside. Swiftly he opened it, the elegantly precise handwriting of course belonging to her. His heart plummeted at the first sentence, then rose to impossible heights at the second.

My Own William,
To my endless regret, I cannot come to you this night.
But my sister A. having been called away to the
country, you may come to me, late, if that pleases you
instead.
　Yours forever, my love,
　B.
Writ at dawn
Penny House, St. James's Street

He read it again, just to be sure. So she hadn't disappeared from his life like the Bethany in his nightmare. She still wanted to see him, tonight, at her house. She'd called him her own William.

She'd called him her love.

"Bad news, guv'nor?" Twig asked, shuffling his feet with sympathetic concern.

"Not at all." Quickly William refolded Bethany's note and tucked it inside his shirt. He pulled two chicken legs from the basket and handed one to the boy. "Here. For being such a fleet messenger."

The boy nodded solemnly, taking the chicken leg as his due as he sat cross-legged at the end of the bed.

"Tell me, Twig," William said as they both began to eat. "What do you know of love?"

Twig screwed up his nose. "Is that what Miss Bethany wrote about?"

"In a way," William said. He wasn't sure why he'd asked that question of the boy in the first place. Was he so pathetically reluctant to be left alone that he'd ask such a question to keep Twig's company, or was he truly interested in the boy's philosophical opinion? "But I asked you first. What advice can you offer me about the ladies, eh?"

"I've no use for them, guv'nor," Twig said succinctly. "Excepting in the usual ways, for washing and cooking and such."

"Miss Bethany's as good a cook as any in the kingdom."

"Amen to that," Twig agreed, taking another bite of his chicken leg. "Which means that I warrant you should love her."

"Is that reason enough?" William broke a muffin in half for Twig, wishing his decision could be as easily made.

Twig licked his fingers, thinking. "I'll wager there's more to it than that. Before he was 'pressed, Da swore that Mam loved me more'n she loved anything else until she died."

"I'm sorry, lad," William said, handing the muffin to him. "I didn't mean to call up old sorrows for you like that."

"Oh, it's not sorrowful, guv'nor, on account of I can't recall her," Twig said with resigned cheerfulness. "I was only a babe when she died. But knowing she loved me like that—that's something I can keep hold of, like she's watching down over me with the angels. Being loved like that's a fine, comfortsome thing, wherever you are."

William looked down, the chicken suddenly tasteless in his mouth. He had never known that kind of love from anyone in his family, and certainly not from his mother. He'd never had it from anyone, not really.

Was that why he couldn't tell Bethany now? Had his family done this to him, too? Had they made this most beautiful of words so foreign to him that he couldn't say it now, when he most needed to?

"I'd wager Miss Bethany would be like that, too," Twig continued, not noticing that William hadn't answered. "Not that I'm wishing her with the angels or anything, but if she had someone she loved, why, Miss Bethany'd love them like that."

"Fine and comfortsome?" William asked, remembering last night.

"Aye, like that," Twig agreed. "Like that. Maybe you should tell her first, just to be sure."

William sat back, his hands on his knees. "Why in blazes would I do that?"

"Because she sent you this breakfast, guv'nor," Twig said with patient logic. "She wouldn't have done that if she didn't fancy you. Now you say you love her, an' she'll say it back, and there you are. If'n you don't, some other bloke will, likely one of them princes or dukes playing hazard upstairs from her. If one of them says it first, she'll be gone, guv'nor, and so will you."

"Fine and comfortsome," William said again, softly, thinking how well the words suited Bethany. "Like that?"

"Aye," Twig said, shaking the now-bare chicken bone for emphasis. "Fine an' comfortsome, and you'll have more food than a Turk has wives. But you have to say that one word first, guv'nor. You have to say it first."

Gratefully Bethany sipped from the goblet of lemon-water that Pratt had brought her, and let her glance wander around the near-empty front room. Amariah had been right. Acting as the Penny House hostess wasn't nearly as challenging as she'd thought it would be, at least not tonight. The crowd hadn't been as thick as it would be in the middle of the Season, and the gentlemen who were here seemed all to be on their most restrained behavior. There'd been no quarrels over politics or fights over mistresses, no outraged accusations of cheating at cards, not even any too-loud renditions of bawdy songs.

Granted, Bethany hadn't tried to equal her sisters' triumphs—she couldn't imagine standing on a chair and improvising witty recitation in verse, the way Cassia had once done—but she was proud that, so far, she'd managed to hold her own in Amariah's absence.

And soon, only a little longer, she'd be with William.

"How is Letty faring in the kitchen, Pratt?" she asked, more anxiously than she might have wished. "The goose seems to have found particular favor tonight. The last time I looked, the carcass was nearly picked clean. I do hope she has the next one ready to be brought up, even if by now they're closing and tidying for the night. Perhaps I'll duck downstairs, just to be sure."

"Forgive me, Miss Bethany," Pratt said sternly, "but that is not possible. You know that without my telling you. For tonight your place is here, not in the kitchen."

Still she glanced toward the hall and the kitchen stairs with real longing. "No one will miss me if I'm quick about it."

"They will, miss. Trust me, they will," he droned as if making the gloomiest prediction possible. "And if you do, I shall feel it will be my duty to inform Miss Amariah that you were unable to delegate your proper responsibilities."

"Oh, a pox on you, Pratt," she said, knowing he was right, yet still turning away from the crowd just long enough so she could stick her tongue out at Pratt behind her fan without being noticed. "I know you won't tattle."

"You know nothing of the sort, Miss Bethany," he answered with a bow, allowing himself the very slightest hint of a smile in return. "I'll convey your concerns regarding the goose to Letty directly."

She grinned as she watched his old-fashioned powdered head glide among the other men as he moved along the hall. They'd inherited Pratt along with the rest of Penny House, and he was as indispensable to their success as the tables for hazard and faro, even if he could be fussier than the fussiest old maiden aunt.

She smoothed her kidskin gloves over her wrists and up her forearms and glanced at the case clock near the doorway. Past midnight now, almost one. No wonder this room was nearly empty now. Amariah had advised her to begin visiting the gaming rooms upstairs now, for that was where the remaining members would be gathered. Not to make them leave, of course—gaming members were fed and cosseted and permitted to remain at the tables beneath the managers' watchful eyes as long as their pockets held one last coin—but simply to show an interest on behalf of the house. After two, she could retire for the night any time she wished. She straightened the blades of her fan before her trip upstairs. Not much longer at all, and then William would—

"They said you were here, Miss Bethany, but I didn't believe 'em until I saw you for myself." Lieutenant Macallister seized her hand to bow over it, the stench of strong drink drifting around him. "Charmed, as always."

"Good evening, Lieutenant," she said, using her fan as a strategic barrier between their faces. Surely she'd spoken too soon and tempted fate to cross her, for here was her greatest challenge of the evening. "You have just joined us?"

"Are you glad to see me, Miss Bethany?" His eyes were watery and unfocussed, his face mottled over the tight collar of his dress uniform coat. "I'm glad to see you, you know, deuced glad."

"Indeed," she said, as noncommittal as she could be. Uneasily she glanced past him. The room was empty now, with even the guards having gone upstairs to watch the gaming. She could shout for help if she needed it, of course, but to do so would be an admission that she'd failed to control the situation, and failed as Amariah's substitute.

Instead she smiled, and took a graceful step backward to widen the distance between them. "I know you are a lucky man at the tables, Lieutenant," she said, nodding her head toward the stairs. "I've heard there are several excellent games in progress this evening. I can arrange to find a seat for you at any table you please if—"

"You didn't want the pearls," he said abruptly, and tapped the medal on his chest. "I'm a hero, you know, for bravery and valor, yet still you didn't want them. But I can be a generous man to the right lady. A chaise, a pair, a house and servants. Deuced generous, y'see."

"Your contribution to Penny House's charities was most appreciated, Lieutenant." Amariah had advised her on this, too. She wasn't permitted to become indignant or outraged. No matter what kind of suggestions he made to her, she must pretend she didn't understand and ignore them as charmingly as she could. "Everyone says you're a most generous gentleman."

He scowled, and shook his head. "D'you think I care about a pack of filthy beggars? It's you I want, and I mean to have you, too."

She took a deep breath, her smile still pasted in place as she struggled to keep her temper. "Would you like something sent up from the kitchen, Lieutenant? A light supper, or—"

"That's right. I forgot." He leered at her, leaning so close that she could see little flecks of spittle in the corners of his mouth. "You play at being a fine lady, but it's the beggars you want in the back alley, isn't it? The dirtier the better."

She told herself that he couldn't possibly have seen her with William last night, but now she was more afraid than angry.

"The poor folk who come to the kitchen door of Penny House are always welcomed, Lieutenant," she said, "and none are turned away."

"Especially not by you." His red-rimmed eyes gleamed, and he jabbed his finger into the blades of her fan. "Callaway's mad. Did you know that? Put in an asylum by his own father, they say."

Bethant gasped, unable to help herself. "Pray—pray remember yourself, Lieutenant, and where you are."

"What I remember is you ready to spread your legs for a dim-witted, crippled bastard like Callaway," he said, his bitterness spilling over. "How would you like me to tell that to your noble membership, eh? That their innocent Miss Bethany lifts her skirts in the alley for any scoundrel who wants her?"

She gasped again, shaking her head. "That is—that's quite enough, Lieutenant."

"No, it's not," he said, pushing closer to corner her. "But I don't have to tell. Make it worth my while not to tell, and I won't. Give me what you've been wasting on Callaway, and I'll consider it."

She flushed, floundering. "You've no right to say such things."

"Drunkards, thieves, madmen—that's what you want instead of me?" he demanded, and his eyes widened as some fresh insult jumped into his head. "That's why you know Callaway, isn't it? You knew he still lived, while I believed him dead. Yet somehow you *knew*."

"No!" she cried, with no notion of how to answer. "That is, I didn't know!"

"Callaway's mad as they come," he insisted, breathing hard. "He's only fit now for the straw at Bedlam with the other idiots, or fit for serving sluts like—"

"That's enough," a tall man said, suddenly looming up behind Macallister and grabbing him by the shoulder. "The lady doesn't need to hear that, and neither do the rest of us."

Macallister tried to twist about in the man's grasp. "Who—who the devil are you," he stammered with more bravado than sense, "to interfere in my—my private conversation with this woman?"

"I am Eliot Fitzharding, Duke of Guilford," the tall man

said, "but more importantly, I'm a man who expects a certain civility in a drawing room. And you, sir, have offended not only this lady, but me as well."

Belatedly Pratt now appeared with two of the house guards hustling after him. "Forgive me, Your Grace, forgive me if this man has been ill-mannered."

"I'll tell you who's being ill-mannered, Pratt," Macallister sputtered as he flailed vainly in the other man's grip, "and it ain't me."

But the house guards had already taken him by the arms and were hurrying him toward the door, with Pratt following to make certain he was properly tossed down the steps and into the street.

Her heart racing, Bethany took a deep, shuddering breath to calm herself. She'd nothing to fear from Macallister now, or ever; for what he'd just done, he'd be banned for life from the club. Amariah had warned her about the occasional disrespectful gentleman who confused the gaming club with a brothel, and Macallister had certainly done that. But it frightened her that he'd insulted William, too, frightened her badly. She already worried about William's safety as he hunted the murderer; he didn't need Macallister after him, too.

"Are you feeling unsteady, Miss Bethany?" asked the duke, holding his arm out to her. "Should I send for your maid?"

"Thank you, no, Your Grace, I am fine, quite fine." She forced herself to muster a smile, and curtseyed the way she should have earlier. "And while I'll thank you for your assistance, too, I must apologize for needing it. You came to Penny House for enjoyment, not to have to play the gallant and rescue me."

"Oh, but perhaps I did," he said, and to her surprise he winked. She'd first met him earlier, when he'd arrived, and he hadn't seemed like the sort of gentleman who'd wink at all. Although he couldn't have been much past thirty, there was a world-weary air about him as if he'd long ago done and seen anything of any interest anywhere, and the rest was now just tedious gravy. "Your sister told me to watch over you, and I suppose it's a good thing that for once I did as I was told."

She laughed, finding it very hard to imagine him obeying anyone, especially Amariah. "My sister told you that?"

He nodded, the twinkle in his eyes sharing her amusement. "Miss Penny tells me a great many things, you know. Not so many as she must tell you, but a great many nonetheless."

"Indeed." Strange that in all their conversations about the club's members, Amariah had never once mentioned the Duke of Guilford.

"Indeed, yes." He leaned forward and lowered his voice in confidence. "In fact I am a great admirer of your sister and her martinet ways. There is nothing more enchanting than a woman who can give orders that are so instantly obeyed. If only His Majesty would send Miss Penny to France to confront General Buonaparte, why, the war would be over in a fortnight. Though you must swear to me, Miss Bethany, swear most solemnly, never to reveal that to her, or she'll lose all respect for me."

"I wouldn't dare, Your Grace." She laughed again, picturing her sister in a general's uniform as she reviewed the troops. Of course she knew the duke was saying such outrageous things to make her relax and forget Macallister, but still she liked him all the more for doing it. "Amariah would have my head if I did."

"Exactly," the duke said, nodding sagely, "and mine, too. But tell me, Miss Bethany. Who is the fortunate gentleman that's claimed your affections?"

She blushed, thinking at once of William.

"Oh, come, Miss Bethany, you can tell me," he said easily. "And I won't tell your sister, either. But every time I've looked your way this evening, you've been searching about for *someone,* as eager as a spaniel. Your night's almost done. High time he appeared. So who is the lucky rogue, eh?"

Her cheeks grew hotter still. "I cannot tell, Your Grace, not even to you. My sisters and I do not wish to distract from the club by becoming centerpieces for gossip and scandal."

"'Gossip and scandal'?" He gazed up toward the heavens, beseeching, and shook his head. "I'm not your aged granny, Miss Bethany. You don't have to protect my ears, I assure you. But I won't pry. Keep your rascal secret, and pray he keeps you from his wife, too."

"Your Grace!"

Now he was the one who laughed, and he patted her arm. "Go on, away with you, and find your lover. I say you're excused, and no one will question me."

"Thank you, Your Grace." She didn't need his permission, but she still flashed him a quick grin and a curtsey of farewell, folded her fan and hurried up the stairs. She passed through the gaming rooms, taking care to be seen without causing any interruptions, whispering good-nights and encouragements, taking one last look that everything was as it should be. Then she practically ran down the back stairs to the kitchen, feeling like a girl freed at last from the schoolroom.

"Did you survive tonight, Letty?" she asked. "Did everyone behave as they should?"

"'Course they did, miss." Letty wiped a weary arm over her forehead. Only one footman remained downstairs, drying and putting away the last of the outsized platters into the wooden racks overhead, and one of Fewler's guards was sitting half-asleep on a stool by the door. The fires were banked, the tables wiped, and the leftover food put into the safes for the night. Any other plates left upstairs now would be collected and washed in the morning. "And even if they didn't, old Pratty kept coming down to poke his nose about to make sure."

"He did that because I kept fussing." She came and rested her hand on Letty's shoulder. "Not that I needed to. You did splendidly, Letty, and I thank you for it."

"Thank *you,* miss," she said, pleased. "I've checked over the market list again for tomorrow, and everything looks as it should be. There should be more than enough in the purse you gave me earlier."

Bethany nodded, thinking how this would be the first morning since Penny House had opened that she hadn't gone to Covent Garden for the day's provisions. But she wanted to be able to linger with William without watching for dawn, and sending Letty in her place was the only way.

"Since you must rise so early, Letty, why don't you go up to bed now? I'll lock the doors."

"I'll see to that, miss," the guard said, yawning as he slipped from the stool. "'Tis my job."

"'Twas mine long before it was yours," Bethany said, dropping her fan on the table. "You go. I'll close."

The guard opened his mouth to protest, then turned it into a yawn. He shuffled off back up the stairs, and the last footman soon followed.

"You are certain?" Letty asked as she hung up her apron. "You look so beautiful tonight, miss, that I hate to see you down here where you might spot that lovely gown."

"And if I do, then I'll be the one who must clean it off." She hugged the other cook at the base of the stairs. "Good night, Letty, and sleep well."

As she waited for Letty's footsteps to fade away, she

glanced at her reflection in the back of a polished pot, smoothing her elaborately dressed hair beneath the curled white plume. In her blue Penny House gown and the glittering paste necklace and earrings that she'd borrowed from her sister, she looked more like another Amariah than her familiar self, and uneasily she hoped William wouldn't mind the difference, considering how little attention he paid to his own clothes.

She peeked up the stairs one last time to make sure she was alone, then caught the ring of keys from the hook. Her heart beating with anticipation, she unlocked the door and stepped outside.

"William?" she called softly. Since she'd told him to come late, she wasn't even sure he was here yet. "William?"

She caught the shadow of the motion from the corner of her eye, and turned just as he swept her into his arms. She laughed with happiness, and kissed him, and laughed again, pushing herself back against his chest so she could look at his face.

"How long have you been waiting for me, sweet?" she whispered. He'd washed and shaved, his heavy dark hair for once combed neatly back from his forehead.

But he wasn't laughing, not the way she was. In the pale light washing through the kitchen windows, his face was as serious as she'd ever seen it.

"How long have I been waiting?" he repeated. "All my life, lass. All my life."

"Ohhhhh," she whispered, overwhelmed. "Oh, William, I don't know what—"

"I love you, Bethany," he said, his voice raw with emotion. "That's all. I love you."

Chapter Thirteen

William woke slowly, savoring the last few moments of sleep as he hovered between consciousness and sweet oblivion. He was just awake enough to realize that this room was not his, nor was the bed, yet still so drowsy as not to care. Late morning sun streamed in through the open windows, and a lazy bee buzzed through the red flowers in the box outside. The fine linens were redolent of lavender and lovemaking, and as he rolled over he curled his arm around the bare hip of Bethany Penny, soft and warm and just as sleepy beside him.

"I love you, William," she mumbled with an endearing lack of diction, and wriggled back against him. "My… own…love."

"I love you, too," he said, whispering against her cheek. Gently he pulled her closer, her bottom pressed against his belly, and marveled at what a change such a simple word could bring.

Love, love: before this he'd always dismissed it as mawkish and sentimental, the stuff of cheap novels and swooning maidens. But Bethany had changed that. Because she'd trusted him, he'd trusted her, and magically love, *this* love, and all the rest of it had followed. It was as simple and as complicated as that, and if he could spend the rest of his days in this bedchamber of hers, squirreled away from the dangers and cares of the world, then he was quite sure he would die the happiest of men.

He smoothed aside her hair, lightly kissing the place just below her ear that he'd already learned was deliciously sensitive for her.

She sighed, and smiled without opening her eyes. "I thought you wished to sleep late."

"We agreed we'd stay abed as long as we pleased," he said, beginning to slide his hand back and forth along the curve of her hip. "There was nothing whatsoever said about sleep."

"Ha." She rolled onto her back and opened her eyes to look at him. In their haste last night, they'd neglected to pause to remove her necklace, and the gaudy paste stones that had showed so fine under the chandeliers looked incongruously decadent against her lightly freckled chest, here in the morning sun. "You're as sly as any barrister, William Callaway."

He leaned over her to kiss her, taking his time, letting her make him forget everything he needed to forget. "I'd say I'm ten times as sly, and a hundred times better at pleasuring you."

"Oh, please." She laughed, her bare breasts shaking below the sparkling necklace. "I trust you're not expecting me to go to the Old Bailey to make a comparison."

"I don't expect you to go anywhere," he said, "at least not without me. You know, I like you in those jewels. Diamonds, and not a stitch more."

"They're very grand for my station, aren't they?" She pursed her lips and tipped her head to one side, pretending to preen. "Fancy what they'd be worth if they were real!"

"You deserve real ones," he said, thinking of how one day soon he'd surprise her with some special bauble. "You're worth it to me."

"That is very kind of you to say, William," she said softly, clearly dismissing his offer as empty gallantry and no more—assuming that he could never afford to be so indulgent. One of her most endearing qualities was that she loved him for himself, not for the title or fortune that he'd never quite brought himself to mention. "But I don't need diamonds to be happy, especially not from you."

She looped her arms around his neck and drew him down to kiss her again, sending charming little moans between his parted lips.

"So you like where you are, Major?" she asked. "You find these lodgings agreeable?"

He made a great show of looking around the room as if appraising it, and she laughed, though he had the distinct feeling that this morning she'd laugh at anything he did or said. Which was, really, quite fine with him.

"There might be a shade too many flowers here for a military man," he said, trying to scowl at the pink roses that patterned the wallpaper on the wall behind the bed, "but the food is markedly better."

"Oh, is it?" She struck his chest with her fist in mock protest. "Is that all I am to you, then? The best galley-cook to be had?"

"The best to be had for love or for money," he teased. "If you'd rather starve me, then you shouldn't have brought me that special tray from the kitchen in the middle of the night."

"I'd rather you kept your strength up for other activities," she said, her whisper now a husky purr. "Besides, if I'd waited until now to fetch you breakfast, everyone else would be in the kitchen, and they'd all *know*."

She was tracing her finger in lazy small circles over the dark powder-burns on his chest. He still couldn't quite believe they didn't disgust her, but here again was more proof of how special she was.

"I'd wager they know already, pet." He understood why she'd wished to keep his presence here a secret as long as they could: not because she was ashamed of him, but because she wanted to hold on to this little world of theirs for themselves as long as they could. He understood because he did, too. The four days until her sister returned would pass like nothing.

"I'll have to go down those stairs some time." He took her fingers and kissed each one in turn. "But I'd wager they're guessing now."

"Let them." This time her laugh became a throaty chuckle as her free hand slipped down between their bodies. "If you're willing, that is. If you'd not rather *sleep*."

By way of an answer he took her firmly by the waist and rolled over on his back, bringing her shrieking with him. She pushed herself up so her face was over his, her hair falling down around them like a tangled, coppery curtain.

"How much do you want them to guess?" he asked, easing her legs over his hips so she was straddling him. "You've never been one to shy away from a bit of work, have you?"

She grinned wickedly, touching him, but still unsure of what to do next. He loved that about her, too, how willing she was to try whatever he suggested.

He raised her up, adjusting them both so his hard length was barely nudging her open. She was still wet and slick and swollen from last night—or whenever it had been— and it took all his willpower not to plunge in deep. Wide-eyed with expectation, she sat poised, ready, her tangled hair falling down her back and her breasts raised before him in a wanton, tantalizing display.

"Trust me," he said, his voice strangled from the effort of holding himself still. "Just—just slide down."

"Trust you," she whispered. "Oh, William, I've always trusted you."

Then she eased her legs down and gasped with the new sensation of being filled by him this way. He raised his hips upward, meeting her, and felt the shudder of her pleasure ripple through her body to his. Tentatively she pulled back, then slid down again with excruciating slowness, and now he was the one who gasped.

"Ha," she said breathlessly, her smile giddy. "Now you must be the one who trusts *me*."

He settled his hands on her hips, his fingers splayed wide to guide her pace and lift her upward.

"It goes both ways, lass," he said, easing her back down. "You trust me, and I'll trust you."

She whimpered with delight, her eyes squeezed shut and her head thrown back as together they found a rhythm that pleased them both.

"You are *wicked*, William," she said, rocking with him.

"I try." He chuckled, and reached up to cup her breast, teasing the nipple with his thumb until she moaned, and he felt her tighten inside around him. He could be wicked, yes, and so could she, but as much as both of them might want, they could not make this game last forever. He quickened the pace and she matched him, until, finally, with a cry of release she collapsed on his chest, and he arched up and finished, too.

"There," she said later, still lying on his chest. "How could I not trust you when you do that?"

He laughed softly, his arms around her. "Because I love you."

"You mean because *I* love you."

He laughed again, happier than he could ever recall. He

had reached the point where he could not imagine his life now without her in it, though he still hadn't decided what he should do to make sure she remained with him.

"Because I love you," he said, "and you love me, and let that be an end to it."

"Yes," she said, and when she propped herself up to kiss him, he could see the tears of joy in her eyes. "I cannot imagine it any better than that."

Macallister slumped down in the most encompassing wing chair he could find in the reading room at White's. He'd turned it so it faced the window instead of the center of the room, and then had opened a newspaper in front of him to make it doubly clear that he did not wish to be disturbed.

Not that any of the other gentlemen had tried. He knew he wasn't imagining it, either, how they were avoiding him, looking away, purposefully waiting until he passed so they wouldn't have to speak to him.

It was all the fault of that bitch Bethany Penny. If she hadn't willfully provoked him last night at Penny House, then he wouldn't have lost his temper, and said and done the things that were being repeated today all over London. He knew they were; he could practically hear the tongues clacking as he'd walked down the street. Everyone knew. Guilford must have spread the tale, even if the Penny woman hadn't.

Though he hadn't received a letter yet from the club's governors, Pratt had told him to expect one. His membership would be revoked, and he would be banned from the club for the rest of his life, refused admission at the door even if he came as the guest of another member. The Penny women had made it clear from the first day that they didn't believe in second chances, not even for a gentleman like himself.

But he could cope with the disgrace. Yes. In a few days, every scandal was forgotten in London. He gnawed at a hangnail on his thumb, trying to convince himself. He was above their petty insults. There were other gaming clubs who'd be damned glad to add him to their membership. It might even be easier to hunt Bethany Penny now, without her hiding behind the rules of her sainted club. And she would be his eventually; he didn't doubt that. Even the most virtuous woman had her price, and he meant to keep raising his offer until he discovered hers.

His only real mistake had been to mention Callaway. What demon had possessed him to link her to Callaway like that? Bethany Penny had certainly understood, and likely Guilford had, too. Now if Callaway were to meet with an accident, a misfortune, then Guilford would certainly remember Macallister's tirade against the madman last night.

He closed his eyes, trying to concentrate. Perhaps he was overreacting. More likely the Penny chit was like every other woman, so focused on herself that she wouldn't remember what he'd said about Callaway, just as Guilford was more concerned with being so deuced helpful only because he wanted to find his way into the woman's bed.

Unconsciously he touched the medal on the front of his uniform, the one for bravery, the one that everyone noticed. With this on his chest, he would always be a hero, and no one would ever dare call him a mealy-mouthed little coward again.

Yes, yes, he *was* overreacting. Really, he had nothing to worry about. Better to stay with his original plan, and move Callaway to the top of his list. There were only two men on it, anyway, and after he'd disposed of Callaway, those others would be nothing.

And then his secret would be safe forever.

* * *

"Miss Bethany, a word, if you please." Pratt stood waiting in the front hall, his hands pressed flat against his sides. "Now, while there is a moment free."

"Surely." Bethany smiled. Although the club's doors would open to members in the next quarter hour, they were alone for now, and not likely to be interrupted. "What word did you wish to ask, Pratt?"

He cleared his throat delicately. "It's more of a concern, miss. I'm sorry to disturb you, but I fear it must be addressed before Miss Penny returns."

"And what concern could that be, Pratt?" she asked, turning to straighten the white plume in her hair. She still hadn't acquired Amariah's knack for keeping the quill in place, and she constantly had to adjust it throughout the night to keep it from drooping over her forehead. "I was under the impression that everything had gone quite well, excepting that one unfortunate incident with Lieutenant Macallister."

"The lieutenant will not be troubling us again, Miss Bethany." Pratt looked down to the polished toes of his shoes. "It is another matter, miss, one that has disturbed both the staff and Mr. Fewler as well. It is the, ah, the gentleman that has been, ah, visiting the private rooms in the evening."

At once Bethany turned to face him, unable to keep from instantly blushing.

"I didn't realize that my personal affairs were of concern to the entire household, Pratt," she said, struggling to appear unconcerned. William had predicted this moment would come, and he'd been right. "I thought I was entitled to that much privacy."

Clearly as miserable as she was, Pratt didn't look up. "I most heartily regret the intrusion, Miss Bethany, and if it were my decision alone, the subject would never have been raised. But Mr. Fewler is concerned for your safety, miss, as well as the welfare of the club. He says this man is the same one who accosted you in the park."

"'*Accosted*' me?" Bethany exclaimed. "We were walking together in conversation along the public paths. There was never any *accosting*!"

"I am very sorry, Miss Bethany, very sorry indeed. But Mr. Fewler says the man is not quite respectable, nor worthy of your regard, and he worries that he might be a danger to your—your person."

"I believe that is my decision, Pratt, not Mr. Fewler's," she said warmly. "The gentleman in question is a former officer in His Majesty's army, of impeccable honor and regard."

Finally Pratt raised his troubled gaze to hers. "I regret to report that Mr. Fewler has his doubts, miss, as to the man's character, and to the veracity of his claims regarding his service to the king. Mr. Fewler fears he is a scoundrel, miss, preying upon your—"

"No, Pratt, I'll not listen to another word," she snapped, turning away. "Please inform Mr. Fewler that I am satisfied with the gentleman's character, and that I have not a single fear for my person while in his company. And tell him, and everyone else under this roof, that I expect to hear no more regarding this—this matter."

She began to walk away, her heels clicking on the polished marble floor, but Pratt stopped her, resting his hand on her arm with more familiarity than he'd ever dared before.

"Then pray answer me this, Miss Bethany. Is Miss Penny aware of this—this man's visits to you?" he asked so earnestly that he was almost pleading. "Does she know that he is a guest in your rooms? If Miss Penny has been told that you are, ah, are entertaining him here in your apartments, and she does not object, why, then, I shall be content."

Bethany looked down at the fan in her hand, absently smoothing her fingers over the blades. These last nights that she'd spent with William had been the most idyllic in her life, and she wouldn't have changed them for anything. But with her sister due home tomorrow, the idyll was nearly done. If she wanted it to continue in any way, she was going to have to decide how to introduce the man she loved into her other life.

She sighed unhappily. "I promise I'll tell my sister as soon as she comes through the door, Pratt," she said. "By supper tomorrow, she'll know everything."

William was whistling.

Because the tune was a march, he'd fallen into step without thinking, as if Bowden Court were his own private parade ground, but the truly remarkable thing was that he was whistling at all. For the past two years, he'd had so precious little in his life to whistle about that he'd almost forgotten how, and the fact that he was doing it now—a little flat, without much melody, but still an honorable and cheerful effort—was indeed worth marveling over.

And the reason, of course, was Bethany.

Her sister's return today had cast a bittersweet cloud over last night, and when they'd made love for this final time in her bed, he'd tried to be especially tender. But while he had long ago learned to take each day for what it offered, bad or good, she'd still been too worried over what she would say to her sister to enjoy the night as much as he would have liked. Although he had offered to stay with her and greet Amariah at her side, she'd refused, saying that she must do this by herself for her sister's sake. He hadn't understood that, but he would respect her decision. There would be time enough to meet Amariah Penny, as well as Cassia and Richard Blackley.

For now, his greatest concern was loving Bethany, and letting her know how much she meant to him. That was what mattered most: the two of them together. The rest would come later.

He was whistling still as he climbed the stairs to his rooms and opened the door, tossing his hat on the bed.

On the bed beside his sister.

"Why in blazes are you back here again, Portia?" he asked with exasperation, his cheerful mood punctured in an instant. "I thought I'd made it clear to you last time that I wanted no part of your scheming with Father."

"And good day to you, too, William," she said, sailing his hat back at him. "How fortunate that your landlady is more agreeable to my visits than my own dear brother!"

"She has no right letting you in here without my permission, if that is what you mean." He sat in the chair to his desk, pointedly putting as much distance as he could between him and his sister. "Don't say you didn't come here wanting something, Portia. I know you too well for that."

She tipped her head back and laughed, twisting her fingers in the long strand of pearls she wore looped around her throat. "You've grown wiser with age, brother, or perhaps with experience. But I won't deny what you say. Why else would I come to this grim little street without a purpose?"

She reached into her reticule and pulled out a creamy white card.

"There," she said, handing it to William. "There's my reason. Aunt Helen is inviting the family to a box at Vauxhall tonight to celebrate our cousin Sarah's betrothal to some marquess or another. Your presence is requested."

"The *family*." He barely glanced at the card before he tossed it back, much as she'd tossed his hat. "Portia, I can scarce recall this cousin of ours, and what I do remember of Aunt Helen gives me no incentive whatsoever to attend."

"Oh, when was the last time you went to Vauxhall?" she asked, ignoring the discarded invitation. "It's so wonderfully tawdry, all those apprentices and milliners aping their betters."

"Is that supposed to entice me?"

"I'll be there," she said. "And my long-suffering Andrew."

"Your husband? How droll." The room was warm and he was tired. He shrugged out of his coat, rolling back the sleeves of his shirt. "Portia, I really don't believe that I—"

"And Father will be there, too." For once her face was unreadable. "He would like to see you, William."

William groaned, and leaned back in the chair to stare up at the ceiling. "Why, Portia? So he can try to convince me to wed that pitiful halfwit girl?"

"He's done with that," she said with a careless wave of her hand. "Besides, the girl's family lost patience, and married her to another."

He yawned, not bothering to cover his mouth. "If you do not tell me soon, Portia, I will fall asleep before your eyes without hearing you."

"Father wishes to see you, William. That is all."

"What, to see my infirmities for himself? To decide which madhouse will suit me best?"

"It's not like that, not at all." She sighed, twisting one of her rings around and around her finger. "Father's not well, William. He'll likely live another year at most, and he wishes to reconcile with you."

"One invalid to another?"

"Hush, William, and stop being so provoking," she said crossly, scowling. "I've told him how much progress you've made, how you're much improved with your recovery."

"I'll never recover," he said bluntly, thinking of the scars that would be with him forever. "I can't turn back the clock to return to what I once was."

"But you are so much better than you were, William!" she exclaimed. "It's not just your leg. You seem happier, more even-tempered, less angry with the world. I remarked it at once."

He knew the reason, but he wasn't about to confess it to Portia. "The surgeons said it would take time."

"The surgeons have nothing to do with it," she said. "It's that girl, isn't it? Miss Ha'Penny? There's nothing that improves any man's health than the release that comes from pleasuring a woman."

He signed, resisting his first inclination to deny it all. "It is Bethany Penny, yes," he admitted. "She has changed everything for me."

"Why, *you* are in love!" Portia's eyes widened with curiosity as she leaned forward to inspect him more closely. "I didn't think I should ever see the day."

"I do love her," he said. He still wasn't accustomed to saying it aloud, and he felt his mouth twist into an idiot grin of its own doing. "I always will."

"I am shocked, William, shocked." She was, too, shocked and disbelieving, the same as everyone else in his family would be. "I hope at least the chit returns your ardor. I've asked after her, William. She's practically a virago. I'd no notion she was one of those Penny House Pennys. They say that club practically mints money, it's so successful. She won't be easy to pry from there."

"I haven't decided if I'll try to or not," he said. "I doubt she'd be content without it."

Portia sniffed. "Of course she wouldn't be content if you ask her to live *here*."

"I wouldn't," he said, all he'd admit. He already knew she loved him for himself alone, not that Portia could ever comprehend such a concept. The real question was not where they'd live, but how: as lovers, as friends or as husband and wife?

"Well, then, the least you can do is bring her to us tonight." She took the invitation and went to prop it on the narrow mantel over his fireplace. "I promise I shall keep everyone on their best behavior."

"Not possible," he said, appalled by such a suggestion. "Our best behavior is the rest of the world's worst. I don't think she's ready for that, Portia, and neither am I."

"Of course she is. She's already met me and survived, hasn't she?" She made a graceful turn, almost a spin, swinging her skirts out around her ankles. "Promise me you'll consider it. For Father, and yourself, and your shiny little Penny. If she's going to love you as much as you deserve, then she needs to know more of who you are. And that includes us."

He shook his head, not wanting to admit how eerily similar Portia's suggestion was to his own thoughts. Bethany had accepted everything else about him, hadn't she? And just as he must meet Bethany's sisters, at some point he in turn would have to introduce her to his own family. Hell, he still had to tell her they even *existed*.

But the more he thought of such a reunion with his family, the less awful it seemed. He wouldn't take Bethany with him, not yet—surviving Portia was one thing, but facing down Father and the inspection of those villainous old harpies, his aunts, was quite another—but perhaps him joining this party at Vauxhall would not be so very bad.

Maybe this was another way that being in love with Bethany had changed him. Maybe somehow she'd made him strong enough, sure enough, that he could see Father again without it becoming a shouting battle of wills.

Besides, Vauxhall being Vauxhall, he could always disappear if things went badly, and no one would notice. And he could still reach Penny House before Bethany had closed the kitchen for the night.

He glanced back at Portia, who was watching him with the same predatory intensity of a cat with a mouse.

"I'm not bringing Bethany," he said. "I won't do that to her."

Portia's painted mouth curved with triumph. "But you are coming yourself, then?"

He groaned, and shook his head, realizing how deftly he'd just been played. "You planned that from the beginning, didn't you?"

"Yes," she said, without a hint of remorse. "All's fair in love and war."

"At least it is among the Callaways," he said, not so much disgusted as resigned.

"Particularly Callaways in love." She winked slyly. "And I'll wager a hundred guineas that your little Penny would not have you any other way."

Chapter Fourteen

When the carriage arrived from Greenwood Hall, Bethany was in the kitchen, rolling pastry and crimping it into pans for the evening's pies. But though she didn't hear the carriage's return, there was no missing her sister skipping down the stairs into the kitchen to greet her.

"Bethany!" Amariah flung her arms around Bethany, heedless of the clouds of flour that now blotched her traveling clothes. "Oh, duck, I'm so happy to be home! You cannot know how much I missed you!"

"Nor I you," Bethany said, hugging her in return. And despite the time she'd spent with William, she truly had missed her sister's company. "But how is Cassia? Is she recovered from whatever was ailing her?"

"You may ask her yourself," Amariah said as she untangled herself from Bethany's embrace and turned back toward the stairs. "She's more cautious now, that is all."

"Cassia!" Bethany hurried to hug her other sister. "Oh, Cassia, how good it is to have you here, too! Let me look at you. You do not look ill, not at all. What was Richard fussing about, anyway?"

Amariah made a dismissive little *huff*. "He is being a

foolish, worrying husband, that is all, when he is the only cause of her so-called illness."

"He's not foolish, Amariah, only concerned for me," Cassia said, untying the ribbons of her hat. "But that's why I hadn't told him yet, to keep him from fussing."

Bethany gasped. "So you *are* with child? How happy I am for you, Cassia, you and Richard both!"

"Thank you, sweet." Cassia leaned forward to let Bethany kiss her cheek. She was beautifully and expensively dressed in a dark plum dress that complemented the coppery hair the sisters shared, but there was also an elegant self-assurance that Bethany didn't remember from before. Perhaps it came from being Richard's wife, or perhaps it came from her coming status as a mother, but to Bethany, Cassia now seemed infinitely older and more sophisticated, and no longer the same sister who'd stood on a chair in the front room to entertain the guests, or had fashioned wood chips into decorations for her bonnets. And as happy as Bethany was for Cassia, in a way she missed the old version of her sister.

Had William changed her, too? Did love alone have the power to do that, or was it the man?

"But that is why I brought her with me, you see," Amariah said, slipping her arm around Cassia's waist. "Here she can have some quiet and peace, and her last jaunt to London while she still can travel. Think of it, Betts. The first Penny babe!"

And the only one for now, Bethany hoped, hurrying to bring a chair for her sister.

"Here now, Cassia, you must sit," she ordered, putting aside her own worries. "Are you uneasy in the mornings, or would you like your regular dish of tea with lemon? Though I've heard a posset of honey and cream with a dash of rum and cinnamon grated fine is most healthful for mothers and their growing babes, too. Shall I fix that for you, or something else you'd prefer?"

"Stop it, Betts," Cassia said, laughing, as she sat in the chair. "You're being every bit as bad as Richard ever could be. Tea would be nice, thank you, but what I really crave is all the news of Penny House. What's the latest scandal, Betts? Who has insulted whom? Who's lost their inheritance at hazard, and who's won a new one? I want to hear everything!"

"Yes, yes, Bethany, you must tell us all." Amariah perched on the edge of the table, nibbling sugared cherries set aside in a bowl for the pies. "Pratt couldn't wait to hint darkly at every manner of mischief that had occurred while I've been away."

"Oh, you know how Pratt can exaggerate." Bethany took up her rolling pin again, looking for any distraction she could. She was acutely aware of how the servants around them in the kitchen had slowed at their tasks, every ear straining to hear what she said next. Doubtless they all knew about William, and likely her promise to Pratt as well, and now they couldn't wait to hear how'd she start.

For that matter, she couldn't wait to hear it herself.

"It was very quiet while you were gone," she began, as noncommittal as possible as she began to roll out another circle of pastry dough. She knew she'd promised Pratt she'd tell Amariah as soon as she could, but not before so many witnesses. "The only thing close to scandal was one night when Lieutenant Macallister caught me in the front room alone, and said a great many things he shouldn't have."

"I heard, and I'm sorry." Amariah lay her hand on Bethany's arm. "Thank God Lord Guildford was there to help you, as he'd promised to me he would. He wrote all about it to me."

"He *did?*" Bethany asked with surprise, then remembered how the duke had seemed to be on such close terms with Amariah. She'd thought he'd been pretending to comfort her, but maybe he'd been more truthful than she'd realized. "I hope he wrote how he rescued me when no one else was there. Why haven't you mentioned him before?"

To Bethany's delight, Amariah blushed. "Lord Guildford is a very amusing gentleman, and that is all," she said, too quickly. "He often keeps me company when no one else in the room is sober."

"He's also the Duke of Guilford, Amariah," Cassia said, teasing, "and he's quite handsome and entertaining, *and* he's most outspoken in the House of Lords. What a perfect match he'd make for you!"

"Don't be foolish, Cassia," Amariah said as the blush in her cheeks deepened to betray her. "Why should I be dreaming of such foolishness when we've Penny House to occupy us?"

But Bethany knew what the servants were thinking all around her: yes, a handsome duke would be a perfect match for Miss Penny, just as Miss Cassia had married that dashing, wealthy Mr. Blackley. They'd never know William's generosity, or his kindness, or his bravery, or how he could make her laugh one moment and cry out with pleasure the next.

All they'd know were the shameful lies that Fewler had concocted about him. And then what a pity that Miss Bethany can do no better for herself than a crippled soldier from her flock of paupers. How could they understand that William was worth more than the entire high-born membership of Penny House put together?

"But the Duke of Guildford, Amariah," Cassia was saying, shaking her head in amazement. "Perhaps we'll see him tonight at Vauxhall."

"At Vauxhall Gardens?" Bethany asked. "Are you going to Vauxhall, Amariah?"

"*We* are going," Amariah declared, now the one relieved by the change of conversation. "The three of us in an open carriage, out for show and for amusement, just like the days when we wanted the gentlemen to recognize us before we opened the club."

Cassia nodded eagerly. "And to thank you, Bethany, for sparing Amariah so she could come for me. We won't stay late—I weary so early now!—so we shall return in plenty of time for the club's busiest hours. But to hear the orchestra, and see the dancing and the fireworks with both of you—can there be anything finer?"

"Not at all," Bethany said softly, touched. This could well be the last time the three of them would have this sort of outing together. She'd tell them then about William, tell them everything, there under the fireworks that would remind her of him. She could see no further ahead into the future than that.

And whether she wished for it or not, everything in her life was changing…

William left the boat that had brought him across the river, and joined the throngs of revelers climbing the steps that led from the water to the entrance of Vauxhall Gardens. Just as Portia had predicted, he was surrounded by clerks and lady's maids in hand-me-down finery, and he smiled to think that he was absolutely no better.

Portia had seen to that, too. Not wanting him to make a sad show before Father, she'd sent a servant to Bowden Court with a selection of the old evening clothes he'd long ago left at the house.

It had been no choice, really. He'd caught his breath at the sight of his old regimentals, the rows of buttons newly polished and the bouillon braid buffed to a golden sheen there among the dark superfine coats that civilians wore at night. He couldn't believe that the uniform had survived, that it hadn't been discarded when Father had sold away his commission when he'd been so close to death. Everything was there, from his boots to his sword to the horse-hair bristling from his hat, and he felt a tightness in his chest at all it represented, all that was gone.

The man had silently helped him dress, refreshing William's memory as to the intricacies of tying a neckcloth and the ridiculous small pleasure to be found in having the wide heavy sash wrapped around his waist. He shaved him twice to make sure no hint of a beard remained, trimmed his hair before he combed it back from his forehead, and even bent to smooth the tassels on the fronts of his boots. Finally he nodded with satisfaction and stepped back, letting William admire his finished handiwork in the looking glass.

Yet it wasn't so much admiration that William felt as he stared at his reflection, but shock. He hadn't dressed like this in years. The once-closely tailored clothes were a shade too large for him now, the fabric hanging loose around the waist over the sash, but still fit him well enough to transform him again into a man with squared shoulders and a back as straight as a rifle's ramrod: an officer, a lord, the son of a peer, a gentleman of authority and breeding and wealth.

A man he wasn't sure still existed.

Now as he entered beneath Vauxhall's arching trees, the fairy-lights twinkling in the branches overhead against the shadowy dusk sky, he was acutely aware of how his dress set him apart. It was as if an invisible circle had been drawn around him that no others could cross, a warning that they could only gaze at him in speechless awe. He couldn't remember if it had been like that before, too, and he simply hadn't bothered to notice then, or if he were just more conscious of the distance now after taking such care to be forgettable, to blend in with the others in the crowd.

He made his way slowly toward the music, taking his time so his limp would not be as noticeable. He knew that his family always took a private box near the orchestra and the dancing. It wasn't so much because they enjoyed the music, but because Father liked to be noticed by others. He wanted to be remarked as having the most fashionable box, the most expensive seats, the most beautiful and beautifully dressed women, and he wanted those facts to be duly noted in the scandal sheets the next day. In all things, Father wished to be envied, which was why a crippled, half-mad son had not fit into his plans for a glorious life.

"William!" Portia called, dressed in a bright spangled saffron gown waving her handkerchief over the railing of the box to get his attention. "William, here!"

It was done now, no turning back, and he forced himself to walk toward the box, up the handful of steps, to stand at the head of the long, narrow table. Faces ranged up and down each side, faces that he knew he should remember and greet as members of his family, but faces that now seemed only an indiscriminant haze. How could they be otherwise, with Father himself, sitting at the head in an armchair that was more like a throne?

"Where's your cane, boy?" Father demanded, his voice booming the question as the only greeting he'd offer. Portia had said he was unwell, but he looked much the same as William remembered: a handsomely arrogant older man with a boiled red face punctuated by the family's pale eyes, his white hair cropped fashionably short and brushed forward over his forehead. His mouth was the same, too, hard and unyielding and intolerant of any weakness, a mouth that could never bring itself to venture any word of sympathy or understanding.

"Have you gone deaf as well?" he demanded, jolting William back to the present. "I asked you what had become of your cane."

"I no longer require it, Father." He refused to smile unless the old man smiled first, and he would not sit unless invited by him, no matter how long Portia continued to flutter and beckon near the empty chair like some yellow moth. "How perceptive of you to remark that I walked here without it."

"That's a damned impudent thing to say to your father, sir." The rest of the table fell pointedly silent. "I thought the army had taught you to respect your superiors."

"It did, Father," William said. "It also taught me the necessity of thinking for myself."

"Is that why you refused the bride I found you, eh?" the old marquess asked, scowling up at William. "A pretty thing, with a prettier fortune."

"I prefer a bride of my own choosing," William said, thinking of Bethany. "A bride who'll want me for myself, and of her own will."

His Bethany, his bride. Nothing would ever sound as right to him, and there in one sentence, he realized he'd made up his mind. Tonight, after this, he would go to her and ask her.

"Is that why you've taken up with that common hussy from the gambling den?" Father demanded. "You prefer a wife with a will instead of a fortune?"

"Miss Penny is neither common nor a hussy, Father," William said. He'd done his part by coming here, but the old man hadn't changed and never would. "And what I prefer most in a wife is a woman who loves me."

"*Love,*" the old marquess, ladling such scorn on the word and the emotion that it could have curdled. "How far will that take you in this world?"

"It's already taken me farther than I'd ever hoped to go." William bowed curtly. "Now it will take me from this place. Good evening, my ladies."

"Not yet, sir, you don't." Father stood, his legs so unsteady that he needed to lean onto the table for support, and for the first time William saw the weakness that Portia had mentioned. "So you are determined to wed her?"

"If she'll have me, Father."

"Bah." The marquess smacked his open hand on the table. "Of course she'll have you, if you'll have her. Now come here and sit by me." He waved his hand imperiously at the empty chair beside his. "Damnation, *sit*."

For an endless moment William hesitated, his conscience battling with his pride. It would be simple enough, and satisfying, too, to turn on his heel and leave and never see any of them ever again.

But the greatest lesson he'd learned from war was the finality of death. He'd no memory of his father showing him anything but scorn and contempt, just as he was doing tonight. There was no way to dip his memory in sugar to take away the bitterness and make them what they were not.

But did he really wish this to be the final way he thought of his father? Did he want that same bitterness to color how he treated the sons of his own that he hoped one day to have? For the sake of the love he'd discovered with Bethany, couldn't he show a bit more tolerance to the man who'd sired him?

And before his father could ask him again, he made his way to the far end of the table, and his father's side. He took his place before the empty chair, but did not sit, waiting for his father to sit again first. His father noticed, and grunted, the only recognition his respect would garner, and dropped heavily back into his chair. William followed, and at once the conversation rushed back to life around them, full of relief and forced merriment to match the orchestra's jigs and hornpipes.

William drank from the glass of wine the waiter filled; even with the best of intentions, this was going to be a long night.

Father leaned toward him, jabbing his arm with his finger to get his attention. "Is she willing to breed, this sturdy, common bride of yours? She'll give you children? So many of these fine-bred ladies with tea for blood don't know their duty. Look at your own sister. Though if she dropped one now, I'd give fifty guineas that it wasn't her husband's."

William tried not to choke on his wine, thankful his father could not read his thoughts and see the image of Bethany riding him with her head thrown back and the paste jewels bouncing over her bare breasts.

"She is most willing, Father," he said finally. "Her father was a country minister, and she knows every duty a good woman should."

"A parson's daughter?" The old man's bristly white brows arched with interest. "Pious women are always the randiest once you convert them to it. Go forth and multiply, eh?"

William took another gulp of the wine, the most civil answer he could muster to such a question.

Beside him his father laughed, then bowed his head and fell so silent that William wondered if he'd nodded off. Sitting side by side, he could see the dark purple freckles that mottled the old marquess's hands, how corded with age they'd become, the bones of his wrists hard knobs beneath his lace cuffs.

"I want more grandchildren, William," his father said suddenly, without raising his eyes. "You knew your brother lost three of his brood last spring? The girl and two boys?"

"I didn't," William said, shocked and saddened that he

hadn't known, and that Portia had not bothered to tell him. Death belonged on a battlefield, not in a nursery. "I am sorry."

"Smallpox." His father shook his head, the wisps of white hair gliding back and forth. "Now he has just the one boy left. The only certain thing in this life is death, William. Ask your parson's daughter to preach you that sermon."

"I'm sorry," William said again, feeling helpless. "I'm sorry."

"At least the bastards didn't kill you." He squinted up without raising his chin, his pale eyes watery and red-rimmed. "I sold you out of that regiment to save you, boy. Can you understand that? It would have broken me to see you go back. The Spaniards took your best, and I'd be damned before I gave them a scrap more of you."

So there it was, laid out as plain as the cloth on the table. He was one more of Father's possessions, the same as a painting by Titian or a prize racehorse, that he could not bear to see devalued by others. Father had had him rescued from Spain to save his own pride, and then had hidden him away to recover—or not—where no one would see him. His father would rather have sent him to an asylum than be shamed by his strange lapses, a madman's weaknesses. If he'd ceased to have a son to make him proud, why, then he'd cease to have a son at all.

For the briefest of seconds, the old marquess rested his hand over William's, the candlelight dancing off the cabochon ruby ring he always had worn. To the others, it could have been a sign of affection, father to son, but after the rest, William recognized the gesture for what it was: a claim of ownership, and nothing more.

"Marry your sturdy wench, William," Father was saying, "then fill her belly as fast as you can. Be a Callaway man, eh? Get yourself some sons by her, and then we'll buy her off and bury her in the country. Now tell this infernal hovering waiter if you want the ham, or the beef."

But the last thing on William's mind was dinner.

"Don't speak of her like that, Father," he said curtly. "She'll be my wife, and I'll thank you to regard her as such."

The old marquess grunted impatiently. "Don't be a fool, William. We both know there's only one reason for a man to marry."

"I'm marrying her because I love her," William said, his temper just barely in check. "That's the only reason that matters to me."

"Then you are a bloody idiot, William," Father snapped. "For love—for *love*! I should have you locked away in Bedlam after all."

"Better there than in this family." William shoved his chair back from the table. Nothing had changed; nothing ever would.

"For God's sake, sit," his father ordered crossly. "I won't have you making a damned fool of yourself like this."

"That's because you won't have me at all," William said with a curt bow. "Good night, Father, and goodbye."

He turned before his father answered, before any of them could try to make him stop. Not that they could: his life with them was done, and his future with Bethany was only beginning.

And the sooner he asked her to marry him, the better.

"That must be our box there, Amariah," Bethany said, pointing with her fan to the last empty seats overlooking the orchestra. "We'll be able to see simply everything."

"That's the point, isn't it, duck?" Amariah linked her arm through her sisters', and together the three of them cut across the dance court to their seats in the private box.

Bethany paused at the railing while her sisters arranged their chairs, enjoying the scene spread before her. When the three of them had come to Vauxhall before, it had been early spring and chilly, and they had not known anyone.

But now the evening was lushly warm, and the countless tiny lights in the branches of the trees seemed like stars dropped down from the velvet sky, with the music floating so lightly through the air that she felt as if she could reach out and touch it. The crowds of dancers seemed lighter on their feet, the laughter around them more joyful and the conversations wittier. Even the allegorical paintings that decorated the backs of the boxes seemed to glow like the work of the finest old masters.

And now the Penny sisters themselves were recognized as part of the gaiety, too. Dressed in variations of the sapphire blue they'd made their own, their famous copper hair dressed high on their heads, they had become celebrities, greeted warmly both by members of Penny House and by those others who wished to belong. The "Three Graces of Gaming," one wag had dubbed them, and from how many well-wishers had slowed their progress through the gardens, it wasn't far from the truth.

"Are you counting the handsome men, Bethany?" Cassia teased, coming to stand beside her while Amariah ordered their supper. "Why, I don't believe I've ever seen so many bachelors together in one place!"

"You've lived in the country too long, Cassia," Bethany answered, swatting her arm lightly with her fan.

"All I wish is for you to be as happy as I am with my Richard."

"As if you found Richard beckoning from a box at Vauxhall," she scoffed. What did she need with a sea of bachelors when she already had found the one that she wanted to keep forever? Of course, Cassia wouldn't know that any more than

Amariah did until she told them, tonight, on the ride home, when they were all jolly and relaxed after supper.

"Clearly seeing only cows and sheep in your vistas has dulled your eyesight," she said instead, teasing back with no mention yet of William. "Otherwise you will notice that most all of those handsome men are already in the company of equally handsome women."

"Oh, I'm sure there are a few rogues to spare here and there." Cassia grinned, with one hand shading her eyes like a sailor scanning the horizon. "Ahoy there, ahoy! A handsome man for my sister Bethany!"

"Stop it, Cassia!" Bethany said, giggling. "Don't *do* that to me, I beg you!"

Her sister grinned wickedly. "I'll do whatever I please," she said, still surveying the crowd below them. "Oh, look, Bethany, there's a girl selling bunches of violets. You know I do love the scent of violets. Do you think we can have her come this way?"

"She'll never hear us over the music," Bethany said, reaching for her reticule. "I'll go fetch you a little bouquet myself."

She skipped down the steps and along the edge of the dancers, humming the tune that the orchestra was playing. A young man tried to catch her hand, begging her to dance, and she only laughed and shook her head. How could she be more severe on such a night?

She dodged a waiter with a full tray of plates, then had to pause behind a cart full of wine bottles.

"That be the Marquess o' Beckham's party," one man was saying to another. "A filthy rich lot they are, too. They've asked for more wine for toastin' the fair little bride on the end, there, the one with th' yellow curls."

The second man tucked a bottle beneath each arm. "Is the military man th' groom, then?"

"Nay, that be the th' marquess's son," said the other man. "Though fine blokes like him have more'n their share of th' skirts, don't they?"

Curiosity made Bethany look to where the man was pointing. At Penny House, she saw many titled gentlemen, but never any of their ladies, and she wanted to see a high-born bride for herself. She stood on her toes, craning her neck, just as the cart moved from her path.

Now she, too, could see the girl with the yellow curls, and a woman that must be her mother, and the tall gentleman that was the marquess's son, an officer in a uniform that glittered with gold braid and brass buttons, leaning over to say something to them as he made his way to the steps to leave the box. Though she could not make out the son's face in the shadows, there was something oddly familiar about the man that she couldn't quite place. Perhaps he'd come to the club as the guest of another member; the son of a marquess would always be welcome, particularly an officer like this one.

She began to turn away, back to find the violet-seller, and just as she did, the tall man straightened, and she saw his handsome face, a face she'd believed she knew and loved better than her own.

A face she now feared she didn't know at all.

William blinked, not trusting his eyes. How in blazes could Bethany be here at Vauxhall tonight, too? She would have told him, wouldn't she?

He stared at her, unable to look away, and she stared back over the dozens of heads between them. She was a spot of bright blue with copper-colored hair, her dear, lovely face unmistakable among so many others.

She couldn't be here, yet she was. She *was*, and then she turned away and was lost in the crowd.

He lunged through the jostling crowd, seeking only one face among so many. He knew she was here. He had to find her, and he would. Then he could ask her to be his wife here, now, without waiting another minute longer than he must.

He crossed to where he'd first seen her, then back again, his desperation growing. She couldn't have vanished into the air, yet as he dodged among the dancers, he began to wonder. Maybe he had imagined seeing her in the shifting light. Maybe she'd been so much in his thoughts after his conversation with his father that he'd looked at another's face and seen hers, or maybe he'd—

And then she was there, not five feet before him, hurrying toward the steps to a box with her head down and her arms full of bundled violets.

"Bethany!" He caught her arm, gently pulling her around to face him. "You *are* here, love. I didn't dream it. You're here."

Yet when she gazed up over the violets, her eyes seemed shuttered against him, her lips tight.

"Look at you," she whispered miserably, as if to someone else. "Your gold braid, your sash, your beautiful sword. Oh, look at you!"

"What is it, lass?" he asked, taking her by the shoulders. "What has happened?"

"You tell me." She closed her eyes and took a deep breath as if marshaling her strength, then opened her eyes again, fast, before she lost whatever she'd gathered. "Are you the William I love, or the son of the Marquess of Beckham?"

"Is that all?" He smiled with relief, grateful that her question hadn't been something more difficult to answer, and brushed his fingers across her cheek. "Who told you?"

She pulled back, away from his touch. "I overheard two waiters discussing your—your family in your box, and they pointed you out," she said, her words coming out in a tangled rush. "Oh, William, is it true? Are you really this nobleman's son?"

"I'm afraid I am, lass," he said with a lopsided smile. He'd never meant it as a secret to be kept from her; it was more of a wish to be his own man, separate from his family, a continuation of how he'd been in the army. "The Callaways are a disreputable lot, I know, but that's no reason to—"

The rocket popped and sizzled and soared overhead, and exploded over their heads in a great falling starburst against the night sky. Almost in unison, the crowd looked upward, exclaiming and cheering and applauding.

William looked up, too, his heart racing with dread of what would inevitably come, fighting to keep the old nightmares at bay. But then the second rocket shot up, and a third, and for the first time since they'd brought him back to England, all he heard and saw were fireworks on a summer night.

In amazement he grinned down at Bethany. "Look, lass. Fireworks, and nothing else. Nothing! Can you believe it?"

"I don't know what to believe anymore, William," she said, and he saw the white bursts reflected in the tears in her eyes. "I thought you were poor, uncorrupted by money and power, and I thought you were different from all the other gentlemen at Penny House. But you weren't, were you? You're just as dishonorable as the rest of them. I trusted you with everything, yet you couldn't even tell me who you—you are."

Her voice broke, and she turned away, her hand pressed over her mouth.

"Bethany, please, it's not like that, not at all!" He reached for her, gently turning he back to face him. "Bethany, look at me, please. I love you, and I want to marry you. Will you be my wife, Bethany?"

Her eyes squeezed shut with misery as the tears slipped down her cheeks. "I can't, William. Not now, not after tonight. I *can't*."

And before he could catch her, she'd run back into the crowd, leaving nothing but a scattering of violet petals.

"Ooh, sir, look'ee at that one!" The tipsy girl with the black hair sighed with delight as she stared up at the fireworks, her arm still looped his shoulders so she wouldn't topple from his lap. "I've never seen none so fine an' pretty here in the Gardens, sir, have you?"

But what Macallister was seeing wasn't pretty, and it certainly wasn't fine. He twisted around in his chair so he could be sure, hoping against hope that what he'd glimpsed was wrong.

Another white flash of the fireworks, like a giant lantern to show what he'd never conceived as possible: Major Lord Callaway, no crippled madman at all, with his arms around Bethany Penny. One flash, no more than a second, but time enough to see that they were unmistakably lovers.

No time to guess how such a terrible union could have come about, or the ruin that, together, they could bring to him. He'd have to move swiftly, without hesitation. He couldn't afford to do otherwise with a man like Callaway. There was only time to look ahead, to make plans to save himself and his honor and the bright medals on his chest, whatever the cost. At least there was real justice still to be had in this world, if only one was willing to pay for it.

The girl nuzzled the back of Macallister's ear and giggled, her breathe ripe with gin.

"I know another way t'make a rocket rise, sir," she said, her unsteady hand reaching for the buttons on the fall of his breeches. "If you'd like a bit o' sport, sir."

He caught her wrist, stopping her hand. "There'll be time enough for sport later, sweetheart," he said, still watching the other couple. "Time enough and more."

Chapter Fifteen

The next night, William climbed the polished white steps to the front door of Penny House for the first time. He had sent one letter here this morning, and it had been returned unread and the seal unbroken, as had the second, and the third, too, this afternoon. That had been enough, and so he'd come himself.

He'd chosen plain dark evening dress instead of the dress uniform, not wishing to draw any attention away from his purpose. The army was his past, Bethany his future. Unlike the other gentlemen who were arriving at the club with friends, William came alone, nor was he laughing or joking or boasting in anticipation of a night of success at the gaming tables inside. His business inside the club tonight was deadly serious, and as for success—he'd no reason to be sure of it at all.

"Good evening, sir," the club manager said, bowing, as William entered. "Are you a member, sir?"

William shook his head. Strange to think that this must be the famous Pratt. He'd heard so much about him from Bethany that William felt he knew him, too.

"Ah," Pratt said, ever discreet, his expression unchanging. "Then are you the guest of a member, sir?"

"I am Major Lord William Callaway," he said, "and I am the guest of Miss Penny."

Pratt hesitated only a moment, likely just long enough for him to appraise William's clothes and his manner, and to judge whether or not his title and rank were truly what William claimed.

"I shall tell Miss Penny you are here, my lord," he said, ushering him into a small private office, little more than a closet, to one side of the hall. "This way, my lord, if you please."

William didn't have to wait long. The door behind him opened and he turned quickly, expecting Bethany, and was just as quickly disappointed. Still, the elegant young woman smiling at him now was remarkably like Bethany, with the same hair color, the same features, the same height to her figure, and yet at the same time so different, in the little ways that were impossible to describe.

"Good evening, my lord, and welcome to Penny House," she said, smiling as she held out her hand to him. Around her throat was the same necklace of glittering paste diamonds that Bethany had last been wearing with him under very different circumstances, reminding him of things that weren't wise to remember right now.

"I've heard so much about you from my sister, my lord," she continued, blissfully unaware of his thoughts, "though clearly she has left a great deal more unsaid."

"Has she?" Could there ever be a more ambiguous statement than that? What the devil had Bethany told her sister, anyway? Worse yet, what *hadn't* she said? "You are Miss Amariah Penny?"

"Forgive me, my lord, how remiss of me not to introduce myself," she said with a self-deprecating little pat to her cheek. "I am indeed Bethany's sister Amariah, and I am so glad that you have finally come to us. I know you are not a member of Penny House as yet, but I do hope to-night you will enjoy yourself, and make our house yours."

"How kind of you, Miss Penny." He wasn't about to tell her that he'd already had a pretty fair go at making her house his own, and enjoying himself, too. "But it's your sister I've come here to see."

"Have you now, my lord?" Her pleasant half smile told him less than nothing. "At this time of the evening, my sister is generally quite busy with her responsibilities in the kitchen."

"I know she can be summoned upstairs, else I can go to her."

"I know that, too, my lord," Amariah said. "But what neither of us can tell is what my sister's decision in the matter will be."

"Then why must you be so confoundedly protective?"

"Because I *am* protective, my lord," she said with a sudden smile. "We have no parents left to guide us, you see, and she is my youngest sister. I remember quite clearly the afternoon when she was born."

"But Bethany's a grown woman now, and I don't—"

"If my sister wishes to see you, my lord, then she'll come upstairs to you as soon as she can."

She was maddeningly deliberate, firmly polite. Her manner was also night and day from Bethany's impulsiveness, which was perhaps why Bethany preferred to stay downstairs and away from the club's company.

"That speech has the sound of one that's often repeated, Miss Penny," he said, more sharply than he intended, and sharp enough that she cocked one brow, questioning.

"That's because my sister and her cookery have had many admirers, my lord," she said. "If she took time away from her kitchen to acknowledge them all, why, then we'd all of us upstairs go hungry. Now if you please, my lord, I must attend to my other guests."

"Damnation, not yet." He stepped in front her, blocking her path. He hated being relegated to this phantom legion of Bethany's admirers, just as he hated being kept away from her now.

"You say Bethany's told you about me, Miss Penny," he said, unable to keep the urgency from his voice. "What is her humor toward me now? Does she love me still, as she swore she always would?"

"Do *you* love her, my lord?" Amariah's smile disappeared, her expression turning icy. "To me that's the far more important question. Do you love her as she deserves, or only desire her?"

"What the devil has she told you?"

"To be truthful, she's told me precious little," she admitted. "But I know my sister well enough to understand what she doesn't say along with what she does. You're lovers, aren't you?"

"Yes," he said. "I love her, and I've shared her bed, and now I want to make her my wife. Has she told you that?"

Amariah shook her head, clearly surprised. "You have already asked for her hand?"

"She refused me," he said, not hiding he bitterness. "I have offered her everything I am, and everything I have, and it wasn't enough. Damnation, she won't even see me now."

Amariah frowned, her expression thoughtful. "Yet I do believe she loves you, and with all her heart, too."

"Then why in blazes won't she have me?"

"You had best ask her yourself, my lord," she said. "I'll fetch her. She must stop hiding, and resolve this for both your sakes. You may wait here alone, or join the others in the public rooms."

She sidestepped around him with a soft *shush* of silk and left him. Swearing to himself, he followed her out of the little office, and into another room, a beautifully appointed parlor set aside for dining, and filled with gentlemen talking and drinking.

No one seemed to recognize him, though he caught a few glancing curiously at him when they'd thought he wouldn't notice. Well, let them look, and let them talk; it wasn't often a man had the chance to return from the grave. He helped himself to a glass of port from the sideboard, and patted the front pocket of his waistcoat again, to reassure himself for the hundredth time that the small jeweler's box remained safely inside.

He hoped she liked sapphires and diamonds, real diamonds, the only kind she deserved.

Hell, he hoped she agreed to see him first, so he'd have the chance to find out.

"My lord?"

Reluctantly William turned, and faced a officious man with slick black hair in a pieced-together excuse for a uniform.

"My lord, a word with you, if you please." The man radiated officiousness. "My name is Fewler, my lord, and I am responsible for keeping things as they should be here at Penny House. This will come as a shock to a gentleman such as yourself, I know, my lord, but there is a rascal afoot in this city, the worst sort of beggar, who's taken your name to use as his own."

"Is there?" Impatiently William looked past Fewler, searching for Bethany. Why the devil didn't she come? Wasn't he more important than some infernal pie crust or roast chicken?

"Yes, my lord," Fewler said, rocking lightly back and forth on his heels. "Bold as brass the scoundrel's been about it, too, coming to the back door of this house in his rags with the other beggars to play upon the tender mercies of these fine ladies."

"Oh, that fellow," said William. "I know him well."

"You do, my lord?" Fewler's eyes bulged with excitement. "Then perhaps you can assist me in apprehending—"

"Not now," William said. Bethany had suddenly appeared in the doorway beside the footman who'd brought her up from the kitchen. She was briskly drying her hands in the hem of her apron, her cheeks flushed from the heat of the fires, while her plain cap and linen gown seemed incongruously practical among so many gentlemen in silk-embroidered waistcoats.

And he'd never seen her look more charming.

In four long steps he had cut through the others to reach her, stopping so he stood directly before her. She gasped, but didn't back away, keeping her hands clasped in her apron.

"Bethany," he said. "We must talk, lass."

She raised her chin, defiant. "My sister didn't tell me you were here."

"Would you have come if she had?"

"No," she said without hesitation. "I would not."

Damnation, had he truly wished to hear that?

All other conversation in the room had stopped, all heads turned to watch their little drama, and he knew all of fashionable London would speak of nothing else over their breakfast tomorrow. He was half aware of Amariah standing to one side of Bethany, and another copper-haired woman that must be the third sister Cassia, beside her, the three of them in a row together.

To protect Bethany? To support her? To make this three hundred times harder for him than it was already bound to be?

"You should go, my lord Major," Bethany said, her uncharacteristic formality reminding him again of how badly he'd erred. "Leave now. There is nothing more for us to say to one another."

"But there is, Bethany." He reached into his pocket, his fingers betraying him and turning clumsy as old sticks. Somehow he opened the box, turning it in his hand so she could see the diamond and sapphire betrothal ring tucked inside.

She did see it, too, her gaze flicking down to the ring. One of her sisters gasped, but Bethany's expression didn't change.

Undaunted, he plunged ahead.

"Bethany." He cleared his throat, the words he'd planned wobbling on their way from his brain to his mouth.

"Miss Penny. You know how much I love you and respect you. You know you are not only my lover, but my dearest friend, and you would do me the greatest honor possible for a mortal man by becoming my wife as well. Will you, lass? Will you marry me?"

She took less time to consider than he'd taken to propose.

"How could I possibly marry a man I do not know?" She reached out and closed the curved lid of the ring box, then looked back at him. "I am sorry, William, but my answer is no."

He could not—would not—believe she'd end it like this. "Bethany, wait, please, let me—"

"Don't, William. Just—just don't." She blinked, made a stiff-backed curtsey, and fled.

Leaving him with a ring that felt heavy as lead in his hand, and a heart that felt like a stone in his chest.

Two days later, Bethany was slicing loaves of bread on the kitchen table, the long knife sawing back and forth, when Amariah reached around and propped the letter against the loaf.

"This just arrived for you," her sister said. "He brought it to the door himself."

"He should not have wasted his time." Bethany pushed the letter aside with the tip of the knife. "You may tell him that, too."

"He's already gone," Amariah said. "I suppose he hadn't much hope after you refused the last two."

"Then he won't be surprised to see this one returned, as well," Bethany said. "Please have one of the footmen take it directly."

"But now this one's dusted with bread crumbs," Amariah reasoned. "So William will know you saw it."

"He can know whatever he wants." Bethany cut away the heel of the loaf, and stacked the slices in a basket to be given out with the soup to her flock. "He won't change my mind, Amariah, and neither will you."

With a sigh, Amariah folded her arms and leaned against the edge of the table, tapping the rejected letter against her wrist.

"If that is so, Bethany," she began, "then why are your eyes so red and puffy from weeping the night through that I wonder you can see to use that knife? If you truly don't care, then why do you bother to return William's letters to him? Why not simply toss them into the fire, and be done with it?"

Bethany bent her head, trying to hide the fresh rush of tears that burned her eyes. A pox on her sister for mentioning them, and making her cry all over again!

"He deserves to know how I feel, Amariah," she said, sniffing.

"What the poor man deserves, Betts, is for you to let him plead his case to you in person," said her sister, for once ignoring Bethany's tears. "You've always prided yourself on being fair and just in everything. Now you're not being fair at all to the man you once claimed you loved with all your heart."

"That was before he—he revealed his true colors to me."

"Oh, yes, those famous colors." Amariah nodded. "I have heard of many women who have broken off with lovers because they proved to have more paltry fortunes than they'd professed in the heat of passion. But you, Bethany, must be the first in history to cast aside a perfectly good man because he had more worldly riches than he'd led you to believe."

"I told you before, Amariah, that that is not the reason. I have broken with his lordship because he was not—not honest with me." She dropped the knife and groped in her pocket for her handkerchief, wiping furiously at her eyes. "He—he let me believe all manner of nonsense about himself, and played me for the silliest fool possible. He even disguised himself as a pauper, dressing as if he hadn't a cent in the world!"

"And yet you managed to fall in love with him anyway," Amariah mused. "William Callaway has asked you to marry him, Betts, and asked you twice. That is not foolish, or nonsense. That is quite, quite serious. Not only for you, either. What if you're carrying his child? Doesn't that poor innocent deserve to have his or her parents wedded?"

"I am not that ignorant, Amariah!"

"Then stop moping about as if you were," Amariah said. "I should think his devotion should make some amends for your wounded pride."

Bethany blew her nose, feeling thoroughly miserable. "It's not my pride that was wounded, Amariah. I trusted him with everything, and he couldn't trust me enough to tell me his name."

"But he did trust you with a good deal more, didn't he?" her sister asked softly. "Didn't he tell you things, dark, painful things, that he'd never shared with any other?"

"Then why couldn't he tell me his name, or who he was?" she asked, wadding her handkerchief into a tight ball in her hand. "If he could tell me of the war, then why couldn't he tell me of his family?"

Amariah reached out to cover Bethany's hand with her own. "Not everyone is blessed with the parents we've had, duck. You must remember that. A title and a fortune are no guarantees of a happy home."

"But I still do not see how—"

"Hush, and listen until I am done," Amariah said firmly. "War is supposed to be fearful and grim, and a man is applauded for surviving. But what if his family and his home were worse than any battle? What man could admit that, without feeling as if he'd somehow failed?"

Bethany stared down at her hands, and remembered how little William had ever told her of his boyhood, how he would always change the subject or withdraw if she asked. She thought of how shocked she'd been by his sister's behavior, and of the strange tensions she'd sensed between them.

"You say William cares deeply for the men he commanded," Amariah went on. "Perhaps he has decided they are more worthy than his own family. Perhaps that is why he chooses to live where he does, and dress in clothing similar to theirs. Perhaps he wished to be a part of their families, their lives, instead of his own."

"Oh, Amariah," Bethany said, her voice breaking as she thought of what her sister was saying. "It took William so long to tell me he loved me! It was as if he'd never had anyone love him—as if he did not know how even to say the word!"

"And yet two nights ago, he said it to you aloud before scores of witnesses," her sister said. "You might not have listened, but he said it. For you, Betts, he learned that most perilous word for men, and what it means. Just for you."

She set the letter back on the table before Bethany. "It's your decision to make, and I'll not tell you what to do. You can wed him or not. But remember how Father always told us to think of others and not only ourselves. And if you love William as you say, then you will think of him as well."

She kissed the top of Bethany's head, and left her to stare at William's letter. The first time he'd written to her— had it really been less than fortnight ago?—she'd been so excited she'd nearly danced with joy, tucking the folded sheet beneath her pillow when she'd slept that night.

Now he'd poured his very soul into this letter before her, not trusting it to another but bringing it himself, yet she had not been able to make herself read it. She stared at her name written on the front, picturing him sitting at his desk with the pen in his hand.

Maybe this letter wasn't again asking her to marry him, but instead withdrawing his offer. Hadn't Amariah said he'd left after he'd delivered it, not waiting for a response? She touched the front of the letter, imagining William walking down the front steps without looking back. What if she never saw him again? What if she'd driven him away, and she never again saw him smile, or heard his laugh, or tasted his kiss?

What if she'd lost him forever?

It wasn't just that she'd thought of herself first. She hadn't thought of him at all, just as Amariah had said. She'd said before he'd made her feel like a fool, but now—now she was the greatest fool in the world, and it was all her own doing.

She reached for the letter before she lost her nerve, and slipped her finger along the edge to break the seal.

"Forgive me for interrupting, Miss Bethany," Letty said tentatively. "But would you like me to begin serving the soup from the door? Mr. Fewler's guard isn't here yet, but there's a great long line of people today, miss, and if we don't begin soon, then we'll have—"

"I'm coming, Letty." Swiftly she tucked William's letter into her pocket along with her handkerchief, determined to read it later alone, and hooked the basket with the sliced bread over her arm. "And Mr. Fewler's man can join us whenever he chooses. No one likes to be kept waiting when they're hungry."

Letty had been right. The line was long, curling back and forth through the yard to the alley, waiting patiently for them to begin. Bethany was glad of the distraction of greeting and feeding so many, and forced herself to smile and laugh as if William's letter were not weighing heavy as lead in her pocket.

Yet still she couldn't help looking back to the end of the line as it snaked past her. That was where William had always stood, waiting until everyone else was fed before he'd take her time. Over and over she caught herself hunting for his familiar battered hat and dark coat, part of her vainly hoping that she and William could go back to where they'd once been.

"Thank'ee, miss, thank'ee." The old woman named Maude gave her familiar gap-toothed smile as she clutched the bowl to her chest. "So there's to be another wedding at Penny House, eh, miss?"

"Another wedding, Maude?" Bethany asked as she filled the next bowl, working hard to keep her voice even. "Wherever did you get such a notion?"

"They was talkin' nothing else at the market," Maude declared, delighted to have so much attention. "They say you was goin' to marry some great lord. They say he asked for you right here at Penny House, before all the other lords an' dandies."

"Then they should have finished the story, Maude, and told you I refused him." She dipped her ladle back into the kettle of soup. She'd made her refusal as public as possible; she shouldn't be surprised at how quickly news of it had spread through London, or how humiliated William must be feeling to have the whole city speaking of how she'd rejected him. "No wedding."

"You can't marry, Miss Bethany," Twig said, popping up next in line. "Who'd look after us if you married some bloke and went away?"

"Who, indeed?" she said sadly. "Good day to you, Twig. How have you been faring?"

"Middling, Miss Bethany, middling," he said, tugging on the front of his cap, "but I thank you for asking. Have you seen the gov'nor, miss? He's been missing for a few days now."

"Haven't you heard, Twig?" she asked. "He's not your governor at all. His proper name is Major Lord Callaway, and he's the younger son of the Marquess of Beckham."

"Nay!" the boy exclaimed with amazement. "He be a lord?"

Bethany nodded. "I suppose he foxed us both, didn't he?"

"Him a lord," Twig marveled. "Who would've thought it?"

"Miss Bethany!" a red-haired man in a short green jacket shouted from the alley gate, and everyone in line twisted around to look. "Miss Bethany, come quick! My friend what you just fed—he be sick, miss, retching an' heaving an' writhin' about like he been poisoned!"

Poisoned. The word rang like a shot through the yard, repeated over and over with panic and horror. At once the line began to break and scatter as people started to flee, some running as if poison could chase after them, while those who had just received their meal dropped their plates clattering to the ground. Children were crying, sensing their parents' fear, and a woman screamed.

"No one's been poisoned!" Bethany shouted. "Please, please! I promise you this food is safe to eat!"

But no one was listening to her as the crowd became

more and more panicked, pushing and shoving as they all tried to get through the gate to the alley to escape.

"I'm going to find this sick man, Letty," she said, dropping her ladle back into the kettle of soup. "You stay here."

"You can't go alone, miss!" Letty protested anxiously. "Wait for the guard!"

But Bethany was already hurrying across the now-empty yard, picking her way through puddles of abandoned soup and dropped apples. The sight of so much waste for no reason made her furious. She knew no one had poisoned her food, and the only way to keep her name clear was to find the man who'd accused her. She would *not* let him ruin her, or Penny House. She ran through the gate, searching for the man who'd called to her first.

"Here, Miss Bethany, here!" The man in the short green jacket was calling to her from down the alley beside a stack of storage barrels, waving his arms frantically for her to join him. "My friend's here, right where he fell, an' he's sufferin' bad!"

Bethany quickened her steps, her apron flapping over her skirts. She remembered the man in the green jacket, a new face to her though one of the first in line today, and she was eager to see if she recognized his sick friend as well. Most likely the man was suffering from too much gin, or some other illness that had nothing to do with poison or her food. Whatever ailed him, she would not let him from her sight; as soon as he recovered, she intended to have both him and Green-Jacket testify at her back door that her food had not caused any harm—the only sure way to restore her reputation.

"Like an angel you are to come to him, Miss Bethany," Green-Jacket said, yanking off his hat as she neared. He certainly seemed to care for his friend's welfare, for his own eyes were wide with anxiety and his face slicked with sympathetic sweat as he glanced again down to where his friend must be lying, behind the barrels. "I've never seen anyone suffer like this."

"Then let's see what we can do to ease his troubles." Strange how for all the sick man's great suffering, she hadn't heard so much as a whimper from him. A stoic fellow indeed, she thought, and slipped between Green-Jacket and the barrels. "I'm here to help you as best I can, sir, if you'll but—*what is this?*"

There was no one sick waiting for her behind the barrels, no one suffering who needed her help. She had the briefest glimpse of a large man lunging toward her, a coverlet or tarp in his hands. She gasped with fear and twisted away, trying to escape, but Green-Jacket was waiting to catch her, to grab her hands behind her back while the other man gagged her with a dirty cloth that smelled like old fish. Still she fought, twisting and trying to break away, until a sharp pain struck the back of her head.

And then her world went black, and she felt nothing more.

Chapter Sixteen

With his old broad-brimmed hat pulled low and his shoulders hunched inside his worn coat, William walked slowly down the line of impoverished folk, waiting for the scraps from the Lord Mayor's dinner the night before.

"What ship, friend?" he asked, and listened patiently to the blind sailor's tale, the heroics and the injustices rolled together in experiences as complex as the tattoos inked onto the man's arms. When he was done, William pressed his usual coins into the man's hand, closing his fingers over them to make sure none were lost. He was generous, as he always was, but he knew that listening to the man's story with a sympathetic ear had been as valuable to him as the coins.

"God watch over you, friend," he said softly, clapping the elderly sailor one last time on his shoulder before he moved on to the next man.

It was the old routine, as if nothing had changed, when in fact everything had. When he listened now to the stories of bravery and daring, bad officers and worse orders, disastrous wounds and bungling surgeons, he thought of how Bethany had done the same for him. Though he couldn't really remember what he'd told her, he knew it had been things that he hadn't been able to say to anyone else, words and experiences that had been dragged from deep inside of him. She hadn't made him forget—that would never happen, nor would he wish to, not really—but she'd helped him ease the pain and the shame, enough that he could see a future to his life, and not just a past.

Most of all, she'd taught him about falling in love. The sorry part was that she'd left before she'd explained how to fall out of it.

Bitterly he thought of the ring he'd bought her, sitting on his desk where he'd tossed it last night. Unacceptable and unwanted, rejected with the same thoroughness as she'd rejected him. Three times was supposed to be the magic charm in all the old stories and ballads, wasn't it? So why had she refused him not once, but three times after that, for a reason he still could not comprehend? He'd never once meant to deceive her, or trick her into believing he was something other than he was, yet now she would not even let him begin to explain.

How in blazes had this gone so wrong? One minute he was convinced he'd found the secret to more happiness than he'd ever expected in life, and the next he discovered he had nothing.

With a groan, he bowed his head, determined to forget. He reached out to the next man, his remaining leg balanced between makeshift crutches. "What regiment, friend?"

"Guv'nor, guv'nor, there you be!"

Twig came bounding toward him like a loose-limbed puppy, and William couldn't help smiling at the boy. "What brings you here, lad? This isn't your part of town."

"I was—I was huntin' for you, gov'nor," he said, out of breath. "Something bad's happened, an' we need your help!"

William took him by the shoulder, guiding him away from the others who were unabashedly eavesdropping.

"What bad thing has happened, Twig?" he asked. "Calm yourself, now, and be brave. And who is this 'we' who needs help?"

"It's—it's Miss Bethany, guv'nor," Twig said. "Someone came to Penny House an' ate there, an' then they pretended that they'd been poisoned, an' everyone was scared and ran away, excepting Miss Bethany. She went to help the man what was sick, and then she got taken."

William felt the lurch of fear low in his belly. "What do you mean, she was taken? Taken ill, too?"

"Oh, no, guv'nor," said Twig, swiping his sleeve across his nose as his voice rose to a squeaky wail. "I mean th' men took *her* away. They kidnapped her, guv'nor, an' gave me th' note for Miss Penny. She's the 'we.'"

This was worse than he'd feared, far, far worse. "What kind of note? For ransom?"

"You'd have to ask Miss Penny." The boy pointed to the street, where Amariah was waiting, leaning anxiously from the window of a cab. "It was writ to her."

"Come with me." William grabbed the boy by the shoulder and hurried him to the cab. Maybe the boy had misunderstood, or was exaggerating. True, with all the money that Penny House was taking in, any of the sisters would make a prime target for ransom. It was true, too, that because of her work among the poor, Bethany would be the easiest to kidnap, but still the thought of her suffering and in danger because she was too kind, too trusting, made him furious.

"Oh, my lord, I am so glad we found you!" Amariah cried. "I would have hunted all over the city for you, but Twig knew exactly where you'd be found."

William nodded curtly. "Where's the note?"

"It's so short, it's not very useful at all," she said, handing it to him through the window. "Why would anyone want to steal Bethany away from us?"

"Money." Quickly William scanned the note. Amariah was right: it was neither long, nor revealing, and the handwriting had been purposely disguised.

We have Miss Bethany Penny. If you want her returned unharmed, send Callaway to us at the east door of Fulham's Chandlery, near the Tower. Nine o'clock this night. Do not wait or seek other help, or she will suffer.
 You decide her FATE.

"Does it mean anything to you, My Lord?" Amariah asked, her self-possessed voice suddenly sounding more like an unsure girl's. "I shall never, ever forgive myself if anything happens to her!"

"I'd say something already has, Miss Penny." He frowned, his mind racing ahead. "Where were the hired guards?"

Amariah's lips pressed tightly together. "Mr. Fewler's man was late coming to his post in the kitchen. My sister chose not to wait, though others in her staff asked her to, she went to aid the sick man unattended."

That was Bethany, through and through. "This note is all you received? There was no demand made elsewhere of a ransom?"

Amariah shook her head. "Just this," she said, handing him another letter. "I suppose it's to prove that they actually do have her as their prisoner. She must have had it in her pocket."

He barely managed to bite back an oath. The letter was the last appeal he'd written and delivered to her himself, his last offer for her hand.

And because this one had been opened, it must also have been read...

He couldn't consider that now. Whether Bethany had read his letter or not, even whether she had changed her mind in his favor—all of that paled beside the need to rescue her now.

He turned back toward Twig. "Did you recognize the man who gave this to you, lad?"

"He was in line at Miss Bethany's kitchen, him an' the other one, but I never seen them there before today," the boy answered with an extra sniff. "I was at the other end o' th' alley when I seen one man carrying off a something all wrapped in a bundle—I know now that must've been Miss Bethany herself—while this other man called to me, an' gave me these, an' told me to take them to Miss Penny if I knew what be good for me."

William nodded, his anger fueled by the image of Bethany bundled like old laundry. They'd pay for doing that to her; they'd all pay.

"I should've known he was a bad one, guv'nor," the boy was saying, "because he was the villain what said Miss Bethany was giving us poison, an' Miss Bethany would've never done such wickedness!"

It was easy to imagine how incensed Bethany must have been to have anyone accuse her of poison in her cooking. Food meant so much to her that that would have been the greatest possible insult. The man was fortunate she hadn't come after him with one of her enormous knives.

"Did they look out of place in the yard, Twig?"

"They didn't look like no fancy lords from th' gaming rooms, if that's your meaning," the boy said. "They was just common folk. But I'd know them again, guv'nor. I'd know them anywhere."

"That's good to know, Twig," William said, "but I'd wager they're just hirelings of another who didn't want to sully his hands. Someone who, it seems, would rather have me than a ransom."

"Someone who is jealous of you, my lord," Amariah said, then blushed self-consciously. "That is, the news of your offer to my sister has been widely discussed in town. This—this man might have heard, and now views you as a rival."

"A rival who'd been refused," he said, not bothering to hide his bitterness, then glanced back at Amariah. "You told me once that because of her cooking for the club, your sister had more admirers than she could count. Is that true?"

Defensively Amariah slipped back into her habitual discretion. "It is a consequence of our position as both the owners and the only ladies at Penny House, my lord, though I won't be so vain as to claim the distinction for our own beauty or wit. Given a sufficiency of wine, most gentlemen among the club's membership can become unduly enamored with any pretty woman."

"Speak it plain, Miss Penny," William ordered impatiently. "Your sister's life may be at stake."

To his surprise, Amariah seemed to wilt, ducking her head beneath the brim of her hat as her nose reddened and tears filled her eyes. "Then—then return with me to the club, my lord. I'll draw a list for you of the members who have been too attentive."

"Now that, Miss Penny, will be useful." He unlatched the door to the cab and climbed in beside her. "Are you joining us, Twig?"

"Nay, guv'nor," the boy said, backing away. "I've got a bit o' private questions to be askin' myself. But I'll cover your back when you need me, you can be sure o' that."

William frowned at him. "Don't stick your nose where it doesn't belong, lad. You won't be a help if I have to come rescue you, too."

The boy grinned, and swiped at his nose again as he bounded away.

"Are you sure he'll be safe?" Amariah asked as the cab started up. "A child like that alone in London?"

"That child is more wise in the ways of this city than you and I together," William said as resettled his hat on his head. "Now tell me which of these 'admirers' would be most likely to kidnap Bethany?"

She sighed unhappily, folding her arms over her chest as she leaned back against the cushions. In one of her hands he could see the soggy ball of her handkerchief, proof that, though she hadn't wept before him, she, too, was worried for her sister's welfare.

"We've had difficulties with Lord Bolton," she began. "He's rather a bully, and he has asked Bethany if she'd like to be put in keeping. Colonel Field has also been persistent, but I'm not sure he's devoted enough to resort to kidnapping. Sir Henry Hackett has the temper for it, especially if there were a wager involved. And if I were honest, my lord, I should add you to the list of unpredictable admirers, too."

William smiled. "You don't care for me very much, do you, Miss Penny?"

He wasn't surprised that she didn't smile in return. "It doesn't matter if I do or not. What should concern you is that my sister does, and a great deal at that."

He leaned forward, watching her. "I thought you wouldn't discuss her affairs?"

"Things have changed since then, my lord, haven't they?" She sighed again, the tears still there but unshed, and twisted the fringe on her shawl around her fingers. "You are going to risk your life to save hers. Given that, it's only fair that you know how very much Bethany loves you."

"She does," he said quietly, not a question, but a statement, because his heart was already sure. "You know I love her, too."

"I never doubted that for a moment," she said, an unmistakable poignancy in her voice.

"You shouldn't," he said, thinking again of how Bethany had had his last letter with her. "And neither should she."

But Amariah wasn't listening. "Wait, my lord, wait, I've thought of another gentleman you must consider! Macallister, Lieutenant John Macallister. He's sent Bethany jewelry, which of course she's returned, and he turned most unpleasant because of it."

"Macallister." He'd had little use for the man before, but once he'd heard how the lieutenant had threatened Bethany at the club, William's contempt had only grown. "Move him to the top of the list."

He'd no real proof beyond instinct that Macallister would be his man. But William had long ago learned to trust his instincts, and already his mind was racing ahead, making plans in his head. He knew Fulham's Chandlery, an empty, ramshackle warehouse down near the legal quays that must be filled with shadowy places to hide a kidnapped woman. He would of course go alone—he wouldn't risk Bethany's safety by taking others—but even though his main weapon would be his wits, he intended to be armed, and heavily.

"I'd wager these people are more desperate than clever," he said. "Especially if Macallister's behind this."

"Oh, I pray you are right," Amariah said, her voice breaking as the tears finally spilling down her cheeks. "Just save her, my lord. Save her."

He looked from the cab's window, his face hard and grim. "I will get Bethany back, Miss Penny. Whatever it takes, I will bring her back. And I'll make those who have her pay dearly for what they've done."

* * *

Bethany groaned, trying to find the strength to open her eyes. It wasn't so much waking as fighting to wake, the effort of reaching consciousness almost beyond her. Finally she managed one eye, then another, forcing them both to focus on the blur of light against the shadows.

A man, two men, crouched before a pair of tin lanterns on the floor. They were quarreling, their voices raised and their gestures exaggerated by the shadows they cast against the bare brick wall behind them.

"I say th' bastard won't show his face or his gold," one man was arguing, "an' then we'll be left with th' woman."

"And I say he'll come, with th' gold, too." The second man spat into the dirty hay scattered over the floor, and turned the collar of his green jacket up over his neck. "Even if he don't, being left with th' chit's not th' worst lot in creation, Matt. We could use her as we pleased before she wakes, then sell her to one o' th' houses. Red hair like that'd bring a good price."

"Are you daft, Tom?" The first man swung his palm and slapped the second on the side of his head. "That woman's gentry! We can't sell her like she was some wench fresh from the country!"

The second man rubbed his temple. "That don't be reason for striking me, Bob," he said indignantly. "All I'm saying is that th' girl's worth money to us, even if her lover don't want her back."

Now Bethany remembered: she remembered hearing this man claim his friend had been poisoned by her food, and going to the alley to help, and having them throw something dark over her head, and then—then nothing.

How long ago had that been? Had she been in this place minutes, hours, days? And was William the lover who wouldn't come for her, her own dear, sweet William?

William, whose proposal she'd refused? William, whose letters she'd returned unread? William, whom she still loved, but who now owed her nothing?

She struggled to concentrate, to make sense of where she was and what she should do next. She knew she had to do something to save herself, or suffer horribly at the hands of these two men.

She was lying on her side, on a blanket that smelled like a stable. Her mouth tasted like dry sand, and her head ached abominably, but when she tried to reach up to feel it, she realized her wrists were tied together.

"Ha, she's wakin' now, Tom!" The man called Matt came over with the lantern, crouching down to peer into her face. "She looks poorly. You should've taken th' gag off when I told you. She won't be worth a shilling if she's dead."

Listen, Betts, listen and think and use the wits God gave you.

"Water," she croaked, trying to lift her head to appeal to him. "Please, sir."

"Th' poor thing's fair parched," Matt said, tucking his pistol into his belt. "Fetch her some o' th' cider, Tom."

"I'm not her maid," Tom grumbled, though he brought the cider, "nor yours, neither."

"Here now, girl, up you go." Carefully he sat her upright, and she struggled to find her balance as the room spun in queasy circles. "There's no harm in cutting her hands free so's she can drink, is there, Tom? She's weak as a half-drowned kit."

Matt didn't wait for permission, but slipped his knife under the cord around her wrists. She pulled her hands forward, falling forward and crying out as the blood rushed into her stiffened limbs.

"Here, girl, drink this," Matt said, holding out a earthenware bottle of cider.

Bethany took it, her hands shaking. The cider was thick and too sticky-sweet, but still it was wet on her parched mouth, and she drank gratefully.

"Thank you, sirs," she whispered, partly because she didn't trust her voice to go much louder, but mostly because playing on their sympathies as a pitiful, unthreatening weakling would serve her better. Besides, they each carried at least one pistol and a long-bladed knife apiece, and she had nothing, not even a hope of being rescued by William, nor did she deserve one. Her fate was in her own hands. "You are…most kind."

Matt beamed, showing the gaps among his teeth. "We *are* kind, aren't we, Tom?"

"Most kind sirs," she whispered, making her voice tremble with sadness. "How hard it is for me to believe that you betrayed me so!"

"Betrayed you?" repeated Matt, confused. "What, because we did as we was told, an' stole you away?"

She sighed deeply, and shook her head. "No, sir, no. Because you said I'd poisoned you."

Tom grinned, and knocked Matt on the shoulder. "That was a good one, wasn't it? Th' man what hired us said poison would make you come to us like a coney to an apple, an' he was right."

"What man was that, sir?" she asked, trying to sound as innocent and guileless as possible.

But not guileless enough. "Th' man what hired us," Matt said doggedly. "Th' man what told us to say you'd poisoned us."

She managed a tiny, frail smile. "How do you know I didn't?"

Tom's smile disintegrated. "Because we wasn't taken sick, not for real. No one was."

"But that's how it's been at every one of the kitchens for the poor, hasn't it?" she asked. "Each time only one man was struck, out of so many who ate. How do you know it wasn't you?"

"I'm not sick," Matt insisted, puffing out his chest as proof. "Hale as a bull, an' always have been."

"For now." She pushed her tangled hair back from her eyes. "Poison doesn't work in an instant, not when it's conveyed through food. It takes time to grow and spread its evil through your body, to sink its claws so deep into you that all help will come too late."

"Then how d'you know?" asked Tom, worried. "If you don't feel nothing, then how d'you know?"

She shrugged. "*If* you'd been poisoned, you'd first have the cramps low in your belly, so fierce you'll wonder if you can bear them. Next you'll begin retching so hard with the black vomit that you'll feel as if your bowels want to turn inside out. Then, at last, when you've no will left to fight it, the convulsions and fever will kill you."

"All that?" asked Tom, his eyes round with horror.

"All that," she said, smiling. "Some men are taken much worse. But only if you're poisoned. You came at the front of the line. I cannot recall who took that one bowl."

She leaned back against the wall and let her eyes flutter shut again, hoping she looked as wan and feeble as possible. She had every right to be tired; if she'd said the right things, she'd just planted enough doubt to fell an army.

Matt slipped his hand inside his coat and pulled out his pistol, setting it on the floor beside him so better to rub his hand back and forth on his stomach. "I have been feeling a mite uneasy," he said. "I thought 'twas just th' heat o' th' day."

"Ahh, you're daft," Tom said, but he, too, was bending over in a peculiar way, his arms folded across his midsection, and there were fresh drops of sweat dotting his forehead.

But Bethany only smiled to herself. In another quarter hour, the two of them would be writhing in agony, convinced they were suffering from the most lethal poison imaginable, and then—then she'd make her escape.

And without any help from the lover she'd sent away, the lover she no longer deserved, the one man she loved most who no longer wanted her, or her poor broken heart.

Macallister stood in the shadows across the street from the old Chandlery, trying to be as inconspicuous as possible. The taverns this close to the quays were full and raucous, their patrons spilling out into the summer evening and so bent on their drinking and whoring and brawling and other pleasurable pastimes that none noticed one more man on the street.

But to Macallister this felt like the most exciting night of his life, and as he paced back and forth along this little patch of the street, he kept patting the bulge of the pistols he wore hidden beneath his coat: for courage, for reassurance, for luck.

Once again he glanced up at the corner window of the darkened warehouse, both hoping for and dreading Callaway's arrival. The plan was simple enough. One of the men who'd arranged the kidnapping would greet Callaway here on the street at the prearranged time, and take him upstairs to where Bethany Penny was being held. Macallister would follow, and pretend to surprise them. The two men had been told to make sure Macallister was the one who rescued Bethany, a hero in her eyes, but also to make sure that Callaway was killed.

Simple, more than simple enough. Three men to one had seemed like favorable odds earlier in the day, but now as the actual time came closer, he was having second thoughts. What did he know of his so-called partners, anyway? Could they be trusted to actually finish what they were being paid to do? All along he'd been picturing Callaway as a half-mad cripple, but from what he'd glimpsed at Vauxhall, the man still looked strong and hideously capable.

He touched his pistols again. Gunpowder and ball always won over mortal flesh, didn't it?

And there were more wrinkles to this tale now than when he'd first concocted this plan to claim Bethany Penny. Callaway had proposed marriage to her, and to everyone's amazement, she'd turned him down. The entire city seemed to be speaking of nothing else. Macallister had been as surprised as anyone, but he'd also soon realized how much this worked in his favor: now Callaway would be perceived as behind the kidnapping, a thwarted suitor driven mad by love.

No one would dream of connecting Callaway's death to the poisonings, or to that infamous day long ago in Spain. It was really a quite perfect quirk of fate. Macallister was still a bit hazy as to what his own explanation would be for coming to Bethany's rescue, but he'd invent something. He always did.

As nervous as he was, he still could smile at the irony of it. Not only would his secret be forever safe, but the legend of his heroism would grow.

And Bethany Penny would be his.

William walked slowly toward the old warehouse, taking his time as he neared the door where he was to meet the kidnappers. Every nerve was on edge, his usual wariness even more acute, and beneath the brim of his coat his gaze wandered restlessly, searching for anything that seemed wrong. For Bethany's sake, he couldn't afford to be careless now.

Across the street he noticed another man loitering, and at once William melted into the shadows of a doorway. The other man was clearly waiting for someone or something, and not being particularly subtle about it, either, kicking at stones and swinging his arms in circles. Most likely he'd come from a rum shop and was waiting for his doxy. William hung back in the doorway, using the pause to check the flints on his pistols one more time, watching until the man turned his back and ambled down the street. Then William hurried to the warehouse's side entrance and down the four steps to the door, picking his way through the old newspapers and trash that had accumulated there, and rapped on the door. At once the door opened, and he slipped inside.

"You've come alone, m'lord?" a man rasped, holding a shaded lantern before him so that while he could see William's face, his own was obscured by the brightness.

"I have," William said. "Where's Miss Penny?"

"In time," the man said, yet William sensed something was wrong. The man's voice was uncertain, almost as if he were in pain, and the lantern wobbled in his hand.

"Damnation, take me to her," William ordered. "Show me she's unharmed."

But instead the man groaned, the lantern slipping from hand to the floor. William grabbed it before the flame guttered out, and swung its light toward the other man. The man was crouched low, clutching at his belly, his face pale and washed with sweat.

"Th'—th' bitch poisoned us," he said, grimacing with pain. "To—to hell with her, I say!"

"Where is Miss Penny?" demanded William, not stopping to make sense of this. "Tell me!"

The man rolled onto the floor, curling himself into a tight ball of pain. "Up—up th' stairs with Matt."

William drew one of his pistols and cocked it, and with the lantern in his other hand, headed up the stairs as fast as he could.

"Don't leave me, m'lord!" the man on the floor croaked, panicking. "Don't leave me to die alone in th' dark! Th' rats will get me, m'lord!"

"You should have considered that before you stole Miss Penny," William said. Poisoned or not, the man was one less for him to worry over.

He paused on the first landing, listening. The warehouse was empty and echoing; they could be holding Bethany anywhere, and he'd no idea where to begin. He closed the door on the lantern so only a glimmer of light showed through, and cautiously shoved open the nearest door. No sounds, beyond the scurry of frightened rats, and the rush of startled bats or pigeons among the beams.

He turned to the second door and opened it. Again nothing, no matter how hard he listened or squinted into the dark. Maybe she wasn't here at all; maybe that poor bastard writhing down there in the dark was the only one here.

But then he tried the last door on the landing, and was rewarded. This time, far off in the distance, he could make out a faint glow of light as if from another lantern, coming from behind a dividing wall. He closed the door on his own lantern entirely, and moved as swiftly and as quietly as he could toward the light. He could feel the old soldier's battle-blood pumping through his veins, ready to battle whatever he found. How many men would be guarding Bethany, he wondered, how many would he have to fight to free her?

He drew closer, close enough to hear a man's ragged breathing and muttered oaths beyond the other side of the half wall. Then he heard a woman's voice—soft, pleading—that he recognized at once as Bethany's. What the devil was happening, anyway? Was the bastard making her beg for her life? He set his lantern on the floor and lowered his gun, ready to charge in.

But suddenly the other lantern's light rocked to one side, and William heard the unmistakable sounds of a scuffling fight. He raced around the wall, and stopped abruptly.

"William!" Bethany cried with relief. She was standing over a man in a green coat, lying facedown on the floor and groaning. Her hair was disheveled, her clothes filthy and torn, but clutched in her hands was the man's own pistol, now aimed at his head.

"I've captured him, William, I did it myself!" She grinned at him, but her grip on the pistol never wavered. "I didn't think you'd come, you see, and I'd have to save myself and—and—oh, William, I'm so vastly glad you're here!"

"So am I," William said. This was the damnedest thing he'd ever seen. The man was at least double her size, and yet she'd obviously bested him, and now he was left standing here all primed and ready to fight with nothing to do. "Are there any more of them?"

"Only one," she said. "He went to open the door for you. I suppose you must have already disposed of him."

"He disposed of himself." William noticed she hadn't released the lock on the pistol, but he didn't see much point in sharing that fact. The man didn't know it, nor did he need to. He tucked his own pistol back in his belt, and crouched down beside the man. Ignoring his groans, William pulled off his neckerchief and used it to bind the man's hands behind his back.

He stood, and looked at Bethany. This should be the place where they threw their arms around one another and promised eternal devotion. But except for what her sister had told him, he'd only her last refusal of his proposal in his ears. He'd come here to rescue her, but she'd rescued herself.

And, of course, she was still holding a gun.

"Bethany," he began, the best beginning he could manage. "Bethany."

"You know how I did it," she said, whispering so the groaning man wouldn't hear. "I let them think I'd poisoned them."

"You?" he asked, incredulous. "Why, you'd never—"

"They didn't know that. I told them all the symptoms and now they've thought so much about it that they're convinced they're dying."

He shook his head, not sure what to say next. He'd predicted that cleverness would win over the kidnappers, but he hadn't expected it to play out quite like this. "Bethany, I—"

"Yes," she said, her grin fading to an uncertain wobble. "If you'll still have me."

Before he'd quite realized what she'd said, she'd dropped the gun and had come and looped her arms around his shoulders and turned her face up for a kiss, and then there he was, kissing her as if none of the rest had happened and as if there weren't some poor bloke groaning on the floor sure he was dying.

"I've never stopped loving you, William," she whispered, feathering little kisses along his jaw. "Not once, not even when—"

"Release her, Callaway," shouted a man's voice behind them. "Release Miss Penny at once!"

Instantly William twisted around, shoving Bethany behind his own body as he began to reach for his pistol. But too late: by the lantern's light he saw two pistols already aimed at him, one in each of the man's hands, and these were cocked and ready to fire.

"What the hell do you want, Macallister?" William demanded.

"You've told her everything, Callaway, haven't you?"

the lieutenant snarled. "About me and the ambush, about the Spaniards. You couldn't keep it to yourself, could you?"

Bethany leaned around his arm. "He hasn't told me anything, Lieutenant Macallister, except that he loves me!"

"Not now, Bethany," William ordered, pushing her back behind him. "You're making no sense, Macallister. What about you and the Spaniards?"

"What, you want me to confess it, too?" He laughed wildly. "You saw me. You were there. We were on the same road, you know, though I hung back because I didn't want your little pack of scoundrels taking my water."

William listened with growing horror. How could he know about the heat and the dust and the tiny bit of water left to skim their canteens? "You don't know what you're talking about, Macallister."

"Don't I, though?" the other man said, his voice turning shrill. "I thought I was safe. I thought I'd reach the coast on my own. But then those wretched diegos caught me, laughing and jeering with no regard at all for me, for an officer of the king of England!"

"They weren't supposed to show us regard," William said slowly. "We were the enemy."

"Greasy little bastards," Macallister fumed, too lost in his own hatred to listen. "They held me down and cut the buttons from my coat, then threatened to slit my throat, too, if I didn't lead them to more English."

"And you did it," William said, though he already knew the answer. "You betrayed us."

"Well, what sane man wouldn't?" Macallister demanded. "My life, or the lives of a pack of faceless strangers from the lowest ranks? How could I know you'd be there in the middle of them, Callaway, ready to disgrace my good name?"

"That would have been the least I'd have done to you if I'd known!"

"But you did," Macallister insisted. "You saw me just as the first of their artillery fired, there beside their captain. I know you saw me, marked me, you and your worthless, low-bred rascals!"

"I didn't," William said hoarsely, all the pieces of that long-ago afternoon finally falling into place. "By God, I thought it was my fault, that I'd led my men into a trap."

"Oh, William, William, I told you it wasn't because of you," Bethany cried softly behind the shelter of his back, her hand holding tightly to his. "Oh, my love, you were always better than that!"

"My life for yours, that was the trap," Macallister said. "You know how it is in war, Callaway. All a man thinks of is saving his own neck. And the devil take me, *I* lived, and was made a hero for it, too. But who would have guessed you'd live, eh? Who would have guessed you'd come back to ruin me now?"

"And so you killed the others, too, didn't you?" William asked, though he already knew the truth. "You found which of my men survived, and then you poisoned them, one by one, to keep them silent."

Macallister cackled. "You can buy any service if the price is right. And who would care about those used-up scraps of human rubbish, anyway? No one but you, Callaway. No one but you."

And at last, after so much time and suffering, the dam of William's conscience broke.

"How dare you?" he thundered, loading each word with venomous scorn. "How can you wear the uniform of an officer of the king? Where is your honor? Where is your loyalty? You're nothing but cowardly, murderous scum, and by God, I will see you broken and hanged for this!"

Macallister's face hardened. "Not if I kill you first, Callaway," he said as he steadied and aimed the pistol in his right hand, "the way I'd always intended."

Damnation, was it really going to end like this? Not killed honorably on the battlefield, but by the shot of a madman's gun? At this range not even Macallister could miss, nor would there be any chance of survival.

At least he could die saving Bethany; at least she would know he'd loved her enough to trade his life for hers…

In the fraction of a second that it took Macallister's finger to draw back the trigger, William shoved Bethany to the floor and lunged forward at the gun. He saw the flash before his eyes, and his nostrils filled with the acrid burn of the gunpowder, but there was no pain, no wound, no impact. Instead William saw Macallister's face contort with pain, and he dropped the spent pistol to grab at the back of his neck.

William didn't care. He threw himself at Macallister, knocking him down, wrestling with him to gain control of the other gun. He was bigger, stronger, and he could feel the other man's helplessness growing.

But desperation gave the smaller man one final burst of strength. He twisted his wrist free of William's grasp, turned the gun toward his own chest, and squeezed the trigger.

"William!" Bethany cried, her voice tortured with agony. "Oh, my God, William!"

"Don't look, Bethany," he ordered, pulling back from the mangled pulp that Macallister had become. As quickly as he could, he stripped off his blood-soaked coat and covered the dead man with it. "Keep back."

Yet she came to him anyway, not hiding her tears as she buried her face against his chest. He slipped his arms around her, resting his cheek against the top of her head and closing his eyes. Exhausted, he could do nothing more. It was done; everything was done.

"He didn't hurt you, did he, guv'nor?"

William turned to look. "What in blazes are you doing here, Twig?"

"I got him good for you, didn't I?" Unfazed by the blood-soaked body, the boy held out his hands: in one was a slingshot, in the other a small pile of the acorns he used as ammunition. "Right smart in the' neck when he was set to fire at you an' Miss Bethany. I told you I'd be watching your back for you, guv'nor, an' I always keep my word."

And at last William smiled. "It's a good thing you did, Twig. The best thing in all the world."

Epilogue

They were married as soon as the date could be arranged, there in the front room of Penny House. For a wedding that was so widely discussed by so many people, from the most fashionable set in St. James's Square to the poorest folk who slept beneath the empty market stalls at Covent Garden, the list of guests was remarkably small, and surprisingly diverse, too. But from the lofty Duke of Guilford to the lowly Twig, resplendent in a new suit of clothes, every guest did agree that they'd never seen a happier groom than Major Lord William Callaway, or a more joyful beauty of a bride than the new Lady Bethany.

Like every wedding, there were the usual unpredictable moments. The elderly minister, a friend of the late Reverend Penny, confused which red-haired sister was the bride. The ceremonial kiss between the new husband and wife became so passionate that the bride's headdress came unpinned and toppled from her head.

And while few brides would dream of baking their own wedding cakes, Bethany had made five. Not only had she created the beautiful concoction of candied fruit, nuts and spun sugar icing that was carried proudly up the stairs like a queen on her throne, but also the three additional cakes that were cut and given out to every member of her flock that wished one.

And later, much, much later, when William and Bethany were finally together in their bed at the inn on the road to their wedding trip in Brighton, Bethany produced the fifth, and most important, of her wedding cakes, this one baked for the groom alone.

"This is for you, my love," she said proudly, handing him the small box tied with a blue bow. "A sweet for my own sweet William."

"You're the sweet one, Bethany, not I." He propped himself up on the pillows as he opened the box, and grinned. The little cake was exactly enough for two, with two interlocking hearts iced across the top. He ran one finger along the edge, gathering a swipe of butter cream, and pressed it to Bethany's lips.

"Now that is sweet," he said, leaning forward to kiss the frosting from her mouth. "Not me, but you."

Her laughter filled their kiss, and helped spread the buttercream across his jaw and her cheek.

"But you are missing the most important part of the cake, William," she said, breaking the cake in two. "I put in egg whites and almonds and all sorts of other good things that are supposed to give us extra vigor."

"*'Vigor'?*" he demanded, though he was laughing again, too, as she slipped a large chunk of the cake into his mouth. "What in blazes are you implying, wife?"

"I'm implying that I intend to spend as much time in my husband's bed as possible," she said, popping another chunk into her own mouth, "and I wish us both to be equal to the challenge."

"Oh, I'll challenge you," he said, rolling her beneath him. "You can be sure of that, Lady Bethany."

She gazed up at him, and her smile softened. "I am always sure of you, William."

"Because I love you, lass," he said, the best and only explanation for everything. "Because you love me."

"Yes," she said, and reached up to lick the icing from his cheek. "Now show me again how sweet I am."

"As you wish, my lady," he said. "Whatever and whenever you wish."

* * * * *

On sale 5th October 2007

TO THE CASTLE
by Joan Wolf

A powerful knight and his innocent bride...

Just weeks from taking her holy vows, Nell de Bonvile
is swept from the convent, and ordered to marry
Roger de Roche, heir to Britain's most powerful earldom.
Lovely and naive, Nell bravely faces her uncertain future.

Roger is prepared to wait for his innocent bride, yet as
he watches Nell blossom from timid girl to courageous
mistress of his keep, his desire grows. But war gives
no quarter to newfound passion, testing every
whispered word and each unspoken promise...

MILLS & BOON

Historical

On sale 5th October 2007

Regency

MASQUERADING MISTRESS
by Sophia James

The war-scarred Thornton Lindsay, Duke of Penborne, can
scarcely believe it when a beautiful stranger comes to London
proclaiming to be his lover. Courtesan or charlatan?
Thorn is intrigued by both sides of this mysterious,
sensual woman. There's a vulnerability beneath her smile
and easy laughter. Could she be the one to mend a life
he'd thought damaged beyond repair?

Regency

MARRIED BY CHRISTMAS
by Anne Herries

Josephine Horne ignores convention. She never
intends to marry, so why should she be concerned
with rules? Then she meets handsome Harry Beverley...
and her ideas about marriage begin to change. Hal must
marry for duty, but his attraction to the rebellious
Miss Horne is ridiculous! They both have a lesson to learn
– and Christmas is the season of love!

ᚎedieval
LORDS & LADIES
COLLECTION

VOLUME FOUR

CHRISTMAS KNIGHTS
Share the magic of a
Medieval Christmas!

King's Pawn by Joanna Makepeace

The handsome Earl of Wroxeter, powerful and
commanding, had no intention of marriage. But when
the king ordered him to take a bride, he had no choice
but to obey. Cressida, a beautiful innocent, caused
fireworks at court. It was the Earl's task to rescue
her…and make her every Christmas wish come true!

The Alchemist's Daughter by Elaine Knighton

A chance meeting in the Holy Land gave Isidora a
means of escape. But she would have to watch her
beloved Lucien continue the experiments that claimed
her father's life. And how would such an exotic flower
fare in the cold depths of an English winter?

Available 5th October 2007

www.millsandboon.co.uk

M&B

Medieval
LORDS & LADIES
COLLECTION

When courageous knights risked all to win the hand of their lady!

Volume 4: Christmas Knights – October 2007
King's Pawn by Joanna Makepeace
The Alchemist's Daughter by Elaine Knighton

Volume 5: Exotic East – November 2007
Captive of the Harem by Anne Herries
Pearl Beyond Price by Claire Delacroix

Volume 6: Mediterranean Heroes – December 2007
Honeyed Lies by Claire Delacroix
Rinaldi's Revenge by Paula Marshall

6 volumes in all to collect!

*Victorian London is brought to life in
the stunning sequel to Mesmerised*

London, 1876

Though Kyria Moreland is beautiful and rich enough to
attract London's most sought-after gentlemen, she has yet to
find love and refuses to marry without it. When she receives a
mysterious package, she is confronted with danger, murder and
a handsome American whose destiny is entwined with hers...

Rafe McIntyre has enough charm to seduce any woman, but
his smooth façade hides a bitter past. Still, he realises Kyria is in
danger, and he refuses to let her solve the riddle of this package
alone. Who sent her this treasure steeped in legend? And who
is willing to murder to claim its secrets for themselves?

Available 17th August 2007

FREE!

2 Books
and a surprise gift!

We would like to take this opportunity to thank you for reading this Mills & Boon® book by offering you the chance to take TWO more specially selected titles from the Historical series absolutely FREE! We're also making this offer to introduce you to the benefits of the Mills & Boon® Reader Service™—

- ★ **FREE home delivery**
- ★ **FREE gifts and competitions**
- ★ **FREE monthly Newsletter**
- ★ **Exclusive Reader Service offers**
- ★ **Books available before they're in the shops**

Accepting these FREE books and gift places you under no obligation to buy, you may cancel at any time, even after receiving your free shipment. Simply complete your details below and return the entire page to the address below. You don't even need a stamp!

YES! Please send me 2 free Historical books and a surprise gift. I understand that unless you hear from me, I will receive 4 superb new titles every month for just £3.69 each, postage and packing free. I am under no obligation to purchase any books and may cancel my subscription at any time. The free books and gift will be mine to keep in any case.

H7ZEF

Ms/Mrs/Miss/Mr ....Initials ....

Surname ....

BLOCK CAPITALS PLEASE

Address ....

....

....Postcode ....

Send this whole page to:
UK: FREEPOST CN81, Croydon, CR9 3WZ